The Doctor, The Plutocrat, and The Mendacious Minister

GLYN POPE

GP

Arizona USA

The Doctor, The Plutocrat, and The Mendacious Minister

Copyright © 2010 by GLYN POPE
Copyrights actively enforced.

First Edition.

ALL RIGHTS RESERVED BY THE AUTHOR. No part of this book may be reproduced or transmitted in any format or by any means, including scanning into a data base, without written, signed, permission of the author and publisher. Rights use requested are logged and actively enforced. Purchasers of this book do not purchase any rights of use other than to read for their own enjoyment and cannot assign any rights. Libraries may only lend, not scan this book. NO ONE may scan this book in full or in part. Contact publisher for permission to use requests: www.CactusRainPublishing.com.

This is a work of fiction. Names, characters, places, and incidents are fictitious or are used fictitiously. Any perceived resemblance to actual persons, living or dead, business establishments, events, or locales is false.

Cover Design by Nadine Laman and Joyce Himes

ISBN 978-0-9829181-0-4

Published by Cactus Rain Publishing, LLC
San Tan Valley, Arizona, USA.

Published November 1, 2010
Printed in the United States of America.

In memory of W. L. Pope

Chapter One

Peter Latymer stepped from the Great Northern carriage at Belgrave Road station. The concourse was unusually busy for late afternoon on a chilly October day. The secure glow of warmth from the fires of the train engines and the heavy smell of oil and coal, bound up with the crowd moving as if all were on a new journey. Peter stood, reflecting for a moment on his new start.

The daylight failing, there were lights shining as hadn't been enjoyed in three years. There had been a brief glimmer of hope earlier that year when the Olympic Games were held in London. But that had been London. In the rest of the country the celebrations hadn't made any difference. The aftermath of the war existed. It was still dark. A new age had yet to dawn.

Latymer heard a piercing scream rise from amongst the general sound of the station. He took it to be the whistle of an engine. As he looked around his eyes set upon a man clutching his arm. Could this be his first patient, so soon after his arrival?

'The stupid sod.' The voice sounded shrill.

'Now sir, watch your language, there are ladies and children present.' His uniform gave the porter the prerogative to sanction.

'Yes, Reg.' The lady with the injured man spoke, attempting an air of authority.

Reg replied, 'Are you standing here with a broken arm?'

'No, it's just that–'

'Shut your gob then,' Reg told her.

'Reg,' the lady pleaded, 'stop the palaver. Don't speak to me like that.'

The porter moved to intervene.

'Fight a man with one arm, would you?'

'Reginald. Calm down.' The woman was firm with her husband.

'What was the idiot doing,' Reg whined, 'slamming the door on a train full of people?'

'I don't know.'

'I bet he's in the station bar,' said Reg, 'cosy with a whisky. That's what I need, a whisky for the pain.'

'I'll get you one.' The lady looked around and shouted, 'Porter!'

'Don't give him anything.' Latymer purposefully strode to the small gathering. Full of self-importance he said, 'I'm a doctor.' Every young doctor has the desire to utter the statement, 'I'm a doctor,' and answer the emergency.

'Thank God for that.' Reg spoke, with a miserable groan, as if his life needed saving. 'A doctor.'

'He may be in shock. No alcohol.' Latymer repeated the instruction while he looked into the man's eyes.

'What the doc means is he may need an operation.' The porter made a sawing motion across his own arm. 'His arm amputated.'

'Oh no! Oh no! Milly, I'm going to have my arm cut off. You'd better get me that drink.'

The porter walked away and left them to it.

'You're all right. Pull yourself together. Let's take you to a seat and have a proper look.' Latymer pointed to a bench.

His wife led Reginald to the nearby seat. At the end of the bench was a narrow space, perhaps large enough for Reg to sit. The rest of the bench was taken by a lady of large proportions with a scarf tied tightly to her head. Next to her was seated a schoolboy.

'Move along and let the gentleman sit down. He looks a bit pale.' The woman gave the boy a nudge.

'Where am I going to sit?' asked the boy.

'You'll have to stand. The train will be here soon,' the lady said kindly, seeking to appease him.

'I'll have to stand on that, as well,' the boy shot back.

'Stop being cheeky. Here you are, sit down, duck.' She gestured for Reg to take the empty place that the boy, flouncing and sighing, had gone to great pains to make.

Reginald made a show of sitting down as if he were a hero.

'Well it can't be because of the war,' the boy gave a sideways nod towards Reg, 'it's been over three years now. Why can't we get proper food? I was reading in *The Times* that they're better fed in Germany and they *lost!*' He stood petulant in his schoolboy's uniform, speaking as if he were talking about a game of football.

'We don't want that kind of talk,' said the lady minding the boy.

Latymer looked at the boy and said, 'You've got a politician there. How old is he?'

'Ten. He sees, hears, and reads everything.'

'Is that so? Very bright,' answered Latymer.

'So his parents say. I'm seeing him back to school.'

What a precocious child, Latymer thought, but doctors are taught to never give away their true feelings. 'Anyway, thank you for letting this gentleman sit down. He's been in an accident.'

Reg nodded his head, affirming the situation.

'Yes, I see that,' the boy went on. 'His arm isn't broken though. At the worst it's a slight sprain. If he moves it carefully, it'll free itself. He'll be right as rain in no time.'

Years of hard work training to be a doctor, Latymer despaired looking heavenwards towards the vaults of the railway station, *and a ten-year-old diagnoses my first patient.*

'His mother and father say he wants to be a doctor.'

The boy confirmed the statement, pronouncing his words as if he had a plum in his mouth. 'I do want to be a doctor.'

'Well, there's a lot more to it than guesswork.' And to show that he was very serious, Latymer spoke in a voice that was a few decibels below his normal one.

'How long have you been a doctor then?' the boy asked.

Latymer ignored the question, but carried on with his explanation. 'There's seven years hard training, difficult examinations.'

'There's nothing wrong with most patients you see as a GP that wouldn't cure itself,' said the boy pompously.

Latymer knew the boy to be correct. 'How do you know that?'

'I read it in *The Lancet* – last June's issue. I can send it to you if you give me your address.'

'You read *The Lancet*?' Latymer gave the boy another look.

'Like other boys read the *Beano*,' the lady told them rather proudly, as if she were his mother.

'Yes, so do I,' said Latymer, foolishly with pride in his voice.

'You read the *Beano*, Doc?' asked Reg. 'I can let you have my back issues.'

'No, *The Lancet*.'

'That's why he knows more than you,' said Reg.

'He doesn't know more than me. This arm could be broken.'

'As a second opinion–'

'I don't think I'll have a second opinion from a ten-year-old boy.'

The gathered crowd nodded sagely as one.

Latymer's confidence took a further knock when he heard someone mumble, 'Doesn't know a lot, that doctor, does he?'

Latymer attempted to renew his authority, 'Right, let's get on.'

'Come on, let's get you on the train and let the doctor work,' said the childminder.

The boy passed Latymer a neatly folded piece of paper. 'Here's my address in case you need to contact me.'

Latymer looked at the paper with suspicion, then stuffed it into his pocket.

Reginald moaned and coughed to focus the attention back on him.

The boy and his nurse turned to look at Reg and stopped in the crowd to watch for a minute.

'Now, Mr–?'

'Call me, Reg.' Looking towards the lady with him, 'Milly, my wife.'

'Okay, Reg. Now, can you slip off your coat?'

'It's a bit cold.'

'The doctor needs to see your arm,' Milly told him.

Latymer turned to the gathered spectators. 'There's nothing to see.'

Nobody moved.

A policeman was leaning against the counter in the refreshments room. Gaunt and thin, Sergeant Simmons spent most of his duty time at the railway station. During the war the duty was particularly important, as it could have been one way for spies to enter the country. Sergeant Simmons never apprehended anyone, mainly for two reasons: one was that he didn't know what he was looking for, and secondly, he spent most of his duty time standing where he was now, chatting to Cyril and Cyril's wife, Dot. Simmons drank tea and ate bun after bun without putting on an ounce in weight. He left his post only when he needed to relieve himself.

'Hey, Sarge?' said Cyril.

Simmons stopped mid-bite. It wasn't often he was interrupted whilst eating.

'There seems to be quite a crowd gathering.'

'Ooh, I wonder what's going on there?' Dot was a nosey woman and didn't miss a trick.

Sergeant Simmons looked in the wrong direction.

'Over there.' Dot pointed with a cup she was drying.

'Ah yes.' Simmons spoke as if he had known all along. 'Best take a look.'

Simmons put his shoulders back, so he looked more like a figure of authority, and strode purposefully towards the crowd.

'Now then. Now then. What have we here?'

'This man has injured his arm. He trapped it in a carriage door. I'm trying to take a look at it.' Latymer told the policeman.

'I see,' said the policeman, full of self-importance. 'You trapped this man's arm in a carriage door? I shall need your name, sir. There may be further proceedings.'

The crowd murmured their disbelief at the crime committed by a doctor.

'I'm Dr Latymer. I didn't trap his arm. I'm trying to help him.'

Carefully scrutinising Reginald, Sergeant Simmons said to him, 'Now I need you to answer truthfully. Did this man,' turning to look in the direction of Latymer, 'who looks too young to be a doctor in my opinion, shut the railway carriage door onto your arm?'

Sergeant Simmons paused for a moment to let the gravity of the situation sink in, whilst the crowd collectively held their breath. 'I warn you that anything you may say could be used in evidence.'

'This is ridiculous,' exclaimed Latymer, wishing he were in a taxi on his way to his first medical practice.

'As far as I know,' replied Reginald, as if he were at the Old Bailey surrounded by aging varnished brown oak, and men and women in grey wigs representing centuries of law, 'it wasn't him.'

There was a sharp intake of breath at the doubt expressed.

'I was in a different carriage. I came here to help him.' Latymer corrected Reg's information.

'He sounds very guilty,' said one of the expanding group of people.

'A terrible thing for a doctor to do,' replied another.

'I saw him, the man who says he's a doctor, get out of the carriage up there. Three carriages away from where the man screamed like a woman,' said one man moving to the front of the pack.

'I did not scream like a woman,' Reginald protested.

'Yes you did,' said the ten-year-old boy as he stepped forward from the other observers.

'Are you prepared to swear to that?' asked the policeman.

'This boy has been taught to tell the truth,' said the boy's keeper.

'Look, Constable,' said Latymer.

'Sergeant,' Simmons corrected.

'Sergeant. I need to see what this man's injuries are. I have somewhere else to get to.'

'Meeting a woman, are we?' Simmons said.

'My practice,' said Latymer growing annoyed.

'What you do in your private life is of no concern to me, as long as long as His Majesty's Law is kept intact.' Simmons glanced at the station clock and saw it was time he was off duty, 'Right, sir, I'll take your word for it. I'll disperse the crowd.'

'Thank you, Sergeant.'

'You could trust a doctor in the war,' said one of the onlookers as she moved away.

'You can never tell,' said another.

'Can you slip off your coat?' Latymer turned to Reg.

'You've asked me that once.'

'So will you do it?'

'It's still a bit cold.'

'Come on, Reg. Do what the doctor wants. He can't look at you.'

Reginald stood up, and with his wife's help, took off his coat, 'Ayah,' he complained as he did so.

'Let's see. Can you bend your arm?'

Reg managed to do that.

'Good. I don't think there's a lot wrong.' Latymer paused as if thinking deeply. 'Hm, you need a doctor to look at this.'

'You said you were a doctor. Were you telling fibs?'

Latymer ignored the question. 'You need your own doctor. Do you have far to go?'

'Stocking Farm. Dr McFadden's our doctor.' He looked at his wife as if it were something to be proud of.

'That's where I'm going,' said Latymer. 'We'll share a taxi.'

***

It seemed miles from the railway station to Stocking Farm.

Latymer and Milly suffered Reg's anguished groans at every bump in the road and his cries to the driver. 'Can't you go any slower? Driver, more carefully, you've an injured man here,' or 'Drive faster, driver, this is an emergency.'

'Make your mind up,' an exasperated Milly told him.

They finally arrived at a housing estate. The houses looked alike, built by the council for the end of the war. They showed lights on in the same rooms; no doubt similar activities were taking place in them.

'Nearly there,' Milly said at last.

'Thank the Lord,' Reg groaned.

The taxi turned into a long drive going slowly towards a stately home.

'Here we are, Doctor. That'll be six shillings.'

'Six shillings?'

'Well, there's the luggage. There's the three of you. I listened to him moaning on, "Drive fast, drive slow." I should have clocked off long ago, been at home to my tea. The missus will be worried. I did this run because you have an injured man in the car that needs dealing with.'

Reg, satisfied the man recognised his plight, nodded in agreement.

The driver went on, 'I would want the spirit that we achieved in the war to carry on.' He looked out of the window as if he was quoting a speech by Winston himself. 'You have to take that into account.' He sounded like a bored actor spouting his lines many times.

'All right. All right.' Latymer paid the driver. He glared at the others. 'We're sharing this.'

Neither of them spoke. Milly nodded and he took it that this was their destination.

***

Latymer stood before a bare bulb sticking out from a wall. It shone onto a door that bore no notice to say where they were. He felt as if he were stuck out in the nether regions of Leicester.

Now, after years of training, he was standing at the door of a new life. As the door opened, he was suddenly taken back to his early days at Northampton University. The bright light reminded him of the dissection room. Their first human post-mortem and all the eager students, abuzz with excitement, filed into the cutting room, prepared for their corpse. A mortuary attendant stood at the door to send them to the correct table. He ran a thumb down a list on a clipboard, 'Latymer? Let's see. Table three.'

Latymer went over to the table, expecting a cadaver, and found a leg stretched out in front of him.

Another student, seeing his surprise, told him, 'I've asked. We've got a leg for six weeks and then we move onto a different part of the anatomy.'

'Do you think it's male or female?'

'Judging by the hairs on it, male, though you never know these days.'

They heard a thud and looked at each other with a smile as one of the students hit the floor in a faint. It was the end of another promising career.

As the trio entered the waiting room at Stocking House, the faces turned to them as if to say, 'You've got a long wait, mate. I shouldn't bother. We were here ages before you and there's only old Dr McFadden.'

'You need to take a disc and wait your turn!' an officious looking woman shouted across to them.

'That's Olive,' Milly whispered to him.

Latymer felt that he'd better go and make himself known.

'Mrs Sharpe for Dr McFadden,' Olive commanded. She wouldn't have been out of place on the parade ground which was surprising for the diminutive figure.

'There's no discs left,' said Reg coming back to where they were standing. He was hobbling now for greater effect.

It was quite late in the evening. There were plenty of patients still to be seen. This practice definitely needed two doctors. Latymer's expectations were to arrive to surgery completed for the day.

Suddenly the whole room was a cacophony of voices, each one giving their ailments.

'My, *you* are going to have to wait.'

'I'm badly injured.'

'I've got the flu.'

'It's me back.'

'I'm expecting.'

'My leg hurts.'
'I've got a migraine.'
'Can't get rid of this cough.'

A door opened and an elderly, but imposing, figure stood framed in the doorway, his crown covered with thick silver hair slicked back with grease à la Clark Gable. He had half-framed glasses, which he took off as if he needed to better see the attended mass. He wore a black three-piece suit with a gold watch chain across the waistcoat. A pleasant smell of tobacco smoke came with him. A sardonic smile crossed his lips.

His natural authority made the patients go silent. 'What's going on here?' he said without raising his voice. 'Anyone who can shout like that is obviously fit and well, and should be on their way home, saving us all a lot of time and money. There are probably genuinely ill patients here who need my attention.'

'And I'm one of them. I'm an emergency,' interrupted Reg.

'Shut up, man.' Dr McFadden glared at Reg.

'Ask the doctor here,' Reg gestured towards Latymer.

'I never said you were an emergency.' Latymer was fed up with the Reg. 'I told you that you needed to see a doctor. There's probably nothing wrong with you.'

'And I've got pneumonia. Try having that.'

'I'll be the judge of that. Shut up. All of you.'

Latymer looked affronted.

'I didn't mean you, Dr Latymer. I'm sorry that you've been welcomed like this. I wouldn't be surprised if you didn't turn heel and get the first train out of this God-forsaken place, faced with this lot.' He smiled and one or two of the patients grinned.

'Miss Riley,' he looked towards Olive, 'show Dr Latymer the sitting room. I'll come see you when I've seen Mrs–?'

'Sharpe.'

'Ah, yes.'

'Why is he being seen before us?' a patient called out to Olive.

'Because, my man, he is a doctor and deserves more respect than you'll ever get. Now if you don't like it, you know where the door is.'

***

Olive led the way to the sitting room. 'Oh, that's good. Bernard's lit a fire.' She turned back to Latymer. 'I'll see a cup of tea is brought.'

'Don't worry, I can see you're busy.'

Olive smiled, and closed the door behind her.

Latymer went to the fire. A pleasant feeling of peace descended upon him. The room was sparse and functionally furnished; two armchairs, a writing desk, and an overfull bookcase were spaced around the room. It hadn't seen a paste or paintbrush in years, and it would have been completely austere without the fire.

A clock ticked loudly from the wall above the desk. At half past seven, time swept by from his first step from the train. Latymer's eyes came to rest on a decanter of whisky sitting on a trolley. He felt tempted to have a glass, but decided to wait and see if it was offered. It wouldn't look good if Dr McFadden came in and found him slugging back the spirits. The Scotsman may be a Presbyterian teetotaller and the drink there for emergencies. Probably a good job that Reg didn't know the about the liquor.

The door opened. He was anticipating the tea, but it wasn't Olive.

'Latymer, young man, welcome. Making yourself at home? Have a whisky. I'll join you.'

'The patients?'

'Don't worry, they can wait. But don't keep the paying guests waiting.'

Latymer assumed McFadden was referring to the private patients.

McFadden went over to the drink trolley. 'I'm sorry the welcome wasn't a little warmer. I wasn't expecting you until tomorrow.' He poured two glasses. 'Water?'

'A little.'

'A threat. Now what happened at the railway station?'

Latymer told him.

'The man's a fool. Probably been drinking.' McFadden took a large swallow of his drink. 'Last week it was his foot. Got it trapped in the door of a lift.' He raised a hand as Latymer went to speak. 'Don't ask. The fire brigade got him out. I would have left him there to starve.'

Latymer winced as he recalled a scene of human starvation.

'Another?'

'No, thank you.'

'Hm, the patients. Better be getting back.'

There was a tap on the door. It opened and Olive's head came round the frame. Both men looked across as if surprised that it was her.

'They're getting restless, Dr McFadden.'

'On my way.' He looked at the empty glass and the decanter.

'Can I help?' Dr Latymer asked.

'Help?'

'Take some of the patients.'

'What a splendid idea, Latymer. You have all you need in your bag? Of course you do. Tell them they can improve on their diet, cut back on smoking and drinking, and take more exercise. Some of them dislike it so much they never come back. We don't miss them, do we, Olive?'

'I think we'd better be getting along,' said Olive without replying to the question.

'Olive, take the doctor to work. I'll just have another of these and follow you in a minute.'

'Don't be too long, Dr McFadden. I expect Dr Latymer is very tired after his journey.'

***

The room Olive showed Latymer into was as cold as ice.

'We weren't expecting you, or Bernard would have lit a fire.'

'Well, let's hope nobody has to get undressed, or they'll die of pneumonia.'

'I'll try and guess what's wrong, and send in the easy cases tonight. There'll be no women patients until Dr McFadden has spoken to you. Do you have everything you need? Don't be afraid to call me if there are any problems.' She added an afterthought, 'Or Dr McFadden. You didn't get your tea. I'll see a cup is sent in to warm you up.'

'I would like that.'

'Good luck. And welcome.' She sounded kind. 'I hope your stay is a long one.'

'Thank you, Mrs–?'

'Miss Riley, but everyone, including the patients, calls me Olive.'

'Thank you, Olive. I'll see that man, Reg, first.'

'That won't be popular. There'll be a revolution out there.'

'No, but he was my first patient in Leicester, so I'd like to finish the job. What's his name?'

'Fantam.'

He raised his eyebrows.

Olive suppressed a smile. 'I'll send him in, Doctor.'

'Doctor.' Eh, it felt good.

Latymer sat for a moment and surveyed his empire. The room was empty of anything resembling warmth and comfort. There was only an examining couch, his desk, three chairs, a lamp, and an empty sterilising tin. A bare bulb hung from the ceiling, its lampshade removed, obviously, to give more light. On the light green-glossed walls was a reading chart to check sight. A pair of scales stood in a corner like a recalcitrant child. Another door led to somewhere in the house. The door opened. A man stood there. It wasn't Reg Fantam.

'Bernard Birtwhistle, sir. Olive sent me to light a fire and here's a cup of tea. I took the liberty of putting a spoon of sugar in it.' He was a big man, too large to be holding a cup and saucer in his sausage-like fingers.

'Thank you. Don't light a fire. Nobody will want to stay in here long.'

'If you're sure.'

'I'm sure.'

'Right you are.'

'Gerrout o' me road. Move. I'm an emergency.'

'All right. Hold your horses.'

Reg barged into the room. 'At last! I'm in great pain.'

'Sit down, Mr Fantam.'

'It's freezing in here. I could die of pneumonia as well.'

'Let's be quick then, shall we, to save you from an untimely death.'

Reg winced at the thought.

There was a knock at the door. 'Yes? What now?'

'Can I come in?' It was Milly. 'See how he is.'

Reg looked sorry for himself as if he were a cocker spaniel.

Latymer nodded. 'Sit down over there.' Returning to Reg, he said, 'Now I know you haven't broken your arm.'

'Without an x-ray? You believe that kid then? Thought *you* were the doctor.'

Latymer ignored him. 'Let me see your hand and fingers.' He turned them over in his own. 'Hm. Hm. Yes.'

'Is it, is it bad?' Reg could barely get the words out. 'Will I need to be rushed to hospital?'

'No.' Latymer suppressed a laugh. 'You'll live. Nothing broken. Just a bit of bruising. Miraculously no cuts.' Latymer looked in Milly's direction. 'Mrs Fantam?'

She nodded.

'He needs to soak this alternatively in bowls of water, one very hot and one cold. That will bring the bruising out, take away any swelling, though I can't see much. Do that for an hour. He'll be as right as rain in the morning. Give him a couple of aspirin, and as he's taking painkillers, under no circumstances drink any alcohol.'

'We was going to the Beaumont Leys when we left here.'

'No, straight home and on with the treatment. A light meal, a few boiled vegetables without meat to help him get over the shock, and then an early night with no undue excitement.'

'I'll sleep in the spare room. We're trying for a baby, you see.' She lowered her eyes demurely. 'But we won't try tonight.'

'Don't I need a medical certificate for a few days off work?'

'Goodness man, of course you don't.'

Reg made a face that gave the message, 'All my earthly pleasures are being taken away from me, sex, booze, and a holiday.'

'Follow my instructions and you'll be perfectly fit for work in the morning. And don't forget to leave the money with Miss Riley,' Latymer spoke firmly to show that he was being serious, 'that you owe me for the taxi.'

Reg was too shocked to speak.

'He will. Thank you, Doctor. You've been very helpful.'

'My pleasure. Tell Olive I'm ready for my next patient.'

Chapter Two

The time was half past five in the morning. Sleep didn't come easy to Latymer, with all of the excitement his first proper medical job had given him going round and round in his brain. As a young man he loved the idea of earning his first wage that he could see and spend. He was doing just that in his imagination.

It was cold in the bedroom. Although the bed was warm under the blankets and an eiderdown, there was no source of heat. He dreaded getting out of bed onto a lino floor to find the light switch and make his way to the bathroom. He used the toilet once in the night when he felt his bladder would burst, and then shivered himself back into sleep.

After the surgery finished the previous night, Bernard's wife, Edna, left him a nameless and tasteless stew, but it was hot and filled his stomach. He'd eaten worse whilst in Europe at the end of the war.

Olive told him that she would arrive an hour before the surgery was to start to 'show him the ropes.' Dr Mc Fadden was nowhere to be found. When he'd asked Olive where McFadden was, she said, 'He has rooms in the town centre, on Charles Street. I occasionally go there when he needs help with private patients.'

'He doesn't live here then?'

'Goodness no, Dr McFadden is old school. Pre-National Health when doctors practised for charity and the rest for money. Angus likes the better things in life.'

'I see.'

'This old house is yours to rattle around in. I'm sorry I have to go.' Olive looked pensive. 'Mother will be beginning to worry. When I get home this late, she thinks I've been in an air raid. It's a habit from the war. I'll see you in the morning.'

***

Latymer finally got out of bed and sat on the edge of the mattress. He dressed quickly and went downstairs. There it was much warmer, so much that he opened a door to the grounds and took a large gulp of cold clean air.

The view out of the back door took him by surprise, as it wasn't the unpleasant tangle of grey concrete that he expected to see. Stocking House was at the top of a hill overlooking the town of Leicester. Judging by the low grey clouds that hung over the town, Leicester was obviously an industrial centre. From where he was standing his view swept down to houses, modern council cement-rendered, three up-three down dwellings, to the two-storey red brick flats. Beyond that were pre-war privately owned brick houses with mock Tudor bay windows, upstairs and downstairs.

He could see and smell the factories, and there was obviously a sewage farm close by. But green lawns surrounded Stocking House, a falling down stable, great oaks and chestnuts that were far older than the house. Latymer heard the noise of hens. He went outside to have a proper look at the building. It could be eighteenth century, perhaps a house that might have been found in a George Eliot novel. He turned back to take in the view. There was a cough behind him.

'Dr– ?' A woman was framed in the doorway, her large bulk filling the space.

'Latymer, Dr Latymer.'

'I'm sorry, Dr Latymer. I was told your name when we was expecting you.' She was smiling, and if there were another human's face to see so early in the morning ,then hers was quite acceptable. She was friendly and awake. 'I took the liberty of making you a pot of tea.'

'Tea. I will drink tea at any time of the day. But at this moment I would die for it, Mrs Birtwhistle,' said Latymer.

'I'd rather you called me Edna.'

'I'd be happy with Peter, but must remain formal with the patients.'

'Oh, don't worry. I understand. I know if ever I wanted to finish old McFadden off, then I'd just have to say, 'How you doing then, Angus? He'd have a stroke.'

Latymer started laughing.

'I'm sorry, Dr Latymer, I didn't think it was that funny..'

'It's just the image. I can see his face,' Latymer replied.

'I can do you slices of toast. What with the rations still, I save the bacon until Sunday, except when I get bit extra off Eric at the local shop. He's a bit of a spiv.'

Latymer smiled. 'I see.'

'I can do you an egg any day of the week. We've three hens here.' Edna sounded proud of the fact.

'I did hear them. Toast, eggs, and tea sounds excellent.'

'Come this way then. You probably don't know your way round the house yet.' She led him to a warm room, with a fire and a table laid for one. 'You'll have all your meals in here.'

He heard noises in the hallway, the door opened and Olive joined him at the table.

'I've eaten. I'll just have half a cup of tea,' she said before any greetings.

Now that he saw her in the day, the excitement of the previous evening gone, he was able to assess her better. He guessed, probably correctly, that she was the backbone of the practice. She was quite a small figure. She wasn't much over five foot two, but her slimness bordering on thinness made her seem smaller. Her hair was tight into a bun, strangely her eyes were olive in colour, matching her name. She wore a neat dark matching suit. He would hardly see her wear anything different. It was impossible to guess her age. She could have been anything from thirty to fifty years old.

Without any preamble she began immediately. 'We have around forty patients in the morning.' She looked at her watch as if they were already pounding on the door. 'The first will be arriving soon.' Taking a sip of her tea, she went on, 'I'm sure you know all this.'

Latymer nodded. 'This is my first post. So best if you tell me everything, then I can't say I wasn't told.' He gave a nervous smile now that he was thrown into the deep end of work as a doctor.

'Yes. Well, they just come and wait to be seen. When we have two doctors on they can choose who they see, but I often just send them to whichever doctor is available. Especially if an emergency comes up.'

'Does that happen often?'

'It depends, sometimes nothing for months. Though that is unusual. And then two or three in a week, say, at one of the factories.'

'Don't they go to hospital?' Latymer asked.

'Sometimes.' Olive replied as if she were holding something back.

'So we do it?'

'We charge them. That is, the factory owners pay as private patients. They're prepared to pay to show that they care. It keeps everyone happy. The bosses show they're bothered and Dr McFadden gets extra money.'

Olive seemed to have an attitude towards her employer. She wasn't in favour of his behaviour as far as making money at every opportunity, but obviously respected his efficiency. He wondered if she liked him.

'Don't get me wrong. Dr McFadden is a very good doctor. I've worked with him for fifteen years. I moved here with him during the war in 1942.'

'Where from?'

'Another time.' Olive looked into her cup and saw it was empty.

'Shall I call Edna to bring you another?'

'No thanks, I don't like treating them like servants. Though sometimes I think they like behaving like they're in the *big house.*' A smile crossed her face. 'Dr McFadden doesn't suffer fools. If there's nothing wrong with a patient, then he'll tell them, but he is caring. He knows where there's money to be made and which fools can afford to part with it for a few scientific words. That's a good lesson to learn.'

Latymer didn't feel convinced. He always wanted to take the right and moral way.

'Anyway, I've gone right off the point. Time is getting on and we'll have our first customers hammering on the door soon. Forty patients in the morning, then home visits just before and after lunch.' She talked quickly now, and he was barely able to interrupt.

'Does one walk or is there a vehicle?'

'A car. Though if it's nearby, try to walk there. We get good petrol rations. And in the evening the same again,' with a toss of her head, 'forty patients. Dr McFadden will tell you the rotas and when each of you is working. You're the only one living here though, so in many ways you're on call twenty-fours hours a day or worse still, night.'

'Is there a telephone?'

'Oh yes, we've caught up with modern times. It's in what I call my office, where all the patients' records are kept. I've been on Angus that there ought to be extensions in the sitting room and on the landing upstairs. You can't be expected to go round chasing after a telephone.

Leave it with me. I'll work on him. You'll have it by the end of the week.'

He knew now where the power was, and who to keep on the right side of.

'There might be hammering on the door at night as well. But be very sure when you answer that you know it's an emergency. It could be anyone standing there.' Olive sounded serious.

'Okay.' He made to move.

'Dr Latymer, something else that's very important. It's a bit sensitive. With female patients, never examine them if they have to get undressed at all, without me being present. I will stop whatever I'm doing. You can sometimes get women who are a bit odd. You are a young attractive man and they'll start accusing you of all sorts.'

He nodded.

'Dr McFadden hasn't suffered that trouble for years. No, in all seriousness, he still gets me in. We don't want any unnecessary problems, so don't take unnecessary risks'

She stood up and Latymer rose with her. 'Bernard is the caretaker and odd-job man. He's very good, so any problems to do with the house, go to him. Edna will see to your meals, and I suppose is like a housekeeper.' She touched his arm tenderly as if she were his mother. 'I just hope you don't get too lonely. You'll make friends. Dr McFadden has five children, all doctors, just about; one still at university. One is at an airbase near here. You'll meet some of them, I expect.'

Latymer was ready to ask if there was a Mrs McFadden when she issued the order, 'Now, let's get to your surgery for your first day at work.' She smiled kindly.

***

After an hour and six patients later there was a tap at his door, and McFadden came in followed by Edna carrying a tray with two cups of tea and four plain biscuits on it.

'I took the liberty of giving us a short break. Important medical stuff to discuss.'

Latymer's face went serious as Edna left the room, carefully closing the door behind her.

'Joking. Rest easy.' The older doctor smiled a benevolent smile. 'The door there,' McFadden gestured towards the corner, 'leads to the house without you having to tramp through the waiting room and the patients seeing you. Should you need the call of nature or ten minutes in an armchair. They'll just think you're very slow or taking great care. Never give them more than seven minutes, you know. Tops.'

Latymer smiled broadly.

'How many have you seen?'

'Five or six.' Latymer shuffled a few papers on the desk to show that he'd been very industrious that morning.

'I've seen twice that. You'll be here all day. You laugh. You're full of energy now, but wait until you get to my age. Drink your tea before it gets cold.' Dr McFadden pushed a cup and saucer towards Latymer. 'I think that's yours. Edna always puts a wee dram in mine. Fine woman.'

Latymer took a sip. Much to his relief it tasted like proper tea.

'Have a biscuit, Latymer. Olive, I gather, has filled you in on the necessary. Anything else though, you must ask her as she has her finger on the pulse.' He laughed at his own feeble attempt at humour.

Latymer nodded, unable to speak, his mouth full of biscuit.

'You'll be all right then in this big house?' asked McFadden.

Latymer swallowed. 'I think so. Thank you.'

'A big house for one man. Get married. Fill the place with children. They'll love it.'

'I haven't been here twenty-four hours and you're marrying me off!'

They both chuckled.

'Yes. Probably is a bit too soon. You won't want to marry anyone from round here, anyway. Milly Fantam?' He raised his eyebrows in question and Latymer smiled. 'Shouldn't talk about the patients like that. Now then, where were we?'

Dr Latymer was beginning to wonder what the point was in Dr McFadden coming to see him, other than for a cup of tea.

The older doctor brought himself back to the agenda. 'We do need to talk rotas and such. I'll try and get us half an hour with Olive before evening surgery. You all right with home visits this afternoon?'

'Yes, I suppose so,' replied Dr Latymer.

'Can you drive?' Dr McFadden asked.

'Yes, I just won't know where I'm going. I'll probably get lost and you won't see me for evening surgery.'

'Can't have that.' McFadden looked genuinely worried. 'I'll get Bernard to act as your guide for your first couple of times. It is easy to find your way around this estate, though. You might find the outlying districts a bit difficult. Bernard will willingly help the doctor in his call of duty.'

There was a knock at the door. It opened and Olive rushed into the room.

'We know. We know there's patients to be seen.' Dr McFadden spoke, rising from his chair.

Unusual for Olive, she said, 'I think that the patients will have to wait. There's been an accident at the school. A child's got his head stuck through the railings.'

'Again?'

'Doesn't that only happen in Ealing comedies?' Dr Latymer commented with a smile.

'Which of you is going?' Olive stuck to her business not amused at young Latymer's attempt to fit in.

'On this estate,' Dr McFadden said, 'you can expect anything, Latymer, you wait and see. Go, I can't abide the children in that place. I'll finish here. Down the drive, then left.' McFadden pointed. 'You won't need the car. A monstrosity of a building - you can't miss it. Willowtree Junior School.'

'I'll get my coat.'

'Ah, Latymer. Emergencies. I've decided to put extensions from the telephone in Olive's office to the sitting room and on the landing. Save you having to run round the house should there be a call for an emergency.'

Latymer found it difficult to meet Olive's eyes, but he felt hers on him.

Dr McFadden continued without missing a beat. 'And I've just remembered. I've booked us a table at my club tonight. Eight o'clock all right with you?'

Latymer nodded.

'Should be finished here by then,' McFadden added. 'Well humans call, if you can call them that.'

***

It looked cold and grey and desolate, so Latymer grabbed his overcoat and put on his gloves. When he reached the end of the drive, which didn't seem as long as the previous night, he came to the main road running through the estate. The artery was Marwood Road. Across the road was a row of bungalows built for pensioners. His patients, then, would be a mix of people from very young to old, and possibly of a different class, should those living on the outlay of the council estate use him and Dr McFadden as their doctors.

Four hundred yards up the road was the school. There were railings surrounding the building, probably to keep the children in rather than intruders out, as if the children were prisoners. As the night before at the railway station, there was a small crowd. It was strange how the human is attracted to another's misfortune for entertainment. He could hear the occasional yells of the trapped child. The rest of the school seemed to have been taken in early from their playtime. A small fire appliance drew up as Latymer strode purposefully towards it, before the fireman could do damage and terrify the child.

'Hello, what have we here then?' Dr Latymer asked.

They could see from his bag that he was a doctor and they parted to let him through.

'Dr–? I'm sorry, I don't know you. Another locum?'

'Dr Latymer. And no, I'm here to stay.'

'We'll see. Mr Beltham, Headmaster.' The man pronounced the name with an emphasis on the 'th' so his name wasn't 'belt'em.' A small, thin man with short hair parted to one side, he extended a hand and Latymer took it. The headmaster didn't smile. 'I don't know why they sent for you. They'll,' nodding towards the firemen curtly, 'soon have him out just like every other time.'

'Do many of the children do this then?'

'Only this one, all the time. Hm,' he paused as if remembering, 'every month or so?'

'That regular? Why?'

'Because he's an idiot. Don't start your psychological nonsense here. The whole family are idiots.'

Latymer went over to the boy. 'Let me see.' He looked closely at the head through the railings and then at the size of the boy, as if he were assessing them. 'Leave him alone,' he said to the firemen. 'If you can just wait over there, please.'

'The other doctor, when he can be bothered to come over, just tells us to grease his ears and pull him out. Like podding peas,' one of the firemen said.

'Yes well, I'm just going to talk to him for a moment. Try and calm him down.' Latymer crouched down to the boy's level and got the smell of stale, unwashed clothes and body odour into his nostrils.

21

'What's your name?'
'Anthony.'
'How old are you?'
'Seven.'
'What happened?'
'I was looking and my head went through.'
'What were you looking for?'
'My mummy.'
'I see. We'll soon have you out. Don't worry. Where's your mum?'
'I don't know.'
'Who looks after you?'
'My sister. Her name's Linda and she goes to the big school. Can you get me out?'
'Yes. Don't worry. Wait here.' He laughed. 'You won't be going anywhere, will you? I'll talk to the firemen. Perhaps they'll let you see the fire engine afterwards.'
'They'll do no such thing or we'll have every child in the school sticking their head through the railings thinking they'll get a reward for it,' said Mr Beltham loudly enough for everyone to hear.
Latymer ignored the headmaster's comment and went over to the two firemen.
'Grease his ears then?' one of them asked.
'No.'
'Leave him then?'
'If you look at him,' the officers looked over as if seeing him for the first time, 'his head is bigger than the width of his body.'
'Yes,' one of the officers said, and the realisation dawned with the rest, 'got you.'
'I read it in *Bleak House*,' Dr Latymer said in hushed tones to himself.
'It's amazing what they put in them medical books,' said a member of the public who overheard him.
'If we turn him onto his side, gently, I reckon we'll get him all the way through. Then there'll be no risk of hurting his ears. The little chap won't think that his head is going to get stuck and be scared.'
In under a minute Anthony was through the railings and standing in the world outside the school.
'Now, that wasn't so bad, was it?' Dr Latymer kindly asked the frightened boy.

The boy shook his head.

'Promise me one thing. You won't go looking through the railings again.'

This time Anthony nodded his head. The group from the school began to move back inside.

'Mr Beltham, could I have a word?' Dr Latymer made to move towards the headmaster.

'Of course. I was forgetting myself, thank you, Doctor, for your help. I'm sure we couldn't have managed without you, and I hope your tenure is a long one.' There was a lack of any genuine feeling in his voice.

'No. It wasn't that.'

'Well?'

'Is the boy being properly cared for?'

'In the school. How dare–'

'In his home?'

'Here we go.' Mr Beltham made a great fuss over sighing. 'You do your job and I'll do mine. Bodies and minds. We have different priorities.'

'Yes and no. The health of the residents on the estate is my concern; that means health and diet. That must also be your concern as far as the children go.'

'You're very new to your job, Dr–?'

'Latymer.'

'Ah yes, Latymer.' Beltham pronounced it as if the name and person meant nothing to him and never would. 'Naïve is what I might call it. Grow and try to be a little more like Dr McFadden.' He turned on his heel and went back inside.

Latymer looked after him, amazed at the man's rudeness.

'Dr Latymer.' A woman's voice sounded decorous and cooing.

'Mrs Fantam. And how is Mr Fantam today?'

'He's right mardy he din't get a day off work.' Latymer didn't completely understand the slang, but he got the gist. 'So he's at work.'

'Good.'

'That soaking in hot and cold water worked a treat. His hand was cured this morning. I went to bed with him, though, I was too cold to sleep by myself.'

'Who you sleep with isn't my concern.' He was aware of blushing. Mrs Fantam began giggling. He was feeling uncomfortable. 'There was really nothing wrong with Mr Fantam's hand,' added Latymer, digging himself a hole now, 'if you see what I mean?'

'Yes, I understand, Doctor. His hand was all right.' She looked coy. 'Well, must rush. Here's my bus. Off to work.'

'Yes, and where would that be?' Latymer saw an opportunity to change the subject.

'Lewis's in town.' She spoke quickly as the bus approached. 'The big store. Sells everything. You know it?'

'I haven't been into town yet.'

'You can't miss it when you get off the bus. Come in and see me. I'm on perfumes.'

'I will, though I don't know who I'll be buying perfume for.'

'Is that right? You surprise me.' The bus drew up to the stop. 'Here I go. Cheerio, Dr Latymer.'

***

From the window in his office Mr Beltham watched the scene between Latymer and Mrs Fantam play its way out. 'He's quick off the mark; she's quite an attractive young woman.' Beltham saw her laugh and Latymer smile, and Mrs Fantam looked away, the way women do when they're flirting. He's certainly one to be watched, with his film star looks.

Mr Beltham put his hand over his hair to flatten it as he sat down at his desk and thought about Mrs Beltham. It was a long time since he'd wanted to kiss Mrs Beltham. He gave her the obligatory peck on the cheek when he left for the school. With her illness there was little else they could do. It was difficult to believe that the reserved, austere, and unpleasant man sitting in his office feeling only angry resentment had once been young, full of the future and a love of life. Life dealt him too many bitter blows.

For all their energies with making love there should have been many children. But there were none. Mrs Beltham blamed herself. She felt she were the non-fecundious fruit, producing nothing. She shrivelled, repelling Mr Beltham's advances. Both man and wife went within themselves. They no longer shared a bed. Mr Beltham became bookish; Mrs Beltham stared out of the window or on other occasions spent hours looking into a mirror without seeing her reflection; only what should have been.

The final blow was Mrs Beltham, after several falls and dizzy spells, once falling unconscious, being diagnosed with a tumour on her brain. The tumour was successfully removed, but it left her semi-paralysed and wheelchair bound. Nursing care was provided. Mr Beltham, even accounting for his cold exterior, loved his wife. He paid for what she needed, so that she was as comfortable as possible.

In his efficiency and with nothing else to use his energies for Mr Beltham climbed the ranks of the teaching profession. By the time he reached his late thirties he was a deputy-head; in his early forties Headmaster of Willowtree Primary School. Positions like this were normally given as rewards for long service, ability often being ignored. This was at least recompense.

His funds weren't infinite, and one day he would need another source of income. How long would it be before he could retire, and they could buy a little place in Devon, where at least they knew happiness on holiday? He felt a determination to buy the house close to the sea and country. He felt an excitement in his stomach at the prospect. He felt he might stop at nothing.

Firstly though, he would find a child to harangue to make him feel better. Judging by the silent hum of work throughout the school, that would be difficult. There must be a brat out of a classroom illegally. He got to his feet and left his office, walking down the long corridor feeling like Gary Cooper in *High Noon*. Soon it would be dinner, when he could knock a few heads together in the dining room.

Chapter Three

After her brief encounter with Dr Latymer outside the school, Milly Fantam got onto the bus to the city centre. As the vehicle progressed she sat and idly watched the scenery. She spoke to no one, smiled if a person smiled at her, then looked quickly away again. She didn't want to talk. She gazed out of the window when the bus drew into a stop. She studied their faces as the queue shuffled forward to fill the bus. She knew where they were each going. The bus only went to one place and few disembarked on the way. But she was curious what these people did when they got there. Work? Shopping? And then back home to a life like hers?

She was only working half a day as she was going in on Sunday morning for a stock take. She was becoming more and more trusted. A post as a supervisor of the perfume department was in the offing. These extra responsibilities were making her think what she wanted, expected, from life. As a young married woman she knew what was anticipated.

The evening before they'd been to Loughborough on the train to visit her mother. Milly's mother was coy and avoided asking the question directly, but wanted to know when there would be the patter of tiny feet, making her a grandma.

Yes, Milly would like a baby. Milly knew everything there was to know about babies. After all, she was married to one. She smiled at the memory of Reg struggling into his trousers and shirt that morning, just to let her know that he was still in great pain. Reg? How did he manage to get his arm shut in a train carriage door? Milly didn't believe it was the other man's fault. Reg somehow put his arm in the wrong place at the wrong time and succeeded in creating an almighty fuss. Last week, he'd come to see her at the department store. He'd got his foot trapped in a lift door. The shop girls now regarded her husband as an imbecile.

Milly wanted the earth to open up and swallow her when the Floor Manager walked over to her and said, 'I think it's your husband that's trapped in the lift, Mrs Fantam. At least the man's asking for you.'

Milly was a few days late for her monthly. There had been other times; but without being able to put a finger on it, this time her body felt different. They were trying for a baby, but in truth, how happy would she be? One wage from Reg. Then Reg working all hours God sends in an attempt to make up for two. She'd spend all day with a baby waiting for Reg to come home from the factory. By herself in the house on a Saturday, and then quiet whilst Reg went through the ritual of listening to the football results. In the evenings he might start going to the Working Men's Club like her dad did. She hated the arguments between her dad and mum when he drank too much – wasting money. She wouldn't want that to happen to her and Reg. Milly decided to say nothing of the pregnancy just yet. She hoped everything would turn out all right.

The bus drew into the terminus. When the passengers began to leave the vehicle, a gentleman paused in the aisle to let her leave her seat. She smiled at him. The conductor was standing on the pavement to help the lady passengers. Milly thanked him and looked up at the exclusive block of flats above the shops on Charles Street. She looked at the expensive façade and reasoned that it must cost a fortune to live there. She believed that Dr McFadden owned a flat in the building. She said to herself, 'I bet he doesn't have any money worries or for anything else. A happy life he leads with no problems.'

She walked on, thinking what Reg would like for tea that night. Egg and chips, his favourite. She liked to give him a treat.

* * *

It was pleasant driving that afternoon with Bernard as guide for home visits. Bernard wanted to take the controls; behind the wheel he was like a child with a new toy. Latymer felt that he would better learn the layout of the estate if Bernard navigated instead. Rather than saying next left, straight on, next right, Dr Latymer asked him to name streets.

So it was, 'We're on Oaktree Avenue now, turn left at Privet Lane and then your second right onto Hattern Avenue.'

The majority of the houses were well kept and clean. A few polished until they shone, 'because the doctor was coming.' And some couldn't be bothered. It was useful to see the inside of the homes; Latymer learnt a lot regarding his patients and their expectations.

One of Latymer's last home visits was a house where the whole being seemed to lack the will to live. There was a child there. The mother told Latymer, 'She's got a bad cough.'

'I'd better have a look,' Latymer said to appear kind and confident to the young woman standing in front of him, unsmiling. She stood in a cold hall, a cardigan wrapped around her, looking as if a few hot meals for her wouldn't come amiss. Latymer bore the burden of seeing far greater suffering in the human state at the end of the second World War in Europe, but this woman was in 1948 Britain after victory.

'Where is your daughter?' he asked.

He received no reply, but was led upstairs to a bedroom. There were no curtains at the window. The room was no warmer than the rest of the house. The child lay staring at nothing. She didn't notice anyone entering the room.

'How long has she been like this?' asked Latymer.

'She's always got a cough,' the woman paused as if the effort to speak was great in itself, 'winter or summer. It never leaves her.'

Latymer leant over the bed to examine the child. He saw that there was only a sheet and thin blanket to cover her.

'She's very cold. Do you have any heating, like a paraffin heater or electric fire?'

'I can't afford the paraffin. It's sitting there all right, just waiting to be filled. I don't have money for electricity.' They both looked at the useless heater standing in the corner of the room.

'You need to get the bed downstairs by the fire. You have one lit?' Latymer asked.

'No,' she replied.

'You need to.'

'I will. I've a bit of coal.' She didn't sound very bothered.

'When does her father get home? You need to move the bed by the fire.'

'Ha!' Her voice was cutting. It was difficult to believe that a person could sound so vicious with one tiny word. 'He doesn't. He doesn't want to know. Just runs the machinery and takes the money. You won't find him here.'

Latymer didn't know what she meant by the last comment. 'Mr Birtwhistle and I will move it now. I can get her comfortable and give you medicine for her. She needs fresh vegetables and fruit.'

'Oh yes? There's no money, I don't know anyone. They don't like me here. They think I'm a...that he gives me lots of money.'

Tears were streaming down her face. Latymer gave her his handkerchief.

'We've nothing. He gives us nothing.' As she spoke, she pulled herself together and recovered her composure.

'Who?' Latymer asked.

'A miracle, they're saying at the school this morning.'

He looked at her and replied. 'Hardly.'

'Will you be able to do a miracle here?' She sounded bitter and Latymer knew she was mocking.

He decided to ignore her sarcasm and be positive. 'We'll try. I'll see myself out. You get the fire lit. I'll ask Olive whether there are any extra benefits you can get.'

Latymer left the house and returned to the car.

'I've just volunteered you for moving a bed downstairs by the fire. A child in there needs it.' Latymer nodded towards the house.

Bernard got out of the car. 'Right you are.'

The two men walked back towards the house.

Chapter Four

Latymer was ready to see his patients ten minutes before he was needed. There was no sign of Dr McFadden. Edna had left a piece of pork pie and two slices of bread on a plate with a cup of tea. He took them by the fire into the living room. He'd managed to tune the radio to listen to some light music. The BBC seemed to be unaware of the music genre Jazz, which he would have preferred. But the music relaxed his mood and he felt content with the world.

After his meal he went to his surgery and sat at the desk fiddling with a pencil. He was thinking that he might as well begin when Olive came into the room. She was smiling broadly.

'What is it, Olive?' Latymer asked her, 'Bernard doesn't want to see me because he's injured his back, does he?'

'No, Bernard's all right. He is going on a bit that now he's a removals man. He doesn't mind really, he just wants everyone to know. Dr McFadden hardly has any patients tonight.' She made as if counting up vast numbers in her head. 'Three at the last count.'

'What's wrong? Is there nobody ill?' Latymer questioned her, surprised and puzzled.

'They all want to see you. The miracle worker.' Olive smiled.

Latymer put his head in his hands and feigned despair.

Olive went on in a singsong voice, obviously very amused at the goings on, 'You pull children through iron railings, take cuts and bruises from Mr Fantam's hands leaving no marks or pain, and the little girl you saw this afternoon has stopped coughing for the first time in months. Her mother is saying all because Latymer laid his hands on her. You're going to be busy tonight, young man, performing miracles. You won't be going to bed until midnight, long after I've gone home!'

'But I'm supposed to have dinner with Angus.' He was taking Olive at her word.

'Don't worry, they won't have a choice.' Olive spoke firmly as she would with the patients. 'They always get this way with a new doctor.'

Latymer felt a little disappointed at that. He liked being regarded as having a talent to cure patients. 'I tell them, Dr McFadden or the door, especially to those who've only come for a look. I've a nose for who's ill and who's just curious.'

'I expect you have by now. Into the breach then, Olive. First patient, please.'

After two hours of non-stop aches, coughs, and pains, Latymer felt he was at the end. Olive came in and said. 'I'm sorry, Doctor, but you have one more. He refused to be seen by anyone but you. He could have seen Dr McFadden an hour ago. He insisted.'

'All right.' He just wanted a hot bath and bed. He didn't feel like facing dinner with Angus, though he knew he would have to. 'Who is it?' he asked.

'Mr Lambert and his boy, Anthony. You know the one?'

'I know. I know. Send them in. Probably a good idea to check that he's all right, anyway.'

She left briskly to tell Anthony and his father that the doctor would see them now.

'I just wanted to shake your hand,' Anthony's father said. The boy was beaming and looked and smelt clean. 'I don't know what you did, but he hasn't been so happy for a long time. It's a miracle. We're going to make more effort as well. We've got to look after ourselves properly.'

'No, I only did what any doctor would do,' Latymer replied.

'The other one,' meaning Dr McFadden, 'wouldn't have been like you.'

Latymer ignored the comment, feeling that it was unfair to Dr McFadden.

'Anthony hasn't been right since his mother died eight months ago. And tonight he comes home from school happy and could talk of no one, but you.' His father smiled. It was obviously a relief to him.

Latymer knew then in that moment that curing illness wasn't just the physical, but the mind as well.

'He drew you a picture. Go on, show the doctor.' The father nudged his son to pass the paper over.

Anthony shyly handed the drawing to him.

Latymer took a meaningful pause to appreciate the drawing. 'That is wonderful. My walls need brightening up. Thank you. How are you feeling? No soreness?'

The boy shook his head.

'Good.'

'He's gone all shy now. We won't keep you. I can see you've had a busy day, but thank you. Anything I can do for you, you ask. Anything.'

Latymer couldn't imagine what that could possibly be, but acknowledged the gratitude.

'Miracle worker,' were the last words Latymer heard as Mr Lambert and son left the room.

***

Dr McFadden was nowhere to be found when Latymer finished with the Lamberts. Latymer wondered whether he'd forgotten that they were to have dinner. Olive was putting documents away in a file whilst Edna waved a duster around the room and she called it cleaning.

'You don't need a meal tonight do you, Dr Latymer?' Edna said as she pretended to dust. It was a statement as much as a question.

'I don't think so.' Latymer didn't want to completely commit himself in case McFadden had forgotten the dinner appointment.

'Yes, I knew there was another matter. It's been such a day. Good job you spoke up, Edna.' Edna smiled proudly at being such a help. 'Dr McFadden wants you to meet him at the Oddfellows Club as soon as you're ready.'

'Oldfellows?'

'No, Odd.' Olive corrected him.

'Old or Odd, either's right,' said Edna.

'Yes, and we ought to keep those kind of comments to ourselves, Edna.' Olive sounded matronly.

Edna pulled a face and curtsied behind Olive's back. Latymer wanted to giggle, but felt that wasn't the correct decorum for the new doctor. Edna apologised, trying to sound like she really meant it.

'How am I supposed to find it?' Latymer asked.

'Book a taxi. The driver will take you straight there.' Olive believed the solution to be manifestly obvious.

'It cost a fortune the other night, six shillings.' Latymer didn't want to waste money he didn't have.

'Don't pay more than two. I'll get you one from the firm we always use,' Olive told him. 'They won't try and get away with more - and if they do, mention Dr McFadden's name.'

'Can I drop you on the way?' Latymer asked her.

Edna looked at one to the other as if she were watching a game of tennis. Fascinated.

'No, I live in the opposite direction. I'll catch the bus.' She looked at the clock. 'There'll be one along in fifteen minutes. Twenty minutes all right with you for the taxi?'

***

On the way, the driver pointed out one or two landmarks that every newcomer to the city should see.

Latymer sat in the back of the car, enjoying the ride as he was learning about his new home. Each piece of information from the man was then punctuated by silence until the driver felt there was something else significant to show him. Latymer instinctively knew he wasn't expected to respond.

'Britley's,' the driver said.

Latymer looked at a big factory complex. 'He owns everything round here. We all work for him one way or another. Even you.'

Latymer felt sure that he was not going to be owned by anyone.

They drove down the empty road. 'The Abbey Park on your right. Beautiful there. That's where that bloke died who was chief minister to that king with lots of wives. Poor bugger.' The driver shook his head in sorrow.

For having many wives, or being buried there, wondered Latymer. History wasn't the doctor's strong point.

There was silence until a tram bore down on them.

The taxi driver swerved out of the tram's way, exclaiming, 'Buggers, those drivers are. Enough to make your hair stand on end. All that noise.' And then more calmly, as if nothing of note had happened, 'On your left, Midland Station.'

'How much is the taxi fare to there?' Latymer asked.

The driver looked puzzled. 'One and sixpence. What do you want to know for?'

'Oh nothing, just wondered.'

The man made another puzzled look at Latymer in the rear mirror. 'This is the main road into town. We crossed the River Soar awhile back. I forgot to point it out to you. We're going to New Walk. Lovely place for a stroll on a Sunday with the missus and kids. You married?' the driver asked.

'No.'

'Or walking your girlfriend,' he mused, and catching Latymer's eye in the rear view window, he winked at the doctor. Bringing himself back to earth he said briskly, 'Here we are then. One and seven pence, please.'

'Two shillings. Thanks for the guide. Keep the change.'

The Club was an imposing building that looked as if it should be made of white marble. There were two pillars outside, giving it a feeling of pomp. Latymer walked up the steps to the Oddfellows Club. A man dressed in footman's livery stepped forward. Another car drew up and he heard footsteps behind him briskly climbing the steps.

'Evening, Sir Brian, sir.' The doorman at the door gave a brief salute.

'Leonard,' he replied without eye contact with the doorman.

'Are you a member, sir?' the doorman asked Latymer.

'No. I–'

'Members only, I'm afraid, or invited guests.' The doorman raised a glimmer of hope in his voice.

Latymer told him, 'I am expected to meet Dr McFadden.'

'I'll see if he's in. I've only just come on duty.'

'I'm having dinner with him.' Latymer was speaking to the doorman's back.

The doorman turned briefly. 'I'll be two minutes. Take a seat, sir.'

'No, thank you.' Latymer stood waiting impatiently. He just wanted to be at home with one of Edna's nameless stews, the radio, a whisky, a bath, and bed, not hanging around the entrance of a club whilst a pompous doorman decided whether he was good enough to be let into an upperclass men's club that he'd never want to join.

'Latymer.' McFadden's voice rang out, sounding as if the old doctor achieved twice the amount of work that Latymer did in a day. In reality it was half, and McFadden was proud of it. Perhaps Latymer would be the same in thirty years time.

Latymer turned. 'Dr McFadden.'

'Come, man, rest easy. My name's Angus. What do you prefer to be called, Peter or Latymer?'

'Either works.'

'Latymer it is then.' McFadden paused as if listening to his own voice. 'Has a ring to it. A drink?'

'Bitter.'

'Bitter it is then.'

The two doctors were standing in a large hallway inside the eighteenth century former paleaceous dwelling. Stairs swept up to a gallery where there were other rooms. Oil paintings, that Latymer assumed to be portraits of the Leicestershire notables, hung on the walls. This was a place of civilised refinement.

'The council wants to turn the place into a museum,' remarked Dr McFadden, 'if they can get the deeds.'

It's nearly one, Latymer decided as he contemplated the room.

Dr McFadden led Latymer into a sitting room which was filled with haphazardly arranged armchairs. On their way to a pair of chairs surrounding a small table, Dr McFadden stopped. 'Sir Brian.'

The seated man stood up and said, 'Dr McFadden, a pleasure to see you,' though his voice sounded otherwise.

'This is our new doctor to the practice, Peter Latymer.'

Latymer and Sir Brian shook hands. Sir Brian's handshake was firm, and he was obviously used to being in authority. 'Also a pleasure to meet you,' he said to Latymer looking him straight in the eye. 'I expect from time to time our paths will cross.' He picked up his brandy glass from the table, gave it a swirl and gulped from it. 'I have to be on my way. There are days when your work never stops.'

Dr McFadden nodded sagely.

Sir Brian put down his glass and left the drink unfinished. 'Angus. Dr Latymer.' He made a short bow and left.

Dr McFadden looked down at the glass. 'Such a waste.' Latymer believed for a moment that McFadden was going to down it.

'Come on, man. Closer to the fire. We'll order our drinks and meal. They have very fine duck here at the moment. Freshly shot, then hung for a day or three.'

They sat in silence. Latymer became aware of a presence entering the room and looking around. A well-dressed man stood for a moment, then left.

McFadden leant over and whispered, 'Joles, our local Member of Parliament. You won't be having anything to do with him. We've never spoken. A nodding acquaintance.'

Sitting over half a duck and rich brown gravy, winter vegetables, crispy potatoes, and a good red Burgundy, Latymer couldn't help but wonder where the food came from when the country was suffering under rationing. In fact, food was in short supply. If this was the fare of a gentlemen's club in a small town like Leicester, then what went on in London? What were the King and Queen and Prime Minister eating tonight? How did this equate with little Amy lying by a fire, coughing out her lungs? Did Amy and her mother have enough to eat, let alone today, but tomorrow as well?

As beautiful as it was, the duck began to leave a bitter taste. They'd been talking medicine all evening, the rota, which of them would do what, when, and so on. Latymer knew that he'd agreed to do too much, as he was working three Saturdays to every one of Dr McFadden's. He was the junior partner; Dr McFadden had a wife and children, different commitments. All evening they'd talked nothing of their backgrounds. Neither knew anything about the other, so Latymer decided to take the conversation in that direction.

'What does your wife do then when you're out on evenings like this?' asked Latymer.

Dr McFadden looked sharply up from his plate. A look of sadness and anger crossed his face. He went pale. 'You don't know, boy?'

'I'm sorry, I don't know what?' Latymer shook his head knowing now that it had been the wrong question to ask.

'No, you don't. You're no fool. You should have been told. Probably by me when we first met rather than when drinking whisky. She died in 1941. Coventry, an air raid. She was in the cathedral.'

'I'm sorry. I'm so sorry. I didn't know.' Latymer wanted to be any where else other than with the bitter middle-aged man.

'No, of course you didn't. In answer to your question, my wife won't be *doing* very much. I don't believe in heaven, so there's an end to it. She won't be anywhere waiting for me. I don't believe in that nonsense. That's why I try to cure the sick to give them as long as possible on Earth. I haven't been the same since she died. *Odd*fellows, hm, right this is the club for me. Don't worry, I know what they say. I'm just an old fool.'

Latymer tried to protest that this wasn't the case.

McFadden put down his glass with an air of finality.

That finished the conversation. They picked at sponge pudding and drank their coffee and brandies. They sat in near silence, Dr McFadden staring off into the distance whilst tamping the tobacco in his pipe.

Latymer's first impression had been that McFadden lacked compassion; now he could see the death of his wife hurt him so much that there were only feelings for himself. The rest of his life was only a burden to be carried.

'I'd better go. An early start in the morning.'

'Yes, your first Saturday. I'll drop by during the morning. You'll be all right.' McFadden called to the waiter as he passed, 'A taxi for my colleague.'

'Yes, and thank you for an excellent meal. I don't remember the last time I ate so well.'

'Taxi for Dr Latymer,' called Leonard.

'Good night man, rest easy,' said McFadden as they shook hands.

Chapter Five

Sir Brian Britley owned most of the industry in the Midlands and a finger in the pie of the rest. The capitalist's chief endeavour was manufacturing cars. He collected vintage models, boasting a Rolls Royce, Bentley, and even a Buggatti. He owned a large factory in Leicester recycling scrap metal, Britley's Plate Metals, which was the employer of most people from Stocking Farm.

The metal was processed in Leicester, then transported by train to Coventry for the manufacture of cars. Britley was determined that within twenty years a good proportion of working class families in the British nation would own the Britley Runaround 1.1. The resolve for Sir Brian was that his employees would drive to work in the vehicles they were producing.

On the evening that Drs Latymer and McFadden were having dinner together, Sir Brian held an important meeting with Lord Wakeham of Budleigh.

Lord Wakeham was a Junior Minister in the National Government for the Defence Department. Britley, with the offer the plutocrat had in mind, expected that Lord Wakeham would be able to arrange for him a great source of iron scrap for his factory in Leicester.

The previous Tuesday, Lord Wakeham held a meeting with the Minister for Defence, Sir Henry Norrington. Lord Wakeham told Sir Henry, 'As any metal machinery arrives back in Britain from the armed forces,' Lord Wakeham put great emphasis on the final statement to show its importance, 'Sir Brian Britley would take it all for the good of the nation.'

Sir Henry had read the papers days before and the decision was already made, but he paused to show that the proposal needed serious consideration. After a few moments he said, 'Yes, I like it. And he will be paying for all of this?'

'Of course, and as well as that, he will be taking anything that the army has as surplus and disposing of it as he sees fit.' Lord Wakeham added the final statement sounding as if it were a bonus, a charitable act that Britley was making.

Sir Henry interrupted him. 'What is the other surplus?' Sir Henry knew it was his turn to play the very grave government minister now. 'You don't mean armaments? That is of paramount importance. Armaments aren't up for grabs.' Norrington made a great fuss of his breathing as he spoke to show that he was being very serious.

'Goodness no, Minister.' Lord Wakeham feigned disbelief that the minister could believe such a thing was in the realms of possibility. 'He will buy everything, except armaments. Uniforms, maps, stationery, foodstuffs, and the like.'

'We don't want him selling armaments to a banana republic. Hitler all over again.' Sir Henry spoke to Lord Wakeham as if the peer were a schoolboy.

Ignoring the overture, Wakeham carried on. 'Also, Minister,' Lord Wakeham knew that now was the time to play the ace of diamonds. 'Sir Brian will pay above our asking price.'

'What do you mean?' Sir Henry frowned, as he felt he was expected to, 'I don't follow.'

'Sir Brian's payment doesn't have to show on the contract that we will have with him.' Lord Wakeham could not help himself smiling.

Sir Henry wanted to make sure he wasn't walking into a trap. 'What are you suggesting?'

'A perk of the job, Minister.' Lord Wakeham's voice was barely audible. Anyone listening at the door would have never heard.

'Is anyone else aware of this?' Sir Henry replied.

'Minister, I wouldn't tell a soul. Your PPS was informed that this meeting was confidential, Government security for the good of the nation.'

Sir Henry felt a smug satisfaction that care had been taken of His Majesty's interests, as well as his own.

'And of course,' Lord Wakeham went on, 'it will create jobs both in Leicester and Coventry and transport on the railways. Britley's factories are in Coventry, but only part of the city. It is a sad place that needs building up after the terrible bombings. The cathedral.'

'Cut the sentiment, Lord Wakeham,' said Sir Henry, quite unkindly. 'Save that for the fools in Parliament. We're dealing with economics and government.'

'It goes without saying that he wants to make money.' Lord Wakeham avoided saying, don't we all. 'But he doesn't, and I can't stress this enough, expect or want government support or grants.'

'I like that last point. Draw up the document. Let me see it. Get this Britley to agree to it. I don't like to be seen with capitalists. And we'll take it from there.'

'The whole operation is set up.' Wakeham rather stupidly said.

The Minister's eyebrows shot up questionably. When necessary he could be very sharp. 'Is it now?' Sir Henry didn't like his ministers going behind his back. He wanted to know everything that was going on before it happened.

Realising his error, Lord Wakeham backtracked. 'I mean, the housing estate in Leicester, I believe it is called Stocking Farm, was built to solve a housing problem, but few jobs were there. Sir Brian has his factory manufacturing sheet metals, but he can easily expand. I mean, obviously, we are waiting upon your final decision, which I know will be fairly taken.'

'Well, I doubt he's running a charity, is he? No doubt expands his pocket as well.' Sir Henry didn't attempt to hide the sarcasm in his voice.

'You're in agreement, then?' asked Lord Wakeham, hoping for the reply he wanted to hear.

'In principle.' Sir Henry sighed as if it took a terrible effort to make the decision. 'Yes.'

***

Lord Wakeham travelled to Leicester by car on Friday. He booked into the Grand Hotel and sat in his suite, warming a glass of brandy between his palms, waiting for Sir Brian.

After Sir Brian arrived and been shown to the plush suite, Lord Wakeham of Budleigh and Sir Brian the capitalist talked and laughed, discussed and joked as if at ease with one another, both aware it was a game of chess trying to out manoeuvre the opponent and avoid any errors in the sensitive negotiation.

After a time they became serious and passed papers between them. It all rested on their shoulders. They agreed there should be no witnesses to the meeting. Lord Wakeham's driver was waiting for him. He was his only staff.

The two men read the words carefully, nodded sagely as if their lives depended on it. Sir Brian made offers, promises. Lord Wakeham looked affronted, but agreed that times were hard in the dark years of the war, and now he deserved his just rewards.

'It will be a service to the country I love,' the big man, Sir Brian, said. 'It will create jobs for our returning servicemen. We failed them after the last war. The nation needs to be economically sound if she is going to continue to be the great nation she is.'

'Quite. *Non sibi sed posteris*,' answered Lord Wakeham quoting the only piece of Latin he knew.

'I couldn't have put it better myself,' answered Sir Brian, having no idea what the Latin phrase meant.

The papers were then signed and exchanged. The agreement, verbal and formal, made. Both men smiled with satisfaction and sat back in their armchairs in Lord Wakeham's suite. The bed wasn't for sleeping. Lord Wakeham wouldn't be staying in the hotel that night.

'Dinner now then,' said Sir Brian. 'Seal the deal.'

'Thank you, Sir Brian, but I must get straight back to Westminster. I hope to see the Minister tonight. You'll hear from me, perhaps as early as tomorrow.'

'Excellent.'

And he did.

***

A few weeks later, Sir Henry Norrington, the mendacious Defence Minister, announced to the House of Commons his achievement for an economic upturn in conquering an unemployment black spot in the Midlands. He said there would be jobs for the foreseeable future, how optimism was rife for the good of the nation after the dark years of the war. Plump Sir Henry Norrington sat down, full of self importance and pride.

Members of Parliament from all sides waved their order papers and there were cries of 'hear, hear!'

Chapter Six

The next morning, Saturday, the surgery was busy. As with Monday to Friday, they could have done with two doctors working. Any belief Latymer held that it was the weekend and people would want to take it easier was unfounded. Of course, most people still worked, as if it were any usual workday. By the end of the morning he would be finished.

Home visits weren't the norm on a Saturday, except for the direst of emergencies. There was one already, so he decided that he would pay a visit to the little girl with the cough, Amy Harshaw. Instinctively he didn't feel sure that if the girl was worse, the mother would have 'let the doctor know.' But he felt pity for her.

Olive came into his surgery with the medical records for the day in the order that the patients would be seen. She was followed by Edna bearing a cup of tea.

She whispered, 'Bring you another later,' as she left the room, knowing that it was wrong to disturb Olive from her important task.

Olive put the papers on his desk. 'Forty-two and one home visit. Honestly, we could do with both of you here on Saturday. Hopefully you'll be finished everything by midday. If I were you, I should ignore the telephone and the door after all this. Have the rest of the weekend off. They know where the hospital is.'

'Which hospital do we use?'

'The Leicester Royal Infirmary.'

'And how would I prescribe penicillin? Would I get that from the hospital?' he asked her.

'You wouldn't get penicillin anywhere. It is for troops only.' She made to leave. 'Oh yes,' she looked at a piece of paper. 'A woman rang, asking for you. Yesterday morning, but with one thing and another, I've forgotten until now. She said it was personal.'

Latymer looked up from his papers. 'Did she leave a name?'

'No, only a number.'

'Okay.'

'What would you like doing with it, Doctor?' Olive was feeling aggrieved with his attitude. Was he cross because she'd forgotten? Fridays were always busy. She was against personal calls in principle. Especially when the caller couldn't be bothered to leave a name.

'As you like.'

'I'll put it by the telephone in the sitting room. Then you can do what you like.'

'Okay.'

She didn't like being there on a Saturday morning either and said so, though she knew she was speaking to the wrong person. Dr McFadden would hear it from her later, 'This practice could do with two receptionists, and now Dr Latymer's in the house full-time, Edna could do with the help.'

'Olive?'

She turned, wondering what his query would be, he'd been nothing but questions that morning. She wanted to get on with her work and be at home with her mother.

'Dr McFadden told me about his wife.'

'Didn't you know?'

'No.'

'He's taken it hard. If I'd known you didn't know, I'd have told you. I'm very sorry. The war caused us all tragedies.' She left the room and Latymer began his Saturday morning patients. The mysterious call went completely from his mind.

The home visit was only a bad cold – a complete waste of his time. There were more important ways for a doctor to use his skills. All he could do was to tell the patient to keep warm, stay in bed, take an aspirin and drink plenty of fluids. It was common sense, and in time he would come to wish that people would use common sense rather than believing the doctor was the cure-all.

When he got to Amy Harshaw's house he was surprised at what he found. The little girl was by the fire in the front room as he'd instructed, but there were two people with the mother.

'I wasn't expecting you, Doctor. I didn't send for you.' Amy's mother was abrupt.

'I was passing. I wanted to see how she was,' Latymer replied on the defensive.

'I think she's all right, don't we, Mum?' Grandma nodded confidently. 'Amy's grandma and grandpa come round to see her.'

'She hasn't woken yet, though,' the man said. He lit a cigarette.

'Put that out. You shouldn't be smoking around her.'

The man was affronted. 'Didn't think it would do any harm. I didn't know.'

Latymer leant over Amy and lifted back one of her eyelids. The pupil showed no reaction, blank, no sign of life. He took her wrist to feel her pulse. It was very weak. 'Have you tried to wake her?'

'No.'

'Why?'

'Isn't sleep the best cure?'

'She's unconscious. She needs to be in hospital. Do you have a telephone?' He looked round the room. 'No, of course you don't.'

'Beryl does down the road. Very la-di-da.'

'I don't need to know her background. Get an ambulance. Run, man,' Latymer shouted at Amy's grandfather. 'Nine-nine-nine. She needs to be in hospital.'

For his age the man certainly could go apace, as the ambulance was with them in less than ten minutes. Ambulance officers came into the room bearing a stretcher.

'I'm Dr Latymer. Girl, aged seven. She's unconscious. Probably pneumonia. Hardly any pulse.'

They put her on a stretcher and very carefully, but swiftly, wrapped her in red blankets. The officers carried Amy to the waiting ambulance.

Women and children came out of their houses at the sound of an ambulance. They stood on the pavement, the women many with their hair in curlers, wearing dirty aprons over grubby clothes. Christmas slippers, once new and fresh, now tatty and faded with socks around their ankles, the onlookers watched silently. The sight of the ambulance caused a distraction and excitement for another dreary Saturday morning.

The Doctor, The Plutocrat, and The Mendacious Minister

'Do you think she's going to die?' a child asked his mother.

The thought had occurred to Latymer as well.

Latymer, Amy's mother, and one of the officers sat in the back of the ambulance with the child. Her mother sat on a bench opposite, stroking her daughter's forehead, holding the child's hand, repeating the mantra, 'She looked asleep.'

Latymer sat and waited, passing a very occasional word with the other medical man. For such a speedy pick-up, it seemed to take forever to get to the hospital. Finally though, they were backing into a covered way and the doors of the ambulance were thrown open. A doctor and two nurses with looks of genuine concern stood waiting.

'She's unconscious,' said Latymer out loud to the hospital staff as the stretcher slid out onto a waiting trolley.

'Yes. We can see that, Dad,' one of the nurses said beginning to briskly walk away behind the moving trolley. 'You look after your wife.'

Latymer chased after them. The nurse stopped and turned. 'I'm sorry, you'll have to wait here.'

'I'm the girl's doctor.'

Realising her error, the nurse apologised. The pair moved quickly forward after Amy, catching up with her before she disappeared into a room.

When they reached a side room a doctor was already examining Amy. Latymer introduced himself, 'Dr Latymer.'

'Dr Racre,' came the reply. The man spoke with an American accent. 'We have one very sick little girl here.'

'Yes, I know.'

'We need to get fluids into her. Her temperature should come down. I don't think there's a lot more we can do except keep a careful eye on her and hope her body is strong enough to fight the sickness.'

'Penicillin? Penicillin would cure her.'

Racre took no notice of him as if Latymer wasn't present. 'Nurse, let's get her up onto McCartney ward and make her comfortable. Then we can let her mother see her.'

Fifteen minutes later Latymer and the American were standing at the end of Amy's bed. She looked a little more peaceful.

'Penicillin. Maybe you didn't hear me, Dr Racre.'

'Augustin.'

'Peter.'

'I heard you, Peter. Penicillin. It wasn't my intention to be rude, I ignored you. More chance of landing on the moon than getting any penicillin.'

'Why?' Latymer asked.

'Oh, it's around and it would probably cure Amy, but there's far too little of it in production. Your government decided 'for troops only,' Racre said with a passable King's English accent as if he were the government health minister, 'That is until the drug is mass produced.'

Latymer reflected for a moment. 'Can't have injured soldiers, ill soldiers, returning and *then* dying.'

'You got it, buddy.'

They never told him this at university. Penicillin was to be the miracle cure-all.

'I can't sit and watch and do nothing. I'm going to get the drug somehow.' Latymer voiced his thoughts out loud.

'Like I say, no chance.' Defeated, Racre sadly shook his head.

***

Dr McFadden sat by his fire, smoking his pipe. It was remarkable, he mused, how all these separate flats contained a fireplace. He was a scientific man, but he found it difficult to imagine how all the fireplaces and flues were connected to one chimney, or perhaps it wasn't one chimney, but many. He would try and look on the roof when he next went out. If he went up to a higher floor in Lewis' Department Store, perhaps he could see the roof of his block of flats.

It was a good flat that he owned. A woman came into clean it once a week. It was large enough for a married couple, so it suited the doctor well for his needs. As well as the bathroom, there was a small kitchen, which he only used to make toast and tea, a living room, and two other rooms which, he supposed, originally were intended to be bedrooms. He used the smaller of these to sleep in, and kept the larger as his consulting room for private patients.

McFadden was expecting one later, a Mrs Armstrong. She insisted that she suffered from a bad heart, and Dr McFadden played along. Just as people worshipped their religion and priests, others worshipped their doctors and a few of them paid a lot to do so. He gave her a thorough examination every time she came. He told her what she wanted to hear and prescribed her harmless drugs. Mrs Armstrong paid fifty pounds for a good half hour of his time. If there were fools around willing to waste money like this, then he might as well be the one to take it rather than another doctor.

Mrs Armstrong hung on his every word. After her visit, off she would go with, 'Mr McFadden said this; Mr McFadden said that.' Mrs Armstrong always called him 'Mr,' as a 'Mr' was higher in the rungs of experience than merely a doctor. When she stood at his door he exclaimed, 'Why, Mrs Armstrong,' as if it were his greatest pleasure to see her.

The telephone rang. He hoped it wasn't Mrs Armstrong cancelling. He wanted to give Gerry, his youngest who was still in medical school, extra spending money at Christmas. If it were her, he could try and wangle a home visit. Perhaps she was definitely ill and unable to see him. There had been a few bouts of influenza and colds that week.

He picked up the receiver. 'McFadden.'

'Dr McFadden?'

He'd just said that. 'Yes.'

'Angus?'

'To whom am I speaking?'

'Dr Latymer. Peter.'

'Hello, Peter. I didn't recognise your voice. It's the first time I've heard you on a telephone. Is there a problem? I'm sorry I didn't make it to the surgery this morning.' He felt a lie was in order. 'Er, er an important matter came up. Did everything go all right?'

'Yes and no. I'll get straight to the point. I need the drug penicillin.' McFadden heard a sense of urgency in Latymer's voice.

'There's no chance. It's for troops only. Government policy.' There are hopes you need to kill dead straight away. McFadden knew this was one of them. No point in running around on a fool's errand.

'I know all that.' Latymer was getting angry at being given the same message and sounded it.

'Rest easy, man.'

This phrase of Angus' was also irritating him, and only a few days had passed since their first meeting. 'I am.'

'All right, all right. What's the problem?' McFadden attempted to sound more kind and understanding.

Latymer explained about Amy.

Dr McFadden's doorbell rang. 'I'm sorry, I'm going to have to answer my door. I'm expecting a patient. You sound in a state. I'll call you back in five minutes, no more I promise.'

'Yes, please do.'

Dr McFadden opened his door. 'Mrs Armstrong,' he beamed, 'a pleasure to see you. Come on in.'

She seemed a little flustered. 'The lift has broken. I was forced to climb the stairs. I don't know what that has done to my heart.'

Probably given it the first exercise in years. But McFadden knew better than to say so. 'Now, don't you worry. Come into the living room and sit down by the fire. Take a small medicinal brandy.'

'I shouldn't. Oh, it's the first time I've been in here.' She looked around the room, taking it all in so that she could tell her friends how privileged she was, seeing Mr McFadden's lovely sitting room.

'A brandy will do you the world of good.' He smiled down on her with authority, thinking I don't have the time for all this. 'Doctor's orders.'

'If you say so, Mr McFadden.' She sounded like a silly little girl.

'Now, Mrs Armstrong, I have an emergency I have to deal with. My new partner, a young Dr Latymer, has a problem. Can I leave you for a few minutes?'

'No hurry, Mr McFadden, if it's an emergency.' She liked the idea of playing her part in a drama. 'I could be here until the Sheriff of Leicestershire's Ball tonight.'

Oh dear, Dr McFadden sighed to himself, *six hours with Mrs Armstrong*, but he managed a smile. 'I may see you there myself.'

'I shall have to watch what I do then.'

He laughed as was expected of him, left the room, and closed the door. He picked up the receiver and dialled the number of the surgery. Latymer answered immediately as if he'd been standing over the instrument.

'Latymer.'

'Angus. Now, what's the problem?' Latymer explained the circumstances in greater detail, that the drug penicillin was the one needed to help Amy. 'I understand, but we can't prescribe it. It's for the forces only.'

'But why? Why?' Latymer was feeling anger and despair that the miracle drug he'd been taught so much about wasn't, in fact, available.

'A political debate is pointless, and being angry isn't going to get you anywhere. Rest easy, man.'

There was a pause as Latymer tried to calm down while McFadden contemplated the problem for a few moments.

'There is one avenue I can try. But I won't make any promises. Patient's name and hospital?' he commanded.

Latymer told him, 'Amy Harshaw. McCartney Ward. Leicester Royal Infirmary.'

McFadden repeated it back to make sure he had it right. 'Wait where you are. I'll ring you back either way. Don't hold your hopes out, though.'

He went back into the living room. 'Mrs Armstrong, I'm very sorry, but I have another important call to make. A child's life may depend on it.'

'Oh, no. You must go and make your call. We didn't fight this war so that our children could die now.' She spoke as if she herself drove a centurion tank during the war and had never bought luxuries off the black market.

Again McFadden picked up the receiver and dialled a number that he knew by heart. He knew that the possibility of a positive outcome here was remote. He should have just told Latymer 'No way,' rather than give him a thread of hope. He should have told him to drink his sorrows away with a bottle of whisky and wake up again for work on Monday morning. But that was his way. He didn't want to blunt the young man's compassion.

'USAF Bruntingthorpe,' a woman's voice said. She sounded very British for an American airbase.

'Could I speak to Captain McFadden?'

'I'll try to connect.' He could hear the clicks and bells and voices 'USAF Bruntingthorpe, hold on caller.' Surprisingly on a Saturday afternoon two years after the war was over, it sounded like a busy base. 'Trying Mess.'

Finally he heard a voice speaking loudly against the hubbub of noise and laughter. 'Mess.'

It occurred to Dr McFadden that they obviously started partying early there. 'Captain McFadden, please. Dr James McFadden. I need to speak to him urgently. I'm his father.'

'I think he's here. Saw a girl on top of him awhile ago. Probably shouldn't have told you that.' The man giggled stupidly.

'I don't care. Please, hurry.' McFadden just wanted the silly man to stop the schoolboy stupidity and get on with it.

'Sorry, I'll see if I can find him.'

49

After what seemed an age a voice said, 'What's wrong? Is it Gerry?' James spoke loudly.

'I can hardly hear you,' McFadden said to his son. 'This is important.' He shouted as loudly as he dared without startling Mrs Armstrong. 'Important!'

'I'll get it transferred to an office. Hang on.' McFadden waited again. 'Dad, what's wrong? Is it Gerry?' Dr McFadden could hear now as if all the party goers had suddenly gone home. He explained the situation to his son, what they needed, and why.

'That's impossible, Dad. That would be stealing drugs, and then morphine goes missing and they'd pin it on me. I'd never be trusted again.' It was as if McFadden could hear his son shaking his head.

'I've got a young doctor here. He's losing faith in the system and he's only been practising a week.'

'Dad, I'll have to speak to the Major. It's too big a decision for me to make.'

'We need this yesterday, James.'

'I know. I'll get back to you as soon as I can.'

Dr McFadden went back into the living room. 'Mrs Armstrong, I'm so sorry.'

'Did you get everything sorted?' Mrs Armstrong asked. 'I thought I heard you raise your voice.'

He ignored her comment. 'I'm waiting for another telephone call. I could start your examination. It could be awhile.'

'I don't mind waiting.'

'Shall we say ten minutes?'

She nodded. 'You have it very cosy in here.'

'Thank you.' McFadden managed a smile. 'Another brandy?' He was pouring the drink, ignoring her protestations, when the telephone rang again. 'I'll have to get that.' He passed her the glass and hurried into the hallway.

'McFadden.'

'Dad, tell your man I'm on my way.'

'Leicester Royal Infirmary, McCartney Ward, Amy Harshaw. Drive carefully.' McFadden guessed his son was under the influence of alcohol.

'No worries, Dad. I've got a driver.'

McFadden put down the receiver and dialled the number for Latymer. 'The penicillin will be at the hospital within twenty minutes.'

'How did you do that? No, don't bother. Thank you. Thank you. I'm on my way.' Latymer put down the receiver. It rang immediately. He looked at it in the dark hallway as he went out of the door. *No, ignore it, I've got to get to the hospital.* Latymer left it ringing as he drove down the drive.

Everybody's on their way to help out a very sick child, mused Dr McFadden, and I'm on my way to examine neurotic Mrs Armstrong.

Latymer drove as fast as he dared. He knew that his getting there now would have little effect on the recovery of the girl, but he wanted to be there, to see that the drug arrived in the correct place.

He ran into the hospital. He walked as quickly as he dared without hurtling down the corridors and injuring anyone. He went into McCartney Ward. It was very quiet. An atmospheric silence hung over the whole place. A nurse in startling blue came out of an office.

'I'm sorry, but visiting is over for the day.'

'Dr Latymer. I'm here to see Amy Harshaw. Has her penicillin arrived?'

'I tried telephoning you. But I could never get through. The line was engaged.'

'What do you mean?' He pushed past her and went to Amy's bed. He stood at the foot of it. The bed was empty; stripped of its sheets and blankets. The child was gone. 'Where is she?' He knew the awful answer before she replied.

'I'm sorry, Dr Latymer. She passed away.'

He became aware of another figure standing beside him. He was holding a small glass bottle. 'I got here as soon as I could,' said James McFadden.

'She's dead,' whispered Latymer.

Chapter Seven

He wanted to know the mistake he'd made in diagnosing Amy. How he could have saved her life. Should he have sent her to the hospital the first time he saw her? Everybody at the hospital seeing his distress was very kind, saying what a saint he was in trying to get the new wonder drug and then succeeding was remarkable. But it was no good. The little girl was dead and he felt responsible. For a ridiculous reason he felt as if he were a child sent to his room for a misdemeanour, excluded from the rest of the world.

He remembered the couple of occasions that had been his punishment. One time he told an irritatingly dull aunt that she was very boring. The boy Latymer felt no guilt as he'd sat staring out of his bedroom window at nothing, furious that it was the aunt who caused him to be there. On another occasion his younger sister, Ruth, unintentionally knocked his train off the table and broke it. He'd shouted at her, 'I wish you were dead!'

Later when everyone calmed down and got over the shock of the boy saying such a terrible thing, his father quietly came up to his room and told him that he shouldn't wish anyone dead. The boy tried to make light of it by saying, 'Even Aunt Enid?'

'Even Aunt Enid,' his father firmly replied. And the boy knew he meant it. It was a lesson he remembered when he saw the atrocities at the end of the war in Europe.

His father would say, 'If the intention is true, then the destination will be the correct one, no matter how rough the road.' If he had put these ideas down in writing, his father would have been considered, certainly in Britain, a religious mystic. Latymer knew his father didn't believe in God in the traditional Christian sense.

Unsurprisingly, Latymer found it difficult to live up to these standards, just as later he came to realise that his father had faced his own difficulties. His father's beliefs were challenged by the war, just as any faith that Latymer felt for mankind was, for a time, destroyed.

***

Back at Stocking House Latymer sat on the edge of his bed, his face in his hands as if he bore the sorrows of the world. It wasn't the first patient who died in his care. Those were too far past living by the time the Allies came across them.

In his room he shivered with the cold, but felt warmer when he remembered the bitter ice of the camps.

There was a banging at the door of the house. It woke him from his nightmare with a start. 'Dr Latymer?' a voice shouted.

'I can't do any more this weekend,' he was at a low ebb in despair. 'I shall stay here in the house, a refuge.' But he knew in his heart that he was here to save lives and that was his duty. With Amy he shouldn't have failed. In self-doubt he believed that he should have been better in his diagnosis. He continued to sit on his bed.

'Peter? I know you're there. Answer the door.' In the state he was in he couldn't think of anyone that knew him as Peter. He went to the window and looked out. There was an army Jeep in the driveway with a soldier sitting in the driver's seat. The man standing at the door looked up as if he sensed Peter looking down. 'I can see you. Come on down.' It was Captain James McFadden.

Latymer walked slowly downstairs and opened the door. He didn't need this.

At the hospital, Latymer wasn't aware that the man standing in the doorway looked like a younger version of Angus. The man would only have to look at the father to see his features in thirty year's time.

'Captain McFadden. Come in.' Latymer at least remembered his manners.

They stood in the hall. The front door was still open onto a bleak grey October afternoon growing dark. The driver sat tapping the steering wheel as if he had somewhere else to go.

'It's cold in here.' The man shivered in his greatcoat if he were a poor actor.

'Some tea?' Latymer asked.

'No. Get your coat. You're coming out,' James ordered.

'I don't feel like it.'

'I'm sure you don't. But you don't need to sit by yourself for the weekend waiting for the telephone to ring for you to go see a patient. They'll only have will be a snivelling cold. They could dose themselves with aspirin and keep warm.' He went on sarcastically, 'You can't save the world by yourself, Peter, and as soon as you learn that lesson you'll make a better doctor. You are here for surgery hours. The hospital is here for the rest of the time. You won't see my dad up here answering the telephone and door at all hours.' He paused, out of breath. 'You're coming with me for a bite to eat, then a party at the mess. We have a driver waiting. We're picking up Racre on the way and you're staying at the base overnight. I've got everything arranged. Go get your pyjamas, if you wear them, and toothbrush, and we'll be on our way.'

Latymer lacked the energy to argue.

***

They collected Augustin Racre from a corner near the hospital. He looked as though he'd been waiting for a while. He jumped into the Jeep whilst it was still moving.

'Where to, sir?' asked the driver.

'A grill. You know anywhere, Racre?' James asked.

'Yeh.' Racre gave the driver directions.

'You leapt in like you knew what you were doing.' Latymer attempted to join in on the occasion.

He made a mock salute. 'Lieutenant Augustin Racre, United States Army Marines.' He laughed. 'Done plenty of that on battlefields in Europe.'

'So what are you doing here?' asked Latymer.

'I'm serving out the last six months of my Army career seconded to your hospital ,then I shall be staying forever. I'm sticking around. I like the pubs and the cops and your half-timbered houses.'

'Ah, I see.' Latymer nodded. James looked at the scenery as if he were bored. He'd heard it all before. He knew what Racre was going to say next.

'And, well, I was going to get hitched, but she was already married. Never did understand her. Plenty of pretty nurses, though.'

They drove on in silence for a while.

'Next left?' asked the driver.

'That's correct, soldier.'

'I've got to ask. Do you know why the little girl died?' Latymer needed to know though it pained him.

'Well, you need to know. You were her doctor,' Racre replied directly to Latymer's question. 'We won't know until a proper autopsy is completed, but I'd say she drowned. Her lungs just filled with liquid and we weren't quick enough to drain it. It was too late for the penicillin.'

Latymer stared blankly at the passing buildings as if they were fascinating, trying to hide the sadness he was feeling.

'But you were a hero trying, and our friend here, the Captain,' James smiled, pleased with himself in spite of what ensued, 'I don't know what he did to get it.'

'The Major's female.' James was smiling.

'No. You didn't?' asked Racre.

'No,' James replied. 'You may meet her later. She makes the Hunchback of Notre Dame look drop dead gorgeous. But no one would turn their back on a child.'

Chapter Eight

By Saturday evening, the news of Amy's death was well known on the estate. A succession of neighbours visited Amy's mother where she sat with her parents without knowing what to do. She wished she could see Latymer. She remembered the kind words spoken to her by the doctor at the hospital, but he was able to do little other than offer her tablets to help her sleep. She might take one later. She might take them all later. That was what she felt like, there was nothing to live for now. Dr Latymer would tell her what to do; she wanted him to know that she still needed him as her doctor. She didn't feel that Amy died because he failed; he was trying to save her life when she died, fighting to get a new drug.

***

At St Matthew's vicarage the Reverend Adam Lewis sat reading the *Leicester Mercury*. He noted that the town's football team had beaten Torquay. He didn't care at all for this victory, but a lot of his parishioners did, particularly the men and boys, and it could be a topic of conversation. He pretended with them that he supported his local team in Suffolk and suffered the banter when they lost.

The headline on the front page of the newspaper gave the news of how there was a strong hint that the local firm of Britley's was on the verge of signing a deal with the government, which would mean plenty of work for the area in the foreseeable future. That news did affect him. A lot of the estate worked for Britley's, and an employed workforce meant content people, fewer social problems for him to handle, and a few more pennies on the collection plate.

The vicar's wife answered the door. Adam hoped she remembered to change her footwear. He folded the paper in half and placed it on the arm of his chair. He listened to the murmuring of the voices in the hallway, but couldn't make out what they were saying. He heard his wife say, 'I'm sure he will. Wait in here and I'll check if he's able to see you now.' He knew then that she'd shown the visitor into the study. Adam got to his feet and moved towards the door.

Two years earlier, Adam took the post as Vicar of St Matthew's at Stocking Farm. When at university he believed that he would have a country church, similar to his father's in Suffolk. But he knew that where the hand of God points, there was where he would serve. His faith was unfailing. The dreadful suffering of the recent war, the horror of the atomic bomb on Hiroshima, the devastation and crimes committed in Europe, all for him were part of God's omniscience guiding the universe to an ultimate perfection, an existence of heaven, rather like Suffolk in his childhood.

Adam met his wife when they were babies. Anne was the daughter of a vicar in an adjoining parish. She was born a few months after him. Their fathers went to seminary together, their mothers obviously knew each other well. Time passed, out of nappies, played, learnt, and in each other's company for almost thirty years. Anne waited for Adam, doing voluntary war work, whilst he trained for the church.

They never spoke of love for one another or their dreams. They accepted what God held in His hands. When Adam came home after being ordained, before being sent to Leicester, he asked Anne to marry him. She accepted without a moment's hesitation. Anne always knew that she would be Adam's wife. So far their little family was made up of one child, Benjamin, asleep in an upstairs bedroom. Anne was expecting their second child. She hoped it didn't show too much; as a vicar's wife, she didn't care to think of such matters. Within a few years, though, she wanted the vicarage full of Lewis children.

Anne came into the room. 'Adam, oh you must have heard us,' she spoke as he was approaching the door.

Anne could only be described as a nondescript woman. She was wearing a full dark skirt and grey jumper to keep out the cold. Her hair was pulled back into a ponytail exposing her featureless face. Anne never wore make-up. On her feet, she wore black mules that she always put on, even when answering the door. She didn't think that a vicar's wife should be seen wearing decorative slippers. Wearing slippers being her only luxury.

Adam was similarly attired. Grey slacks and a dark jumper, usually brown, over his black shirt and clerical collar. He always wore black, well-polished, sturdy shoes so he was ready to go out at a moment's notice. A gabardine raincoat, hat and gloves waited by the front door with a furled umbrella, if needed, when the weather was inclement.

'My dear, I heard voices, but nothing more. I have no idea what the matter is.'

'It is the grandfather of the child who died today,' Anne told him.

The pair of them spoke very correctly to one another.

'Amy Harshaw,' Adam said, 'I've seen her in school.'

'Yes. The grandfather is waiting in your study.'

'I'll see him now. Perhaps you'd better offer him a cup of tea. We won't worry about the rationing today. We will make an exception as he has recently suffered a tragedy.'

Adam behaved as if his whole life was a duty and every action was by arrangement with God. He stood outside his study door and offered up a silent prayer to heaven for guidance in this coming meeting with the distressed grandparent. Anne stood behind him, her head bowed also in prayer.

Amy's grandfather stood up when Adam entered the room. The man was wearing a donkey jacket and a red beret. It was of the type ex-soldiers wore.

'Thank you for seeing me, Reverend. I'm Mr Harshaw, Amy's grandfather.'

'My calling tells me that the Lord's work must be done twenty-four hours each day,' Adam replied.

'You must be a busy man.'

'Of paramount importance is the assistance we offer to our brethren on Earth, than to be constantly in prayer and have our thoughts in heaven.' As he said this, Adam looked upwards towards the ceiling where he believed heaven to be.

Anne nodded. The man tried to look as if he understood what the Reverend meant.

'Sit down. Would you bring us a cup tea each, please?'

The way the woman was commanded by the vicar, Mr Harshaw assumed she was the housekeeper. He never expected her to be the vicar's wife. The woman was obviously expecting. He wondered who the father was and whether the vicar was the righteous man he appeared to be.

She left the room.

Reverend Lewis went to the other side of the desk and sat down. 'Now then Mr–, I'm sorry I didn't catch your name.'

'Mr Harshaw.'

'I'm sorry to hear of the tragic loss in your life. And only this very day, I understand. I have to say, and I know Mrs Lewis would feel the same, how sad I am for this terrible event in your life. I'm sure that Amy is looking down upon us from heaven.' Adam spoke kindly.

So she is his wife, mused Mr Harshaw.

In spite of the circumstances, Mr Harshaw felt comfort from these words. He wished that his daughter were present with him to hear them. Mr Harshaw would try to remember the charitable comments.

'Thank you, Reverend, that is very kind of you. The problem is, we don't know what to do now.'

'I don't understand,' Adam asked.

'When a person dies.'

'Ah, I see. Yes.' Adam put his fingers together. A habit of the Reverend's when he was at the point of giving a person practical earthly advice. 'Mr Harshaw, the death, like birth, must be registered at the Town Hall. But you won't be able to do that until Monday. You may need further information from the hospital as well. You will need to speak to your doctor.'

'Dr Latymer. He was the doctor. Yes.'

'Then,' Adam went on, 'you must arrange for the funeral. Winns and Wutteridge, I believe, is a very good firm. I would be very happy to lead the service.'

'Yes, we would like that, if you could.'

'Would you like me to come and speak to Amy's mother now, to offer her words of condolence and comfort?'

'That would be very nice, Reverend, but the wife was trying to persuade her to take one of the tablets the doctor gave her to send her off to sleep,' Mr Harshaw told him.

'I can make time for you and your family tomorrow. Will you be attending the service in the morning?'

'I think we will, yes.' Mr Harshaw nodded.

'After the service then. We will meet in here.'

The door opened. 'Ah, here's your tea.'

'Thank you, Reverend, but I can see that you're a very busy man. I'll just go home now and tell them what you told me. See if they're all right.' Mr Harshaw stood up.

'I'll see you out, Mr Harshaw,' said Anne.

They left the room. Mr Harshaw wasn't aware of the social nicety of shaking hands. Adam dragged the cup of tea over to himself. He took a small mouthful. It tasted good. An example to his flock there was to be no wastage of any foodstuffs in his vicarage, whilst there was rationing. That his wife might want to drink the tea never occurred to him. As he sipped the tea, he sat and reflected on how he would have to change his sermon tomorrow in the present circumstances.

Anne came back into the room wearing her slippers. 'Ah, you're drinking the tea.'

'Very sad, my dear,' Adam said to her.

Anne wasn't sure whether he was referring to the death of the child or that the beverage wasn't offered to her.

'I'm going to have a look at Benjamin.' Anne liked to sit by the child as he slept.

'I'll have a walk round and see Dr Latymer. He may be in need of my spiritual comfort before supper. I do need to meet him. The walk will clear my head, and help my thoughts concerning tomorrow's sermon.'

'You could invite him to eat with us. I've made a vegetable stew and there'll be plenty to go round,' Anne said.

'I'll do that.'

When Adam arrived at Stocking House, the building was in darkness. He believed there to be nobody home, but he knocked on the door anyway.

Poor man, the vicar shook his head, out on another emergency. There is no rest for vocational work such as his and mine. He walked back to the vicarage, Anne, and his meal.

Chapter Nine

The three doctors ate quietly at the grill, exchanging background information and getting to know each other better. After the meal they went back to the USAF base in Bruntingthorpe. There they drank beer and enjoyed the party.

One of the WAFs told Latymer that he was truly wild as he jitterbugged with her. There was a pianist who could play his Jelly Roll Morton like a true professional. In the end, and before the others, Latymer went to the room allocated to him a few hours earlier, and fell into bed. He was sound asleep in moments. He hadn't consumed too much alcohol. He didn't like to wake to a headache and awful hangover in the morning.

At ten o'clock on Sunday there was a knock at his door, and a man came in carrying a tray saying, 'We don't do this for anyone, even if the President of the United States or your King turned up. Breakfast in bed, I ask you, but Captain McFadden said we should spoil you.'

'I don't know what to say. Breakfast in bed is new for me, too.'

Laughed the orderly, 'Could have sent it in with one of the WAFs, then it would have been breakfast in bed.'

'This is wonderful. Thank you.' Latymer looked at the plate and wanted to know where the Americans got eggs, sausages, bacon, and tomatoes when there was rationing. It did seem that the troops were treated differently.

'When you're ready, go to the Mess, ask for Private Wolfenberger. He will drive you back to your base. I don't think that we'll be seeing much of Captain McFadden today.'

***

The RAF doctor was correct in his diagnosis and the cure that what Peter Latymer needed was a party. Here he was back at his base, Stocking House. The night was memorable, but this was the reality. Latymer wanted to get himself in order. A bath first, clean clothes, then lots of tea. Before he could make a move the telephone rang. Latymer's instinct was to ignore it, but he couldn't justify turning a deaf ear to the telephone again. He did have a duty as a doctor. He picked up the receiver reluctantly.

'Latymer.'

'Ah, you're there. You must be a very busy man. It's a wonder that you have the energy for your duties on a Monday morning.'

Latymer wondered who was this sarcastic caller.

'It is the problem with vocational work,' the voice went on, 'I was only saying to Mrs Lewis last evening over supper, that when there's a call, whether it be from the Lord or man, we must answer that call. You, Dr Latymer, obviously act beyond the call of duty.'

It must be the local vicar, Latymer realised; he could do without him right now.

'I've been ringing you for hours. I called round twice, but you were obviously out healing the sick. Is there a Mrs Latymer to restrain your enthusiasms, Dr Latymer?'

He ignored the question. 'I'm sorry, to whom am I speaking?' Latymer looked at the receiver as if it were itself insane.

'The Reverend Adam Lewis, BA, Vicar of St Matthew's, Stocking Farm. Didn't I say?'

'Good afternoon,' Latymer didn't know the correct form of address, 'Reverend Lewis.'

'A pleasure, I hope. Do you have a moment, or are you off to another emergency?'

'No, things seemed to have settled down now.'

'Perhaps I could call round?' Adam suggested.

'Are you unwell?' Latymer asked.

'No, I'm spiritually and physically very well. Thank you.'

Latymer knew what he must look like, unshaven and unkempt. He cleaned his teeth that morning and splashed a bit of water onto his face.

Now he was badly in need of a bath to rid himself of the smells of the party, cigarette smoke, alcohol, and probably women's stale perfume. The Reverend Lewis would think that he were entering Sodom and Gomorrah.

'Actually, I have a patient waiting.' Latymer knew now his destiny was hell after death for lying to a vicar. 'I would be at least an hour.'

'Ah, later I have an appointment, then evening service. I take it you will be attending?' The Reverend assumed that the doctor, as a pillar of the community, would be seen in church. He was shocked by Latymer's reply.

'I won't make any promises.' Latymer knew where he would be, and it wouldn't be attending church.

'Oh. And later supper with the Bishop.'

'I see.' Latymer felt very relieved. 'Tomorrow I could come to see you at four o'clock.'

Adam replied, 'I will need to check my diary.' There was a short pause and rustling of papers. 'I happen to be free then unless the Lord calls.'

Latymer wondered whether it was vicar humour, but the reverend didn't sound as if he were trying to be funny. 'Tomorrow it is.'

'Was there anything particular you needed to speak with me about?' asked Latymer.

'Of course. I'd like to meet you. Yes, and Amy Harshaw's mother, Mrs Harshaw, I suppose she is, though I haven't heard any talk of the father. He must have been killed in the War. So sad to lose two members of that family like that. It is all within part of God's great plan. Don't you think, Doctor?'

'You were saying?' Latymer ignored the theological discussion brewing.

'Yes. Mrs Harshaw wants you to say a few words at Amy's funeral. I'm sure that will be all right. Until tomorrow then. The Lord be with you.' He waited for a few moments as if expecting Latymer to respond likewise before he put the receiver down.

This was news to Latymer. He didn't feel that it was correct for him to speak at the girl's funeral. He hardly knew the family. He was only their doctor in a professional capacity and he felt it should remain that way. There were other patients and other priorities now. He wondered if the reverend suggested him speaking at the funeral with all his vocational nonsense.

On the other hand, perhaps for Amy's mother there was no one else. She certainly wouldn't feel as if there were anything worth living for. He felt a pang of guilt now. He shouldn't have been partying the night before. But he wasn't responsible; he must separate his professional life from his own. A wife and family would keep his priorities in check. He decided that he would wash, change, drink tea and pay a visit to Amy's mother.

Latymer walked to Amy's house. He took his medical bag, as it was a symbol of the professional visit that he was making. When he arrived at the house, he stood outside for a few moments looking at the drawn curtains. Even for a sombre winter's day it wasn't early enough to draw the curtains. He knew that this was a way to show that the occupants of the house were in mourning. On the day of the funeral the houses close by would do likewise. He went and knocked on the front door. Amy's grandfather opened it.

'Dr Latymer. Very good of you to call. Susan will be pleased to see you. Come in.'

They went into the hall. 'I called round last night,' the man went on, 'after I'd been to see the vicar, but you were out. Seeing another patient?'

'Mm.'

'A young man like yourself should be out enjoying yourself on a Saturday night.' He sighed. 'She's in here.' They went into a darkened room. 'The doctor's here, Susan.' She looked up, but said nothing, hardly recognising that Dr Latymer was in the room.

'Sit down,' Susan's mother said. He perched on the edge of the sofa. 'A cup of tea?'

'No, thank you. Don't trouble yourself. How are you feeling?' Latymer asked Susan.

'How do you think I'm feeling?' She snapped back at him.

'Susan!' exclaimed her mother horrified that her daughter should speak in such a way to the doctor who had been so good in his efforts to save Amy's life.

'It's all right. I ask as your doctor. Is there anything I can do for you?'

Straight to the point her mother said, 'She wants you to speak at Amy's funeral.'

'Do you?' Latymer needed to know whether it was what she wanted or an idea put into her mind by the Reverend Lewis.

'I'm sorry.' Susan dabbed at her eyes with at handkerchief. 'Yes. If you would.'

'I will then.' The decision was taken for him. 'Now then, Susan. Is it all right if I call you Susan?'

She nodded

'As your doctor, is there anything I can do for you?'

'No. I don't think so. That American at the hospital gave me those tablets.' She pointed to a brown bottle on the mantelpiece.

'Did they help you sleep?'

'Well, I slept.' Susan managed a smile.

'Let's have a look at you. Could you pull back the curtains?' Latymer asked Mr Harshaw.

Susan's mother looked startled. How could the doctor be so insensitive?

'Yes please, Mum. Let's have daylight in here. Amy loved the sunshine.'

Susan's mother reluctantly drew back the curtains and let in the grey fading light.

Latymer did all the usual things. He took her temperature and pulse. He listened to her heart. 'Physically, Susan, you're very healthy. Are you eating properly?'

'She's hardly eating. Other than tea, I can't get a thing down her.'

'You must eat to keep your strength up for the funeral. Amy's father, have you told her father, so he can come to the funeral?'

'Oh yes, let's do that,' Susan answered, unable to keep the fury out of her voice. 'He'll come rushing. Probably bring his wife.'

'Britley wouldn't want to know,' whispered Susan's mother to herself.

'Mum.'

Mr Harshaw spoke angrily. 'I only want to spit on the man when I see him at the factory. Of course, I can't. You don't see Mr High and Mighty very often though, stuck up in that office of his or at one of his other factories.'

Latymer found it difficult to suppress his surprise. He didn't want to intrude any further. 'Perhaps I'd better go. I'll try and drop in tomorrow.' He got up to leave.

'No, Doctor, wait. If you know half the story, you might as well know the lot, then you won't take any notice of the gossip,' Susan said.

'Don't worry on that account. I don't gossip.'

'I got her the job,' Mr Harshaw took up the story, 'when she left school. On the factory floor like. One of the girls she was down there. I feel responsible for getting her the job. I was in maintenance, so I moved all over the shop; I could keep an eye on her.'

Susan interrupted and continued, her anger giving her the strength to tell it. 'I worked there for nearly two years. I was just over sixteen. Mr Britley, as he was then, asked to see me. He offered me a job at his house in the countryside. We was well pleased. It was promotion and more money. I worked in the kitchen, cleaned, and did the shopping for them. Ran errands, you know.'

Latymer nodded, wondering whether he wanted to hear this.

'I got on quite well with Mrs Britley and became a sort of friend to her. Though, she did drink a bit. I think she enjoyed having a young person to talk to. I loved it there as well. I loved it. A nice home, good food, seeing well-known people. One day Jack Warner came for dinner and I served him. I got pregnant. Not by him, not Mr Warner. He was a real gentleman. I wish I could tell this better.'

Latymer nodded, encouraging her to carry on.

'What I mean is, Mr Britley is the only man I ever slept with.'

Susan's mother nodded in agreement as if that was something taken for granted.

Susan went on with her tale. 'He, Mr Britley, said that I was a flirt, always making eyes at the men, and that he'd heard men go into my room at night. He was the only one who'd gone into my room at night. He got rid of me. Amy was born a couple of months after my nineteenth birthday. I don't blame him for getting me pregnant. I knew what I was doing. Yes I did, Dad, don't look like that. I was flattered. An important man like him. And I loved him, fool that I was. I thought that he loved me, that he'd leave his wife. It was how he dropped me and, worse still, his daughter, Amy. I just can't understand that and now he'll never know his lovely little girl.' The whole act of telling had been too much for her and she began crying. Her mother went over to comfort her.

'I'll come again tomorrow,' Latymer said to the elder man as he was let out of the door.

***

That evening sitting by the fire built up by Bernard, Latymer was trying to read a novel by Joseph Conrad. He'd only managed the first fifty pages or so. His mind kept wandering.

He was thinking of Susan's story. She was too distraught to be telling lies, and there wasn't any reason why she should. She didn't know of the brief encounter he'd had with Britley at the Oddfellows. She was too naïve to think that he could take any action to help her. Her anger was an emotional outburst, the resentment pent up over the years which caused her to tell all. She was perhaps expressing feelings that her parents weren't aware of.

He was hypnotised by the fire, recognising the primitive need for the glow. Feeling hungry, Latymer went into the kitchen to find bread and cheese. Whilst looking, he found the cocoa as well. The bread was quite dry. There didn't seem to be any butter in the cupboards, the cheese was stale, but he felt sure his supper would be excellent.

In spite of everything, it felt good to be there in the quiet of his new home. He took the plate of food and his drink back into the sitting room. Passing the telephone he saw a piece of paper protruding from underneath the machine. He retrieved it and remembered then the telephone number that Olive had told him of the day before. He wondered about ringing. He decided after supper, if he felt like it. He finished his meagre meal, put his plate and cup on the table. His eyes closed and soon he was sound asleep.

***

The sound of the telephone ringing woke Latymer. He had no idea of how long he had slept. With a start he looked over at the machine, as if it were something he didn't recognise. He stood, gathering his thoughts, walked and picked up the receiver.

'Dr Latymer.' He spoke into the mouthpiece.

'Peter!'

'Ruth?' He glanced at the clock. The time was after nine. His sister must be calling from a callbox. Something was wrong. Father would never let his sister out after dark. 'What's happened?'

'Guess what?' She sounded excited.

'Go on.'

'We've got a telephone!'

'Dad would never allow it.'

'Mummy and I worked on him.'

'You, more like. He spoils you.'

'I rang you on Friday and spoke to a grumpy lady.'

'Olive.'

Ruth passed the receiver to her parents, and they took a turn in speaking to their son. Finally Ruth came back on the line and asked if she could visit him for a weekend.

'Of course. Let me check the rotas and I'll ring you back.' Latymer replaced the receiver. It would be good to show Ruth his new home. He was a new member of a community where already he felt he belonged. After the whirlwind of the weekend, he soon retired to bed. The house was warmer now with Latymer living in it permanently. He slept soundly.

Chapter Ten

Each day Mr Beltham went into the staffroom at precisely quarter to nine. Punctuality was one of the virtues. Otherwise, meetings amongst head and staff didn't happen. Nothing was discussed between the two camps – ever. Mr Beltham issued commands and the staff followed his orders. The teachers knew better than to question him. For Beltham there was no time at all for social chat. He knew nothing personal concerning any of his teachers or they him.

He spent his time in his office or patrolling the corridors looking for those committing misdeeds, whether they be pupils or teachers. There were no discipline problems. Simply to be threatened with being sent to Mr Beltham was all the teacher needed to say. Kinder teachers and those with good classroom control didn't menace with Beltham, as it terrified the children so much. They preferred to deal with the problems themselves.

Each morning, Mr Beltham stood in the staffroom waiting for silence. Any chatter abated within seconds following his realised presence. He never waited for long. A hush fell over the smoky room.

'Good morning,' he said. There were one or two murmurings in reply. He went straight to the point. 'Mrs Bullock, the school nurse, will be in this week looking for head lice and at the general health of the pupils. Miss Penrose, could you send a runner for this morning and this afternoon to collect pupils from their classes?' He waited for a response. 'Miss Penrose?'

'You want the name now?' She wasn't used to him expecting verbal acknowledgement.

Beltham waited, his fountain pen poised over a piece of paper. Speaking as if Miss Penrose were a tedium he suffered he said, 'It would be helpful.'

'Richard Sharpe this morning and his twin brother, Nicolas, this afternoon.'

'Thank you, Miss Penrose. Very helpful.' He didn't bother to hide the sarcasm in his voice. 'That will be all. Get along to your classes so we have an efficient start to the week. Assembly will be in ten minutes. Let me know the hymn number before you leave, Mr Symes.'

Beltham, full of importance, swept from the room.

Miss Penrose picked up her handbag from the side of her chair and hooked it onto her arm. She gathered together her few papers and the all important register. Turning to her colleague, Mr Taylor, who was just about to stand up, she said, 'I don't understand why he has to be so rude. If the children behaved like that he'd go through the roof.'

'Yes,' said Mr Taylor, 'he has his problems, though.'

'Problems? Speak to me about problems with the likes of him.'

'Well, his wife is very ill.'

'I didn't know that.' Miss Penrose frowned.

'Hm, it may not excuse him?'

'But it doesn't help.'

'Come on then,' said Mr Taylor as if he were in charge, 'on our way before we get into trouble.'

***

At around the same time school was getting underway Latymer was speaking to Olive in the reception area of the surgery. He decided over breakfast that he wanted to meet with Sir Brian Britley.

'What shall I say when I'm asked why?'

'As little as possible, Olive. Tell him–'

Olive interrupted him, 'Or more like his secretary.'

'I'm new to the practice and I want to meet important people in the area, such as him, the vicar, and school nurse, and so on.'

'Mrs Bullock is in school all this week. She helps out here when we need her. That is if you want to meet her. She isn't everybody's cup of tea.'

He raised his eyebrows enquiringly.

'You'll see when you meet her,' Olive said.

'Well, there's a challenge. I'll go into school one day this week as well then. No need to make an appointment.'

He went into his surgery and Olive followed him a few minutes later. 'Sir Brian's secretary,' she said, 'has arranged an appointment for you today at four fifteen. He's away for the rest of the week.'

'Excellent, except now you have to contact the Reverend Lewis and tell him I can't make the meeting with him at four.'

'Oh no!' She held up her hands in despair. 'He's always Lording this and Lording that and how everything is God's will. I'll need at least an hour to make the call.'

'Good point. Make my meeting with him for five thirty, then I can say I've got to be back here for evening surgery.'

'Dr McFadden has asked whether you will start home visits at ten this morning and he'll do the rest of the surgery here. Take the car.'

'Fine by me. Show in the first patient. Olive, let's get the show underway.'

She smiled as she left the room. It was good to have a young person with energy and enthusiasm around the surgery.

***

Like many young men, he enjoyed driving and the feeling of freedom it gave him to be away from surgery. The home visits Latymer made that day were straightforward, though many of the cases could have come along to the surgery. It was a senseless use of petrol in time of rationing and waste of his time. It crossed his mind to visit Racre at the hospital, but to be more practical, he had his first meeting of the day with local 'pillars of the community.'

Latymer decided his to visit Willowtree Primary School first. He went through the double doors that led to the main corridor in the school. These doors would be completely out of bounds to the children. The whole building was in silence as if he had discovered the Marie Celeste of schools. In the distance he heard footsteps echo down an otherwise empty corridor.

A boy turned the corner. He was smart and clean. He was followed by a gaggle of children walking in pairs holding hands. One of them let go of his partner and started waving frantically. It took Latymer a moment to realise it was little Anthony Lambert. He returned the wave and Anthony, obviously with pride, told the boy next to him that the doctor remembered who he was. The pupil in charge led them to a door where they waited in silence. The boy carried on walking up the corridor to Latymer.

Very politely the boy asked, 'Can I help you, sir?'

'Yes, please. I'm looking for the headmaster's office.'

'Mr Beltham.' He pointed to a door. 'That one,' then he made his way back to the queue.

Latymer tapped on the door. A voice from inside shouted, 'What now, Sharpe?'

The boy turned to Latymer, 'That's me. He thinks it's me knocking.'

Latymer tried again. The voice yelled, 'If I come over to that door and it's a waste of my time, you blithering idiot.' The headmaster opened the door and Latymer received the full blast of Mr Beltham's fury. 'Why Miss Penrose chose–, Oh, it's you.'

'That's right, Mr Beltham. It's me. May I come in?'

'What do you want?'

'I'd like to introduce myself to Nurse Bullock. I understand she's in school this week.'

'She's down the corridor. The boy will show you.' He pointed to Sharpe.

'I thought it polite, Mr Beltham,' he said loudly so the children could hear, 'to notify the headmaster of my presence when I came into his school. I have always believed myself to be courteous.'

The children were now agog with the exchange between the two men.

'Come in, Dr Latymer.' Both men stood facing one another as if it were a standoff. 'You're very young.'

'Does one become less polite then with age? I'm not aware of a lack of manners with Dr McFadden.' He paused and rather obviously began his introduction again, 'Mr Beltham, I was passing. I knew that Mrs Bullock was in the school and I wanted to introduce myself. I can make an appointment, if you're very busy.'

'No, I'll take you there.'

Both men left the office and walked down the corridor in silence. The children went to attention as Mr Beltham approached. As they reached the door a scream came from within the room and a woman's voice shouted, 'Come here, you stupid child. It'll hurt if I clout you round the ear.'

It was as if Latymer were a visitor to Dotheboys Hall.

Mr Beltham opened the door to the nurse's room and they went in. Both woman and child froze at the sight of the headmaster.

'Nurse Bullock, this is Dr Latymer. He is new to Dr McFadden's practice.'

She nodded acknowledgement. Her silence betrayed what she was truly thinking; another young inexperienced locum that she could bully.

Latymer attempted to smile at the woman. She was like her name, large and fierce. 'Is there a problem?' he asked.

'He won't let me take the plaster off. I need to see the cut underneath that he says is there. I expect it's nothing,' said Mrs Bullock, pulling a face with ease whilst she did so.

'She just pulls it off and it hurts like mad.'

'Don't be rude, Lambert. That is Nurse Bullock.' Beltham gestured in the direction of the Nurse.

Nurse Bullock pulled a satisfied and smug face.

'Anthony,' said Latymer, 'Let me see.' The boy came over to him and the doctor carefully peeled back the plaster. 'Hm, it does look a bit nasty. How did you do this?'

'I fell in the playground. We was playing British Bulldog.'

'Don't worry, I didn't hit him, Dr Latymer.'

Latymer ignored the headmaster.

'Clean it up and apply another dressing, Nurse.' He looked at his watch. 'I'm expected elsewhere.' Without another word he left the room.

Latymer wanted to get off the premises before he became very angry. Standing at his car, he looked at his watch. He had over an hour to kill before he went to meet with Sir Brian. He took a road that led out into the countryside. It was the one that he'd come back along on Sunday, so it must lead to USAF Bruntingthorpe. As he carried on, he could see the emptiness and space for runways on the base punctuated by the odd building and a tower. He pulled into the main entrance. A soldier approached him from the guardhouse.

'Sir?'

'Could you find out if Captain McFadden is available? I'd like a few minutes, if he has the time. I'm Dr Latymer.'

'I'll try for you, sir.'

He went back into his hut and spoke into a receiver, returning moments later. 'Yes, sir, he'll be waiting for you at the building straight ahead.' The soldier lifted the barrier and let the car roll in.

Latymer brought it to a stop outside the building where the captain was waiting with a broad grin, obviously pleased to see Latymer.

Peter got out of his car. 'James,' Latymer said and stuck out his hand for a shake.

'Peter. We sound like the apostles having a get together.'

'Tell the Reverend Lewis and he'll think it's the Second Coming!'

'Don't mention that vicar to me.'

'You know him then?' said Latymer with a smile.

'This is an American base, so they have their own Padre. But the Reverend likes to be in on everything, so he offered to lead a service. Seemed like a good idea.'

Latymer nodded his agreement.

'Never again. Getting rid of him afterwards was awful. The Major, bless her, because she thought he'd prefer to talk to an Englishman even though I'm a Scot, gave him to me for lunch. I don't speak literally of course.'

'Oh dear.'

James went on, 'I asked him if he'd like a beer.'

'And he believes alcohol to be an evil.'

'You got it. So of course, I couldn't have one. Then he ranted on sermonising, the temptation of sin, wanton women, and the evils of drink. Well, you can imagine.'

'I've spoken to him on the telephone.' Latymer raised his eyes to the sky. 'And I'm seeing him later. I think I've heard all I want to know.'

'Make sure you've got a few hours to spare.'

'I've arranged it for just before evening surgery.'

'Anyway, after lunch he wanted a tour of the base and to sit inside an aeroplane. We've got it, he wanted to see it. You get the idea? My so-called friends could have rescued me, said there was an emergency, but no, for them it was hilarious.'

They went inside the building. James asked, 'Cup of tea?'

'Lovely. I've got a good half hour, then I've got to go see Sir Brian Britley.'

'Britley? Don't like the man.' James shook his head in disgust before carrying on speaking. It was as if he had nothing good to say about anyone that day. 'I've only met him the one time, but didn't take to him. I wouldn't trust him with my daughter – not that I have any children.'

'No.' He wondered if James knew the sad tale of Sir Brian and Susan, but decided not to tell as to be overheard. They sat down and a waiter brought tea and biscuits. 'This is the first I've eaten since breakfast.'

'I'll get you sandwiches; you can always eat them in the car.'

'I could do with them. Thank you. How come you are an RAF officer working at a USAF base?'

'Specialism. And they have the facilities I need for my work here, a burns unit.'

'So, we have an English officer here and an American, Racre, at the hospital in the town?'

'That's the way of it. Allies. Say,' James said, 'a week on Thursday I'm performing plastic surgery on a badly burnt pilot. It's what I specialise in. Would you like to watch?'

Latymer felt both surprise and an honour at being asked.

'I would. I've never seen anything like that. I'm always ready to learn.'

'I'll fix it with Dad. One positive thing in the old man's favour, he's a believer in education.'

***

At the factory's receptionist's desk Latymer was shown upstairs by a teenage boy, whose only role in life seemed to be to run messages around the factory. Dr Latymer was asked to sit in a waiting area.

'He won't be too long. He likes to keep his appointments punctual,' said Sir Brian's secretary.

She was true to her word. In a few minutes the door to his office opened. Sir Brian stood for a few moments exchanging pleasantries with a man before shaking hands with him. The man left and Sir Brian strode over to Dr Latymer.

'Dr Latymer,' he said as if it were a pleasure to meet him, 'good to see you. We met briefly at the Oddfellows. You were having dinner with Dr McFadden?'

The secretary looked up and smiled at the young doctor, thinking him good looking.

Dr Latymer replied, 'We did.'

'This way then.'

Latymer followed Sir Brian into his office. Britley paused by the door and told the secretary, 'I'll need the car in fifteen minutes.' Latymer knew precisely when he was expected to take his leave.

'Tea?' Sir Brian asked.

'No, thank you.'

'Now, how can I help?'

'I'm new to the area, as you know, Sir Brian. I'm sure you understand it is a good idea to meet the people of importance here.'

'Very commendable,' Sir Brian answered.

'I understand that we, that the practice at Stocking Farm, come straight out to deal with any emergencies at the factory.'

'Correct. I want the best care for my workforce.'

'Very commendable.' He smiled at his own sarcasm. Sir Brian failed to see anything funny in the remark. 'And what's wrong with the Leicester Royal Infirmary?' Latymer went on, 'I know they are excellent dealing with major or minor accidents.'

'Well, from yours and Dr McFadden's point of view, we pay you. The workforce is treated as one would a private patient. We must give them the best care.'

Latymer didn't believe a word of it. 'And nothing else?'

'You're on the spot to sign any necessary papers.'

'Yes, no one must question the safety of the workforce, must they?'

Britley frowned. He didn't like to be interrogated. People didn't do it; they respected his judgement – knowing their place.

'I just like to know what I'm expected to do.'

'You're very young, Dr Latymer.'

'But qualified as a doctor, Sir.'

'Please, call me Brian.'

Latymer ignored this overture of friendliness, a ploy which had worked many times in the past for Sir Brian.

'Medical training takes a long time. I have seen more of the world than I would've cared to – the war, you know.'

Britley raised his eyebrows as if he didn't believe him.

'But a good doctor will always be learning. It was drummed into us that we are in a position of great responsibility, and we must always be sure of what we are expected to do.'

'Yes, of course I understand. You sign the form,' said Sir Brian as though it was rather obvious.

'But how am I supposed to know whether you are negligent or otherwise? I'm a doctor, I wasn't trained as a factory inspector.'

Sir Brian looked at his watch. He didn't want to start speaking about legal responsibilities.

'Am I keeping you?' Latymer took the hint and asked straight out.

'I do have another appointment.' Britley sighed impatiently. 'It has never been a problem with Dr McFadden, and he has many years experience.'

'I see. I won't keep you any longer.' Latymer got up to leave. Sir Brian stayed where he was.

'Don't worry, I'll see myself out.'

Latymer walked to the door and in the hearing of the secretary said, 'Thank you for your time. It has been very enlightening.' He turned to leave and stopped. Turning back towards Sir Brian he said slightly louder, 'Oh, one more thing.'

Sir Brian inwardly groaned.

'Susan Harshaw?' asked Latymer, looking directly at Britley.

A flicker of recognition crossed the industrialist's eyes.

'Very sad, her daughter died of pneumonia last Saturday. I believe the funeral is next week. I could let your secretary know the date and details.'

'Why would that be of interest to me?'

'Her family works here.' He waited for a response. There being none he said, 'Goodbye, Sir Brian.' He went out leaving the door open behind him.

After an afternoon seeing Beltham, Bullock, and Britley, Latymer was angry. Those with authority or responsibility for others behaved as if they were the ruling class and nobody seemed to have a right to challenge that. There had been times when he'd seen Dr McFadden treat his patients as if he were speaking to a herd of cattle. Even more maddening was they accepted it without blinking.

***

The final meeting before evening surgery was with Reverend Lewis. The Reverend's wife received Latymer at the door.

He introduced himself and she said, 'This is a pleasure, Dr Latymer. Come in. I'll tell my husband that you're here.'

He followed her into the hallway.

She turned and asked, 'Would you like tea?'

'No, thank you. I have, at the most, twenty minutes before evening surgery begins.'

'This way, Dr Latymer.' She was very formal and he played up to her game by taking it for granted that convention was the order of the day. She led him to a closed door and tapped lightly before opening it into the study.

Reverend Lewis sat behind a desk surrounded by books lining the walls. For a moment Latymer caught him as if in a photograph, posed working on the great theological argument of the day; answering the call from the Archbishop of Canterbury himself.

The vicar stood as if he were a great man of the church and came round from his desk, extended his hand and spoke. The voice should have sounded deep, tremulous and with great authority, but it was a disappointment. The tone was thin and reedy as if it were yet to break fully. He would never have been able to command troops. There was little charisma as well, only a thin figure, a little over five foot seven, who could easily dissolve into the dimness of the room.

'Dr Latymer,' he said in a watery voice. 'Welcome to Stocking Farm. May your stay be long, worthwhile, and fulfilling.' The reception sounded prepared and fake.

'Reverend Lewis, thank you for your kind words. I believe you are the first to formally welcome me. Have you been vicar here long?'

'Two years,' he said smugly. He made it sound as if it were a millennia. 'Now then, I expect you would like a drink of tea? In spite of the rationing, I think we can find a little to spare. Dear?'

Mrs Lewis went to speak, but Latymer interrupted her. 'I only have,' he glanced at the clock ticking on the wall, 'fifteen minutes before seeing my evening patients.'

'Those of us who are members of the caring profession, whether it be for the Lord, or the benefit of man or for both, as I like to think of myself, must always be on duty for whenever the alarum should strike.'

'Yes?'

'Sit down, please. Now then?' He dismissed his wife with a wave of his hand. 'That will be all, dear.'

'When would you like supper?' she asked.

'In forty-five minutes, as I have no further duties, as far as I am aware, unless the unseen and guiding hand should make a divine intervention.'

His wife left the study door open when she exited.

Perhaps He would do us the favour of giving this man a fatal heart attack. Latymer felt horrified that such a notion should have occurred to him. The vicar was such a fool, and strangely the doctor was finding him more difficult to handle than Sir Brian.

'Amy Harshaw?' asked Latymer.

Reverend Lewis made a great show of gathering his thoughts as if they flew on a much higher plane and looked puzzled for a moment.

'The funeral?' queried Latymer.

'Ah yes, Mrs Harshaw.' He went back around his desk and sat, placed his forefingers over his nose and contemplated.

Latymer couldn't fathom whether this behaviour was supposed to impress, showing him as a contemplative religious being or whether it was his normal behaviour. Perhaps he suffered with his sinuses, but Latymer wasn't going to ask.

The Reverend wanted to show that he was mediating deeply for Mrs Harshaw when he said, 'A prayer for the child.' He paused again. 'Where is Mr Harshaw?' The Reverend asked completely out of the blue, so that the question threw Latymer.

Latymer managed to answer. 'I have no idea.' What Latymer knew about Sir Brian being the father of Amy he wasn't ready to share with the Reverend, and he felt he would rather not. Reverend Lewis would have blamed Susan for her wanton, temptress, harlot ways, having her cast into the fires of hell that very moment.

'He must have been a soldier, lost in the war fighting for good against evil. That poor woman hath suffereth much, but through it her faith will strengthen and shineth through.' The Reverend nodded sagely to himself.

Latymer attempted to ignore this nonsense. He was at risk of bursting out laughing. 'When is the funeral?'

'The funeral, yes, the funeral. I must prepare my words, so that this soul is raised heavenwards to be with the angels and saints, the Lord and God himself.' He checked a page in his diary. 'Next Wednesday afternoon at two o'clock.'

'Thank you.'

'Would say a few words at the funeral?'

'What?' Latymer asked.

'I know that it would be of a great comfort to her in this terrible time of distress. I'm sure you won't think me too forthright, Dr Latymer, please keep your homage brief. I always find wordiness a great failing in man. A speech should be cut to the quick, neat and tidy, so the point is fired from the archer's bow and achieves its target. Taking all of this, considering your audience, its attention span and the circumstances that not only you, but they as members of your audience, your listeners can achieve,' the Reverend paused for a breath, 'I feel sure that you would agree?'

'I would. Until Wednesday. Thank you for your time.'

'Dr Latymer, I am always here to answer your call as your spiritual guide in any time of need, your benefactor for those moments when you may be in need of healing, *spiritual healing*. Shall we now take a few moments to pray together?' He bowed his head and closed his eyes, no doubt expecting Latymer to do likewise.

Latymer seized his opportunity, silently got up and left the room, letting himself out of the vicarage.

***

At the surgery Latymer slipped into his office as silently as he'd left the vicarage. Olive gave him a look that said, 'You're in trouble.'

He began to see his patients. It was a full evening and the sufferers flowed like a torrent. They never prepared the students at university that so many people would fall ill at the same time. The numbers were so great that he assumed he was the only doctor employed that evening.

The door opened again and Dr McFadden came in and sat down. He looked angry. Latymer was surprised. He'd seen McFadden cross with patients, but not with his equals. He wondered what the matter was. It never occurred to him that he had done anything wrong.

'Dr Latymer, well, you've had a busy day.' The young doctor didn't reply. 'Been here, there, and everywhere I'm told.'

'If I've used too much petrol, I'll walk next time.' Latymer's voice had an edge of sarcasm.

'There's no need to take that tone with me, my boy.'

'I'm sorry if you misunderstood me. I was being serious.'

'It wasn't that.' McFadden looked at his fingers as if he were seeing them for the first time. 'Use the car when you like. I can always fiddle the figures for more petrol.' This seemed to relax the mood a little, but only by an inch. 'No man, rest easy for the moment.' He sighed. 'As I say, a busy day. Your home visits, the school with that despicable Mr Beltham and the nurse whom God must have known what she would look like when he named her Mrs Bullock, though I could think of a more suitable name–'

'And the Reverend Lewis,' Latymer added.

'Have you now? Well, you're welcome. You probably got what you deserved there. Try Father Grundy, next time, at least you get a wee dram from him.'

'You said deserved?'

'Sir Brian Britley telephoned me. I think I've smoothed things over by saying you were new to the job and inexperienced.'

Latymer winced.

'Well you are, man. You are enthusiastic and are prepared to play a full part in this practice. You've already done a lot of sterling work.'

Latymer sat in silence. He refused to be flattered. He was feeling reprimanded in spite of the praise. He wanted to sulk and say, okay I won't bother anymore. I'll just earn the money.

'Do you have nothing to say?' asked McFadden.

'Like what?' Latymer couldn't help sounding sulky.

'Listen to me. You don't approach a man like Sir Brian in the way that you did. He's an important man and important for business in this area. He has friends in government. He'll probably end up in the House of Lords one day.'

Latymer raised his eyebrows as if to say, *God help us.*

'He felt you implied that we sign factory accident forms regardless of the safety procedures and whether they have been breached.'

'*I've* signed nothing yet,' said Latymer, speaking firmly.

'Meaning what? Go on.'

Latymer spoke more carefully. He felt uncomfortable speaking to McFadden like this. 'I wouldn't be happy putting my name to a form that I don't understand.'

'Quite. You *can* ask.' McFadden spread his hands.

Homage to experience was a good idea at this point. 'With your knowledge and understanding, you probably know all there is to know regarding health and safety in factories.'

'Aye, I probably do, but there's no need to be getting round me.'

Dr Latymer could see his ploy was working, even though the older man said it wasn't.

The door opened and Olive put her head round. 'The patients are getting restless, Doctors.'

'They'll have to wait. We're having an important discussion here. A few things need sorting out.'

Registering the tense atmosphere, Olive left, closing the door.

'Listen, young man,' Latymer found that phrase patronising. 'I'm the senior man here. This is my practice and you work for me. I'll say what goes on. I'll deal with the likes of Sir Brian Britley.'

'And me with the death of the likes of Amy Harshaw.'

'A very sorry affair. We've seen enough of death. But I don't see what she has to do with Sir Brian Britley.'

'I'll tell you, and then you can do what you like with what you know.'

Latymer told him the sad tale of Susan and Amy; the poverty that the child had been living in and how Sir Brian had disregarded them.

For a few moments McFadden sat speechless. 'Ah yes. I can see why you are angry. But if you fight him, you're never going to beat him. If he sees you trying to, he'll destroy you. He has powerful friends, and you don't need them as enemies. You are a caring young man, so just do what you can for those you can help.'

'Yes, all right.' Latymer didn't know whether he meant it. He hadn't decided yet.

'Now then, James tells me that you're assisting with an operation this coming Thursday.'

Latymer smiled with pleasure. 'I think it's only observing.'

'He likes hands on. That's why I don't go anymore. He tells me you're a fine man. He doesn't know it, but I trust his judgement. I hope you're staying, Peter.'

'I think I will be.'

Chapter Eleven

The Reverend Lewis was always restless the night before a formal occasion in the church such as baptism, marriage, or funeral. He was very excited that he would be the focal point at the sad ceremony for Amy. Typically, of course, he forgot, the little girl Amy was at the centre of the occasion. His main concern was the central role he would play, how it would reflect on his standing and character in the community. He decided, whilst working on his homily in the early hours of the morning, that he would pile on the grief for Susan Harshaw, or Mrs Harshaw, as he knew her to be. He would lament the death of her daughter and that her husband was a war hero, martyred for the good of the nation fighting evil, and who was now united with his daughter in heaven in blissful union.

***

As he spoke these well-planned words, the congregation listened. Some with respect for the dead child's mother, who wanted the vicar to believe in her married status. Others because, *Why did it matter?* The rest without any knowledge of her background, though these were few.

Sitting like the grim reaper, Mr Beltham almost laughed out loud, an event that few ever remembered happening. He knew the mother to be an unmarried woman. In his opinion, hardly better than a common prostitute and the child, Amy, illegitimate. The young woman by his side was Miss Penrose, Amy's class teacher. Miss Penrose felt sorry and sad that the mother felt that she should tell this lie to the vicar, to pretend in front of the community, when most of the people knew the truth.

The Reverend Lewis smiled to himself when he finished his homily, satisfied with his representation of the glories of the Lord, and that the child's soul was safely cared for. He was wondering whether to organise a memorial service for Amy's father. The Reverend felt he could really shine there.

'After we've sung 'All Things Bright and Beautiful,' which I understand was Amy's favourite,' the Reverend tried to smile sweetly at Miss Penrose and failed, 'Dr Latymer will say a few words.'

***

Throughout the hymn, which many sang with difficulty because of the emotion attached, Latymer planned what he would say. There had been little time to sit at his desk and work out his words. He remembered the ill child and words formed in his mind. If he chose them carefully and took his time, thinking as he went, this could provide a useful platform.

For Latymer and the rest of the congregation, the funeral of the child was a sombre affair. It reflected Amy's life. There had been little fun in the child's life, little food, little warmth.

He could see through the coloured stain of the glass that it was a dull late October day, nearly November, the worst time of the year when nature is dead and cold.

The church was crowded, full to overflowing. The child's death created a feeling of unity in the estate. Perhaps they all knew how she had been wronged. Latymer doubted it; people rarely gossiped their own secrets, only those of others. It was human nature.

Latymer lived death at the end of the war. It was all too painful. His experiences were more than he cared to remember, but this child's death was one of the hardest. He learnt two lessons from it: to avoid being personally involved, and the other to be personally involved because there were repercussions that he both did and didn't regret.

The hymn ended. The congregation sat down with the usual shuffling, breaking the silence. He could hear the sound of soft weeping. He glanced at Susan. She was sitting in complete control. Otherwise there was absolute silence as he got up from his pew and crossed the nave to the lectern. The leather soles of his shoes tapped against the grey concrete floor. He took the three steps up to the lectern where the Bible sat. Latymer surveyed the gathered congregation.

'We are here today to commemorate the death of one little girl, Amy Harshaw. The Reverend Lewis has informed us of that.' He paused; the vicar expected Dr Latymer to pay him a compliment. But he didn't. 'It is not death here that we should be concerned with, but life. We all know that Amy should be with us today. She was a child with her life ahead of her.'

'But Amy Harshaw lived in poverty. I know this because I saw the poverty she suffered two days before she passed away. There was very little money in the house for food. Her home lacked proper warmth, bedding, or suitable clothes for the child. The family relied on hand-me-downs or what her grandparents could afford to spare. That a child should be living like this in these modern times, when Britain is the strongest power in Europe, can only be described as appalling.'

Racing ahead in his thoughts he decided to quickly move away from politics. 'So,' he asked, 'why was she living like that?'

Many in the congregation looked puzzled, as if saying, *Well, it was nothing to do with us, we have our own mouths to feed.*

'What was Amy's mother doing with the pension from her hero husband, the soldier who had died at the hand of evil?'

The Reverend Lewis began to wonder what was going on. Latymer was now painting Mrs Harshaw in a very different light from the one he felt he knew. He wondered if he should take action to stop the proceedings and ask the organist to play the next hymn.

'I'll tell you.' Latymer held the congregation in the palm of his hand. They were hanging on his every word, though most knew what he was going to say. It just felt good to hear a few earnest truths from the pulpit.

Latymer slammed his fist down on the lectern. He was beginning to feel like Lloyd George. 'There was no pension.' He raised his voice as loud as he dared and then lowered it to a whisper. 'Amy's mother wasn't married.'

The Reverend Lewis was appalled and he wanted to clear the church then and there of harlots and evil doers, remembering Jesus' example with the money changers and traders in the temple in Jerusalem. He didn't know how to do it. He could only sit and listen to this doctor, a supposed pillar of the community, like himself, who deserved respect.

Latymer sighed and held onto the side of the lectern as if he were very weary, which was quite close to the truth, weary of the whole affair, but he went on, 'Amy and her mother could have been properly looked after. The man who is Amy's father, he isn't here today.' Latymer looked around as if checking. 'He knows of his daughter's death, though.' He paused for maximum effect. 'I told him myself.'

There were quite a few suppressed gasps from the congregation.

'This man sacked Susan Harshaw from a job, her employment in his house, when he knew she was expecting his child. He wanted nothing else to do with her, or the baby she was carrying. It would be wrong of me to name this man, but he is a powerful man in this community and he employs many of you. I know, and I'm sure I include all of you in this,' he looked directly at Mr Beltham and the Reverend Lewis who was incandescent, 'find it in our hearts as Christians to forgive him. Thank you for listening to me.'

There was absolute silence from the congregation. Nobody knew what to do next.

The Reverend Lewis stood up, appalled that such an event could happen in his church. How to deal with the situation was beyond his experience. He waved his arms about, hoping that would have some effect. He looked at his wife, Anne, who'd attended to see him perform, for support, but there was little she could do. He strode into the vestry, leaving them to get on with it. He'd been made to look a complete fool. His standing in the community swept from under his feet. One of the undertakers came over to Latymer, who now seemed to be in control, and asked him, 'Shall we take the coffin now, sir?'

'Yes, I'll ask the organist to play us out.'

The organist looked at him after the request and said, 'I don't like him. Too pompous for his own good,' and proceeded to play Bach. He never knew whether she meant the reverend, the knight, or the headmaster.

***

As Latymer followed the coffin down the centre aisle, people greeted him and shook his hand as if he were a hero. One man blocked his way and wouldn't let him move on until he had said his piece, 'For six years we fought, believing that afterwards there'd be freedom for the common man, now we are as oppressed as we were in the nineteen thirties. It was a war fought by capitalists.'

'I feel I ought to be outside.'

But the man wouldn't move. 'Fought by capitalists for capitalists, and only they were set to gain anything from it. As their tools, the working man achieved nothing. Now we have to look to our lords and masters and thank them for the victory. Like that toady, the vicar, or that Britley. At least we partly showed them by Winnie losing the election.'

'I'm sure the doctor hasn't the time to listen to one of your political speeches. Save it for your Union,' said a woman beside him, tugging at his elbow.

Outside they stood in respectful silence. The atmosphere of the whole estate seemed to be quiet for a moment as they watched the little coffin put into the hearse. The close family, two or three of them and one or two friends, got into cars following the black hearse as it moved away. The Reverend Lewis pulled in behind them. He realised his responsibility to perform the ceremony to bury the child; but Latymer knew it would be quick and very formal. The little procession made its way off to Gilrose Cemetery.

Latymer turned to leave. The woman he'd seen sitting with Mr Beltham approached him. Out of the corner of his eye he could see Mr Beltham waiting impatiently, standing a few feet away from a man who also looked as though he wanted to speak to the doctor. Or perhaps he was one of Sir Brian's henchmen, and he was here to commit a mob murder, or more likely just issue a few words of warning to Dr Latymer. Latymer smiled to himself as he remembered the films of James Cagney and George Raft viewed at the cinema.

'I'm Miss Penrose,' the young woman said. 'Amy was a pupil in my class. I can't thank you for your kind words, because for Amy, they weren't kind. I will have to think about what you said.'

'I'm sorry. I meant no harm.'

'No, it's not that. Very little happened to her in her life that was pleasant for her, that she enjoyed, and kind words at her funeral would have been…I can't think of the word.'

'I understand. But I didn't know Amy. I couldn't understand why Susan Harshaw asked me to say anything.'

'You're naïve, Doctor. I'm sorry you look shocked. I feel angry.' She searched for her words. 'Perhaps what I mean is, that this should have not been a political platform for exposing wrongs. What do you think Susan Harshaw thinks?'

'I don't know. It's all right.'

'That's the point. Why should we say everything is all right?' Miss Penrose was very forthright in her questioning.

Mr Beltham moved from foot to foot and coughed loudly.

'I'm not angry with you,' she said, 'I didn't mean to sound rude.'

'Emotions are difficult on a day like this.'

'Hm, yes, I suppose so. No, what I wanted to say, you are a pillar of the community. Doctors know everything. You are the new priests, the new religion. They worship you and ever more so now.' She smiled, albeit faintly.

He couldn't fathom why.

'Miss Penrose, we have to be getting along. Mr Taylor can't be expected to look after two classes for a whole afternoon.' Mr Beltham spoke to her as if she were a naughty nine-year-old girl.

Latymer wanted to slap him on her behalf.

Miss Penrose looked as if she wanted to do the same.

She turned to leave, but stopped and spoke again. 'The class has drawn pictures for your surgery. Anthony said you needed them.'

'I'll come over and get them. Thank you.'

She turned and walked in the direction of Mr Beltham, who was already striding away.

'A fine speech, young man.' There he was again, though it didn't sound so condescending this time – quite respectful. 'You rarely hear better in the House.'

Latymer looked at the man quizzically. The speaker was very well dressed in a high quality and well-cut black three piece suit.

'Solomon Joles, Member of Parliament for most of this area. Liberal, if you're wondering how I came to be in the church. That is, Liberal Jew. I'm a Labour MP.'

'Thank you.'

They shook hands.

'There are times when the truth needs to be told, and you were able to see when the occasion demanded it.' Joles said.

Latymer replied, 'I felt the child and her mother were wronged.'

'You may be right. But a person standing on the soap box and speaking can attract the wrong kind of attention.'

Latymer looked at him quizzically for more information.

'The people here this afternoon, with one or two exceptions, supported you.'

'Yes?'

'But they aren't much use to you when it boils down to it, my friend,' and he said this with more than a hint of sarcasm, 'put the food on most of their plates. And they won't bite off the hand that feeds them. Our friend, the Union man, that you've been speaking to, will only go so far. The Church of England is still the Tory party at prayer. Do you see what I'm getting at?'

'Yes, I think so.'

'I'd better go. This isn't the place to hold a conversation.' Joles made to leave.

'I've surgery.'

'We'll be in touch,' the Member of Parliament replied.

'I look forward to it,' Latymer answered and nodded his head.

Chapter Twelve

When Latymer arrived back from the funeral, James McFadden was waiting for him in the sitting room.

'James, what a pleasant surprise after the day I've had. I wasn't expecting you. Whisky?' Latymer asked him.

'No.' James looked horrified as the evils of hard liquor never passed his lips.

'Oh dear,' and sarcastically Latymer went on, 'have I spoken out of turn? Have you taken the pledge?'

'I never drink for twenty-four hours before performing a surgery, usually forty-eight. In this case it's pretty dodgy with the new techniques I'm using. I haven't touched a drop since Sunday lunchtime. Eaten sensibly, bed on time.' James paused as though he didn't want to admit it, 'Actually, I feel pretty healthy.'

'Oh, right. What can I do for you then?' Latymer wondered.

'I'm going to take you away from all this. Dad's going to do evening surgery. You're going to have most of Thursday evening's patients by yourself. The old man wants to get away early. There's a feast over at the Oddfellows, Grand Order of the Boar.'

'Sounds suitable.'

The young doctors chuckled.

'I heard that.' Dr McFadden entered the room and walked straight over to the whisky decanter. James and Latymer stood like schoolboys caught out making fun of a teacher.

'Much healthier for you if you don't drink, you know, Dad.'

'I'll risk it. You two get on your way. Or I'll have you both working tonight.'

'We're going.' They said in unplanned unison, sniggering again.

As they left and walked to the car James spoke regarding the forthcoming operation, 'There are a few things I want to show you – the patient, the operating room, procedures, what I expect from you.' James sounded as if he were starting a lecture.

'Me? I'm just observing.' There was hint of panic in Latymer's voice.

'Like a dummy? No, I won't expect a lot, but it will be active training so that you can be of use to the team. You are a trained doctor. There's a future in plastic surgery, although the money to be made will be in cosmetic surgery, but more of that another time. And then dinner and bed.'

They were driving now towards the airbase. 'We'll make an early start; punctually at seven forty five. We should be finished by early afternoon.'

Three hours later Latymer was ready for bed, except that he knew he wouldn't sleep properly. It was too early. His body would wake at two in the morning and he would lay there staring at the ceiling excited and tense for the coming day. He met the significant people involved, the anaesthetist and the like. James introduced Latymer as if he himself were an important part of the team. Only the Theatre Sister eyed him with suspicion. She probably knew more concerning theatre procedures than the rest of them put together.

Then there was the patient. He looked hardly aged over twenty. His face badly disfigured due to an aircraft crash. The fire caused by the accident had killed the rest of the crew. The pilot knew that in spite of his injuries, he was lucky to be alive.

Unlike the patient, who was nil by mouth, they ate a good breakfast. Scrubbed up and dressed for surgery. Green and masked, they watched as the young man was wheeled into the operating theatre asleep through anaesthesia, so that they could begin one of the many operations that would give him a face again. Skin was to be taken from his fleshy buttock area and transferred.

Latymer didn't contribute a great deal. Whilst he knew operations from textbooks, he lacked experience. He could completely find himself round the theatre, but for him all of this was a learning process, and he knew that James was being kind including him as part of the team in the day's procedures.

Occasionally, he would be asked an open-ended question, to which the answer was obvious and that was designed to make him feel a lot cleverer than he actually was. But more importantly he was talked through the whole of the technique, so that it was a lecture in the most practical of senses. Later he came to realise that it wasn't just for him, but for every person in the theatre, including James himself, who was on a very steep learning curve.

Staff came and went from the operating theatre as they needed breaks from the intense concentration. During the operation a nurse came into the room. She received a nod from James, but didn't respond. All she did was to stand in the background and observe.

Latymer wondered what purpose she served. Was she a specialist, perhaps, for an emergency? An unforeseen event, which may go very wrong, perhaps to assist the nursing sister. But by and large she was ignored. She could only be a very junior nurse, Latymer decided, with special permission to attend such an important procedure. She watched intently. He also noticed the most gorgeous dark eyes looking at him, just the once, from above her mask. He was caught staring when James said, 'Do you want to dress the wound down below? Latymer? Latymer?'

'Oh, yes.'

'Yes, she is very pretty, isn't she?' James' eyes shone with laughter behind the mask. The nurse appeared not to have heard his comment.

'I–'

'No lies here. Come on, a practical job for you.' James was a little more firm now.

Under James' supervision Latymer worked on the patient. When he looked up again, self-satisfied that he'd been an actual part of the operation, she'd gone. In the time of self-congratulation, that all involved felt, Latymer forgot her.

Chapter Thirteen

It was back to reality that evening. The contrast couldn't have been greater. Latymer left Bruntingthorpe on a high after the operation, and arrived back for an evening's surgery of coughs, colds, and backaches. This was the way it was going to be most nights, mundane. His life as a doctor was with people. He would learn to recognise the limitations of his skills.

Coming across James McFadden was a stroke of luck, and being invited to work with him on a groundbreaking procedure that would be written up in *The Lancet*, and read by ten-year-olds everywhere, was quite unbelievable. Latymer chuckled at the thought of the boy with the journal, but in reality he could look at a future issue of the journal and say, 'I was part of that.'

Latymer ate the supper left for him by Edna. He sat by the fire listening to the Light Service. McFadden came into the room and poured himself a whisky, holding up the decanter in Latymer's direction to see if he wanted one. With his mouth full, he shook his head. McFadden took his drink over to the radiogram and stood conducting the orchestra that was playing, waving his glass as a baton.

'I love Mantovani. Do you, young man?'

'I prefer music with a bit more life. Jazz.'

'Hm. I'm getting old. Too noisy for me. My daughter listens. Can't be doing with it myself. The skin graft went well then?'

'As far as I know,' Latymer replied.

'You tired? You must be. The concentration takes it out of me.' He downed his drink in one. 'Have one of these when you've finished and then bed.'

'I intend to.'

McFadden left the room. Latymer followed soon after. He didn't go through the waiting room, but into the back of his surgery. He wanted a few minutes to sort papers before the patients knew he was there. He was learning that they often needed to be dealt with on his terms. Very little was a true emergency. A great deal would cure itself; a sympathetic ear was often all that was needed.

When Latymer went into his consulting room a young woman was sitting there. She was well dressed, middle class, and probably full of airs and graces. Just the type that believed she could get what she wanted just by existing. He knew that she had taken it upon herself to push in front of the common person in the waiting room.

Latymer didn't wait for an explanation. He told her to leave, 'Like the rest, you wait. Report to Miss Riley and tell her you will see me after all the other patients.'

Demurely, she left.

He saw a flicker of a smile on her face, and he was outraged by her lack of manners. He went to the door of the waiting room and opened it. The patients looked at him expectantly for the first of them to be called in, but instead he shouted, 'Miss Riley, a word, please.' He was angry and they all knew it by the uneasy shuffling they made.

Olive came into his room and closed the door.

'Who was that? No, don't tell me, you didn't see her? Surely you know that we don't just let patients wander all over the house, as if they own the place.'

'I–' But Olive was unable to get a word in edgeways.

'There may be drugs in here, and certainly patients' confidential records. Looking at her, it probably wasn't your fault.'

'I–' She started again.

'I'll tell you who she is.' Latymer was in full flow now, 'She's a pregnant upper class woman who wants an abortion, and thinks that she can go to an out-of-the way place on a council estate to get one done on the hush-hush. Well, you can go tell her that she won't be getting one from me–or Dr McFadden for that matter.'

Latymer stopped speaking, satisfied that he'd finished.

'I'll do that, Doctor. Dr McFadden would be very interested to hear that. Although I don't think she is pregnant and looking for an abortion. She has other things on her mind.'

'You know her?' Latymer was puzzled now.

'Yes,' Olive said.

'Well?' He sat down at his desk.

'Gerry McFadden, Doctor McFadden's daughter. She comes up to finals very soon. In a short time we'll have another Dr McFadden.'

'And, I'll be out of a job. Why didn't you tell me?'

'I tried.'

'Yes, you did. Olive, I'm very sorry. What am I going to do? Five minutes in a job and I'm out of it.'

'It's been a long day for you, a very tiring introduction to medical practice. If I can give you a bit of advice, take it easier, or you'll wear yourself out.' Olive spoke to him as a caring mother talks to her son.

'You'd better ask her to come back in.' He stood when she entered the room. 'Miss McFadden. I'm very sorry.'

'Geraldine, but I prefer Gerry.'

He took her hand to shake and held it, looking at her face for a moment too long.

'What's wrong?'

Latymer recognised her eyes, 'You were in the operation theatre today.'

'Yes.'

The door to his surgery opened again. This time it was old Dr McFadden. 'Ah, you found her. Want dinner at the Oddfellows to celebrate?' McFadden taped his jacket pocket, checking for his pipe. 'I've booked a table, Gerry.'

'That's lovely, Dad.'

'Bout eight.' He tapped his pocket again with the palm of his hand as if forgetting he'd just performed that act. 'You are joining us, Latymer?'

'I–' *What I want to do, Gerry,* the young doctor thought, *is to spend the evening having dinner with you. But it wouldn't work having your father there.* 'I'm,' Latymer said, trying to sound convincing, 'very tired after the busy day. I really should get an early night.'

'Very commendable, my boy.'

Latymer felt rather silly with McFadden treating him like a schoolboy in front of the woman he was attempting to impress.

McFadden looked in the direction of his daughter, 'So just you and me, my girl.'

She smiled at her father. 'Shame about you, Dr Latymer–' she said.

'Peter.'

'Perhaps another time, Peter?'

Dr McFadden twiddled his thumbs in the pockets of his waistcoat. 'Well,' he said, 'back to work.' He stood silent for a moment. 'Ah yes, wait for me in the sitting room, Gerry. I'll only be,' he looked at his watch, 'forty minutes tops.'

McFadden left the room.

Gerry stood, not quite knowing what to do.

Latymer's stomach was turning over.

'I, erm–' He had occasionally taken a girl out, but this woman was making him feel light headed.

'Yes?' she questioned.

'I wondered. Well, you can say no. I'd understand. It's not that important. I'm sure you're very tired what with one thing and another, but I was wondering whether you'd like to stay and watch the less glamorous side of medicine, you know, after the excitement of the operation today. I mean say no, say no, if you want.'

Much to Latymer's relief, she replied, 'I'd love to!' as if she'd been invited to a three-week trip on a luxury liner around the Caribbean. 'Shall I sit over here?' she asked.

'Yes.' He showed her to her seat like a waiter in an uptown restaurant. 'I'm sorry,' said Latymer. 'You know, for thinking earlier, you know.'

'Yes, let's just forget it. It's quite funny really.'

After awhile Gerry looked at her watch, and seeing that it was time she to meet her father, she excused herself, leaving Latymer on his own for the rest of the evening's surgery.

As she touched the handle of the door to leave, Latymer said, 'Gerry, I was wondering, you don't have to say yes–'

She interrupted him to spare him the whole rigmarole again. 'The day after tomorrow, I'm down from Cambridge for a few days,' she said. 'I'll come and make a meal for you.'

'I was going to ask you out for dinner.'

'No, I love cooking. I'll shop in town and use what Edna keeps in her cupboards, or maybe have a look in Eric's. What with rationing, we have to shop everywhere.'

As she spoke there was a knock at the door. It sounded wood against wood. Latymer heard a voice he recognised, Milly Fantam, 'shushing.' Then the unmistakable voice of Reg, 'Doctor! Doctor!' as if he were dying.

Olive's voice could be heard, 'Mr Fantam, the doctor will see you as soon as he is able.'

'What do I pay my stamps for?'

Latymer and Gerry looked at each other.

'Friend of yours?' asked Gerry.

Latymer raised his eyes heavenwards.

'I think, I'll leave you to it.'

In some despair, Latymer nodded. Gerry opened the door. Reg filled the frame sitting in a wheelchair, holding onto a walking stick.

Milly stood behind the machine ready to push him in. Just about peeping over her shoulder, stood Olive.

'Mr Fantam,' she said.

'I gathered.'

Gerry was trying to get out of the door. Before she could move Reg said, 'I told you, Milly. They'd heard there was a serious case on the way. A nurse has been drafted to assist the doctor.'

'I'm not a nurse.'

'She's Dr McFadden.'

Gerry and Latymer could see it in Reg's face, he was puzzling, how was Dr McFadden, the grumpy old man, turned into a young, attractive female?

'Don't be silly,' Reg said. 'You don't get women doctors. A joke, eh?'

Now wasn't the time for debate, Latymer said to Gerry, 'Use the door to the sitting room.'

After Gerry left, Latymer turned to his patient. 'Well, Reg, you look as though you've been in the wars.'

Reg remembered to groan. Milly spoke for him as if his injury had robbed him of the power of speech.

'He was playing football.'

'Stocking Farm against Mowmacre,' added Reg, as though this was relevant to the accident. 'We won, two-one.'

A little unkindly, Milly said, 'The winning goals were only scored after you were stretchered off.'

'Let's stick to the events of the accident,' said Latymer.

'I play centre forward, I was running the ball like Don Revie.'
Latymer realised he wasn't going to get the bare facts.
'You know who Don Revie is?'
'Reg, the doctor doesn't care. He's a busy man,' said Milly
'He plays centre forward for Leicester,' Reg said triumphantly.
'Ah, and what happened?'
'I was running the ball like Don Revie–'
Milly interrupted, 'You've said that.'
He glared at her, 'I'm saying what happened. I was running the ball like Don Revie.'

Milly and Latymer wanted to scream. It was like listening to a cracked record. Both realised the fastest way to the end of this recording, was to let it play.

'There I was,' Reg said, 'about to score.'
Milly sighed.
'When I felt this boot in my back. I fell to the earth in agony. The crowd went silent.'

'They were playing on the school pitch. Mr Britley let them have an extra half hour at lunchtime for the match. The kids were watching,' Milly told the doctor.

'Mr Britley loves football. Big Leicester supporter.'
'I see,' said Latymer. 'What happened next?'
'You see, Milly, I told you the doctor would be interested. This should be written up in the sports pages of the *Leicester Mercury*.' Reg sat with a self-satisfied grin on his face.

'No, I meant your back,' said Latymer.
'Oh,' said Reg, 'I was in agony. I had to be stretchered off. The teams could do with you there really, to deal with emergencies.' Reg waited for Latymer to respond in the affirmative, but he wasn't being drawn.

'How did you get the wheelchair?' asked Latymer.
'It belongs one of the player's grandma.'
'Well,' said Latymer, 'I'm sure she needs it back. Let's have a look at you. Out you get. Perhaps Mrs Fantam can help you onto the examining couch.'

'I don't think I can.' Reg spoke, groaning at the same time, his face full of painful contortions.

'You managed to get out for your dinner when you realised the wheelchair wouldn't get to the table,' Milly reminded him.

Reg shot her a look. 'I'll try.'

They got Reg onto the couch. Dr Latymer pressed and prodded. He diagnosed that there was nothing wrong, other than a slight back strain.

'No, nothing broken. You need to move about. If you sit around, your back will become more painful. Two aspirin and a warm bath.'

Disappointment was written all over Reg's face.

'I was going down to the Leys now in the wheelchair.'

'He wanted to be a hero,' said Milly.

'No, I didn't.' Reg was sulking.

'The best action you can take, Reg,' Latymer told him, 'is to return the wheelchair. Walk it there, then have your fun.'

'All right,' said Reg. A doctor's word wasn't to be argued with.

'Are you going to tell the doctor how the centre forward who replaced you scored the two goals that won the match?'

Reg looked back at Latymer without a word and left the room pushing the wheelchair, followed by his wife.

***

After Reg and Milly patient departed Latymer went into the sitting room. McFadden was there with Gerry. They both stopped talking and looked at him as he entered, as if it were him they were speaking about.

'You've been ages,' said Gerry. 'What was wrong with that man in the wheelchair?'

'Wheelchair?' asked McFadden.

'Your friend and mine, Reg Fantam.'

'You don't want to know, Gerry,' McFadden told his daughter.

'Oh, all right.' She paused. 'I gather from Dad,' said Gerry with a smile, 'that you're a great public speaker as well as your many other talents.' She smiled in a way that got Latymer's attention, but he quickly looked away.

'I didn't hear him,' said McFadden, 'but it's the talk of the estate.'

'Well, hardly. I just spoke. It wasn't planned or anything. Only what I knew about the girl and her mother.'

'So,' Gerry asked to confirm that she'd understood correctly, 'Britley was the father and he would do nothing for them?'

'That's right,' said Latymer.

'I wish you hadn't spoken. I hope Sir Brian doesn't hear about it. He's not a person you mess with,' McFadden told them.

'Why?' Gerry asked her father, 'Because he's a bully? Because he can abandon a mother and child? She needed help rather than worry.'

'Just don't get mixed up. It's not worth the trouble.'

'Trouble, Dad? Effort you mean. Anyway,' she said to Latymer, 'this will surprise you. I've stopped him drinking.'

It must take a fairly strong character to stop the old doctor doing anything, and it couldn't be permanent. McFadden couldn't have taken the pledge.

'He's got to drive, and I'm in the car with him.' McFadden looked at her pleadingly. 'Dad, you've got plenty of the stuff at home.'

'Yes.' He sighed as if it were the end of the world. 'Come on, Gerry, let's go. Sure we can't change your mind, Latymer.'

He was surely tempted. 'No, I'll eat whatever delight Edna has left for me.'

'Can't you two call each other by your first names?' Gerry said. 'Are you both still at your public schools? Though,' she guffawed, 'I doubt Peter attended one.'

Latymer felt affronted. 'What makes you say that?'

'A New Age man.' She grinned as if she knew him already. 'I can tell.'

'We're going,' McFadden said, and added a smile. 'Enjoy your meal, Latymer. Sorry. Peter, man of the age, leaving the old ones behind.'

Latymer was sure he heard Gerry giggle as they shut the door.

Chapter Fourteen

On the Thursday that Gerry was due to prepare his dinner Latymer told Edna about the plan when she brought him his morning break of tea and a couple of plain biscuits.

'So, that's all right with you, Edna?'

'If it gives me a night off, I'm happy. I know Bernard will be pleased to have me at home.'

Yes, I'm sure he will, thought Latymer.

'Just tell her,' said Edna firmly, 'not to leave the kitchen in a mess. I'm not coming into a pile of dirty dishes in the morning.'

'I will inform her.'

'Well,' with a grim face and nod of her head, 'make sure you do.'

Edna left the room attempting to look as if she were the older, superior, experienced cook allowing an amateur into her kitchen.

Latymer sat and watched her bulk waddle through the door way. He sipped his tea. He'd been given the wrong one. This had whisky in it. No doubt Dr McFadden would be in to retrieve it soon.

There was a knock at his door and Olive came into the room.

'There's been an accident at the school.'

'Oh, no, we've had this before.'

'Dr McFadden would like you to deal with it.'

Querying her, Latymer raised his eyebrows.

'Nurse Bullock,' she said.

'Has she got her head stuck through the school railings? That could be a difficult one.'

Olive suppressed an outright burst of laughter. It was not professional, no matter who the patient was.

Latymer though, smiled widely at his own joke. 'I'm on my way. I have Dr McFadden's tea here. Can you take it to him?'

***

Gerry and Latymer sat in the sitting room later that day. Latymer assumed that something delightful was bubbling on the stove or perhaps a meat pie was baking in the oven. He felt an excited anticipation.

Latymer told Gerry about his call to the school to deal with Nurse Bullock.

'So what happened next?'

'She'd slipped on an icy patch, as I've said, near the kitchens.'

'What was she doing over there?' Gerry asked, 'Not really in the school with the children is it?'

'No idea. Begging a mid-morning snack?'

'Hm, yes probably.'

'The caretaker and I managed to get her into the kitchen. She was very heavy especially as she couldn't help herself.'

'What was wrong?'

'Well,' said Latymer diagnosing the accident, 'I am quite sure she's broken an ankle in the fall, and probably a wrist, as well.'

'That will put her out of action for a while.'

'It depends how bad it is. She was taken off to the hospital by ambulance. I've heard nothing since, and I can't say I'm particularly bothered.'

'I don't think she will be missed.' She paused in thought. 'So my Father sent you, you do the dirty work?'

'I am the new doctor. I can't expect to have the Harley Street patients. I'm bound to get the Nurse Bullock's of this world.'

'My father's got a chip on his shoulder.'

'Well, wouldn't you have?'

'I don't know whether I can excuse him so easily,' Gerry said. 'He's well off. He has influential friends. He's semi-retired.'

Latymer raised an eyebrow asking what she meant.

'He'll have you running round doing all the work. This bumbling eccentricity, *rest easy, my boy,*' she spoke in his accent and Latymer laughed, 'wears thin when you're working all hours and he's raking in the money from private patients.'

'Should you be speaking like this? He is your father.'

'The others didn't concern me.'

'Others?'

'The other doctors that worked for the practice. Most only lasted a year. A few,' she counted on her fingers, 'less, and the one woman seven weeks and three days.'

She stood looking a little lost, as if she didn't know what to do with herself. 'Forewarned is forearmed. Anyway, I don't think I want you to leave. Come on, let's eat. You must be hungry.'

As they entered the kitchen, Gerry turned and said, 'Did you know I'm a vegetarian?'

'No. Should I care?' asked Peter.

'No, just don't be expecting piles of dead animals on your plate.'

He sat at the table and she served the meal.

'Vegetables,' she said, 'from Edna's cupboard, a few fresh that Eric was selling and a tin from his shop. It was a bit odd. No label, but when I opened it, it looked okay.'

'Sounds great to me.'

'Well, hopefully it won't poison us,' said Gerry.

'If Edna's cooking doesn't, this won't!'

***

Having finished their meal, Latymer wiped his mouth on the napkin that Edna wasn't aware of sitting in the dresser drawer. For Edna, napkins belonged to an entirely different class: only for the King, Winston Churchill, and Fred Astaire.

'Did that have a name?'

'Ratatouille.' Gerry was very put out that there had been no gesture from him that he was delighted with the meal provided from a country under severe rationing.

'Ratatouille. That's a new one on me, sounds like a plate of rats.' Latymer was being funny. 'So, it was a pile dead animals after all.'

Gerry didn't see it that way. She cut him off. 'You didn't like it, you didn't have to eat it. Fine by me, I won't waste anymore of my time making you meals. I suggest,' and here she became very sarcastic, 'that McFadden take the boy wonder, Latymer, to the Oddfellows Club with the load of old men.'

'Gerry, I'm sorry.'

The young New Age man probably wasn't as experienced with the world as he believed he was. He took her hand. She pulled it away. He thought perhaps it was too soon for hand holding, whereas she'd decided that she wasn't going to be buttered up by him.

Latymer was trying hard to extricate himself. 'That was the loveliest meal I've eaten since I've been to Leicester. In fact, I think it may have even beaten my own mother's cooking.'

'Don't go over the top, nothing beats a mother's cooking.'

'I think that did. I shall telephone and tell her now.'

'Don't you dare! She'll hate me forever.'

'Is she going to know you that long?'

'That depends.' Gerry couldn't help smiling.

Latymer went to the receiver and picked it up. Gerry took his hand, forcing him to put it back in the cradle. They stood looking into each other's eyes, each daring the other to make the first move to a kiss.

'Your meal was beautiful. You are–'

The telephone rang. Gerry picked it up before Latymer could complete his sentence.

She spoke, listened, and spoke again.

'A doctor will be with you very soon.'

Gerry gave Latymer an address and told him that an elderly lady was concerned about her husband.

'I'll get my bag.'

'I'll be here when you get back.'

***

The old woman was waiting for Latymer at an open front door, the light from the bungalow's hallway spilling brightly against the street lamps. Most of the other houses were in blackness. There were few signs of life from anywhere other than this solitary house. For the majority of people living on the estate it would be an early start at Britley's, or they worked a night shift and the children were in bed.

'He's in here, Doctor.' The old lady had panic in her voice.

Latymer followed her into the bedroom. The wife was obviously having difficulty keeping him clean. The odour in the room smelled of excrement, vomit, and an unwashed body. It took him back to the camps in Europe where his nightmares began.

'How long has he been like this?' Latymer asked.

'I don't know.' It was as if the lady was trying to be useless.

Latymer was impatient. Emergency calls were a part of the job, but it didn't help if the person calling him was being obstructive. 'You must have some idea.'

The Doctor, The Plutocrat, and The Mendacious Minister

'I'm sorry, Doctor.' She started to cry. 'He won't get better. And we can't afford to pay.'

'You don't need to pay,' said Latymer, kindness in his voice.

An eye flickered from the unconscious patient. Latymer felt for a pulse. 'Who rang me?' Obviously, they didn't have a telephone.

'My daughter. She popped round for a knitting pattern for her little one's new school.'

He let go of the man's wrist, worried with the weak pulse. 'Where is she now?'

'With her kiddy.'

It would never cease to amaze him how people clung to day-to-day life, whilst those around them were dying.

He tried again on a different tack. 'When did this start?'

'Two days ago.' The response was more forthcoming this time, as if she realised the seriousness of the situation.

Latymer saw that she was frightened, and he would have to act as if everything were normal.

'He needs fluids in his body. The only way he can get them is in hospital. Can you go to the phone box and call an ambulance?'

'I don't want him to die.' She began crying.

'I'll do all I can.' Latymer spoke in a kind tone. He knew that he needed to sound positive for her sake. 'Your husband will be perfectly all right, but I must get him to hospital. I'll go to the callbox, I think it may be quicker.' He then stated the obvious. 'You wait with him,' as if there were anywhere else for her to go.

***

At the surgery Gerry washed, dried, and put away the few dishes and pans they'd used. She could see that Latymer, as she called him now, needed a full-time live-in housekeeper. She was set to suggest it to her father. She had the very person in mind to whom her father could offer the job to, the mother of the recently deceased child. Gerry wasn't sure of her name, Susan perhaps.

Gerry spread her hands on the table and stared out at the night. She knew all about losing someone you loved. There were times when she wanted to turn and find her mother standing there. Sympathy for the bereaved actually wasn't that helpful. Gerry knew the woman must be in need of a job, and psychologically, it would be the best for her.

She sat at the kitchen table. Gerry could spend the night at her father's flat before going back to Cambridge to continue her studies, but she was tired and wanted to stay with Peter. Did Latymer want her to stay? Probably any man would. But she didn't feel that Latymer was like that, or was she kidding herself, making Latymer into the paragon he wasn't?

In a few months when she passed her finals, another McFadden would be added to the long line of Dr McFaddens. She wasn't the first woman doctor by any means, but there were few of them. There were plenty of people around like that stupid man in the wheelchair, who didn't believe that a woman could become a doctor. She was enough of a feminist and had an independent spirit. Her education would be used for a positive purpose, but she loved the idea of having children. She wanted family life, a husband, and a home.

Gerry took the course that could not be misinterpreted; if she could find bedclothes, she would make up a bed in the spare room. If she was unable to do that, then she would spend the night with her father.

***

'You're still here.'

'Yes.' As if she meant, *of course*. 'I said I'd wait. Shall I make us a cup of tea?'

'Yes. Please. Good idea.'

She wasn't at all sure whether he was pleased to see her. 'What was it?' Latymer seemed troubled.

'A bad case of sickness, extremely dehydrated. He's an elderly man who is now in hospital on a drip. He'll recover. I hope.' He paused between each statement as if he were very tired.

'I've made up a bed for myself in the spare room. I hope you don't mind.'

'Good idea. It'll be nice to see your face at breakfast.'

'I'm awful to look at in the morning.'

'No, I bet you're lovely.' He was sounding too polite as if he wished he were alone. He mused and drummed his fingers on the arm of the chair.

She wondered what he was going to say, and if she wanted him to speak or would rather he remained silent with his own thoughts. Finally when the atmosphere was beginning to get a little tense she spoke. 'It'll have the neighbours talking. Me staying here, I mean.'

'Especially the Reverend Lewis,' Latymer said smiling.

'You know him, do you?' Gerry said.

'Unbearable man.' Latymer pulled a face that showed his disgust.

'I'm going to have to turn in, Gerry.' He spoke flatly as if his interest, now dissipated from her, was elsewhere. 'Leave the tea. I'll be too tired to drink it.'

Gerry wished that she'd gone to her father's flat. She felt trapped and disappointed.

Latymer gave her a conciliatory kiss on the cheek and left the room. For Gerry, it was a small gesture to make up for the way she was feeling.

As he undressed Latymer knew he and Gerry hardly knew one another, but he felt very natural with her. Because of his lack of experience with women, he was ignorant that she may hold warm feelings for him. He wasn't aware of the coldness in his behaviour since his return from the bedside of the old man. He believed everything to be perfectly all right.

***

Gerry woke to darkness. For a few moments she wasn't aware of where she was. She lay and remembered a dream. The images came back to her quite vividly; the operation on the aircraft pilot, the skin graft. The pilot waking from the anaesthetic was screaming in pain.

Realisation dawned on her that she was at her father's practice and that the screams were coming from another part of the house. It was Latymer. He sounded terrified.

Feeling frightened, she went to see what the matter was. When she entered his bedroom, it was filled with light. He was sat up in bed staring straight ahead looking as if he were ready to scream again.

'Latymer? Peter?'

He turned his head and looked at her.

'I saw them,' Latymer told her.

'Who did you see?' she asked.

She went over to his bed. He was like a child woken from a terrible nightmare, and all she wanted to do was love him as that child. She took his hands in hers. 'Try and tell me, who?'

'The grey living-corpses. So hopeless they should have been dead. I saw them. I was with them.' He was barely audible.

'Where, Peter?' she asked again. 'Where were you?'

'Belsen. I was at Belsen.'

'Peter, I didn't know. Let me hold you.' She laid him back and slid into the bed beside him. She held him until dawn, without sleeping and never wanting to let him go.

Chapter Fifteen

At dawn Gerry left Latymer's bedroom, pulled on a jumper over the shirt borrowed from him. She went downstairs. Sitting over a pot of tea and nibbling her toast, she knew it best that his nightmare was kept to herself for the present.

She went upstairs, washed, dressed, and went out. As she walked she knew that in the light of day, when he was ready, he would talk.

Latymer expected her to reappear, but Gerry was nowhere to be found. He felt disappointed as he sat down for his breakfast.

Edna appeared to be very serious as she gave him toast and tea, and when she spoke, she sounded it. 'Dr Latymer, if I may say, Bernard, that is Mr Birtwhistle, and myself are the souls of discretion.'

'Edna, or should I say Mrs Birtwhistle, as we seem to have become more formal, I have no idea what you are talking about,' Dr Latymer replied to the housekeeper.

'Oh.' She didn't realise that to drop the subject was the best option. 'When I arrived this morning to make your breakfast—'

'And I doubt there's a better toast-maker this side of Birstall,' Latymer interrupted with a smile.

She didn't recognise sarcasm. 'Thank you, Dr Latymer. That's very kind. Anyway, as I was saying, Miss McFadden was in the kitchen wearing one of your shirts and a jumper that reached just below her knees. Bernard didn't know where to look, well I tell a lie, he did until I sent him to chop the firewood.'

'What colour was it?' Latymer asked, his voice full of irony.

'The shirt was a cotton flannel material and the jumper was maroon, quite a dark shade, with very nice ribbing around the neck. Did your mother knit it?'

'No, an aunt,' Latymer said. 'You should have been a detective, Edna. You missed your calling. An eye for detail.'

'Thanks, Doctor.' Edna felt terribly flattered.

'Miss McFadden and I worked late last night.'

'Yes. Of course, Doctor,' Edna said busily.

'As if it's anything to you,' said Latymer.

'It isn't, Doctor.'

'But I'd appreciate it if what you know stayed within these four walls. People can talk and misinterpret the most innocent of events.'

Edna nodded very seriously.

'Where is Miss McFadden?' Latymer asked.

'I think she left,' Edna told him.

'Damn. I need to speak to her.' Latymer shook his head.

'I don't suppose you did too much talking last night.'

'Edna!'

'Sorry.' She went back into the kitchen with a huge grin plastered to her face.

***

After the conversation she had with her father and Latymer the night before, Gerry decided to visit Susan Harshaw that morning. She would have to get on with it as she needed to get back to university later in the day. They wouldn't be sympathetic to extra days taken without permission. She got Susan's address from the records in Olive's office, and went straight to the house. She could say her goodbyes to Latymer later.

She knocked on the door of a grey rendered featureless house that looked like the rest on the estate.

'Who is it?' Susan called from within.

'Miss McFadden. Dr McFadden's daughter.'

'What do you want?' Susan's tone was uncooperative.

'I can't speak through a closed door,' Gerry said.

Finally, as if Susan was making a major decision, she opened the door and stood looking like she was the person people said she was. She looked dreadful. The two women were poles apart. Susan was brandishing a cigarette between her fingers that she took regular drags from, her hair hadn't seen a brush. She was wearing night clothes which didn't look clean. Gerry, though having spent a night away from her own toiletries and clean clothes, could have attended the King's Garden Party.

'May I come in?'

Susan moved away from the door and Gerry entered the house.

'Do you mind if I open the window?'

With no reply forthcoming, she got on with it, and after struggling with the latch whilst Susan stood and watched, fresh air began to leak into the stale atmosphere. There was a bottle of gin on the kitchen table with an inch of the liquid remaining.

'Have you been drinking this today?'

'No. Last night. It helps me sleep.'

'No, good food and looking after yourself will help you sleep.' Gerry sounded pompous. It was the inexperience of youth.

'Have you just lost *your* daughter?' Susan's tone was aggressive.

Gerry defensively took a step back.

'Have you lived like I have to live? No job, no chance of one. They all blame me and hate me. No, you're just Miss La-di-da, the doctor's daughter.'

'Losing a child would be far too much to bear,' Gerry said. 'I'm sorry. More than losing a parent. My mother died during bombing in Coventry. Others may never be able to speak of their terrors.' Latymer and his nightmare came back to her.

'Susan, why don't you have a bath and put on clean clothes?' She was aware now that she was sounding like Miss Pringle, a brisk and busy teacher at her private school, 'And I'll make us a pot of tea. Have you any bread and butter?'

'No.' Susan was sulking. 'Why should I do all this? Do all you're saying? You're a do-gooder.'

'I've got a job for you. It could help a lot.'

'What?' Susan was curious now.

'You keep your side of the bargain,' Gerry replied.

'I haven't made a bargain.'

'Have a bath, Susan, and I'll go to Eric's shop, then come back and tell you where you'll be working.'

Chapter Sixteen

After morning surgery, Olive told Dr Latymer that the hospital wanted to speak with him concerning the man he had sent in as an emergency the previous night.

She was looking at the note she'd scribbled down and read out loud, 'A Doctor Racre.'

'He gets around. Is he the only doctor in that place?'

Latymer rang the hospital, and after the usual whirrs and clicks he was finally put through.

'Racre?'

'Latymer?'

'He's all right, my old man?'

'He'll live,' said Racre.

'That's a relief. What is his diagnosis?'

'I'd say food poisoning.'

'Yes, that's what I expected you to say,' Latymer replied.

'Because of his age, though, there were complications. Have you got a few minutes, Latymer?'

'Yes, go ahead.'

'Mainly his immune system had been weakened. This resulted in–'

'Clostridium difficile?'

'Yes. How did you know?' asked Racre, genuinely surprised.

'It's newly discovered and a professor at university liked to show off that he was up to date.' Latymer felt guilty of the same offence.

'So you know the procedure?' Racre asked.

'I do. Who volunteered?'

'Nobody,' Racre said. 'The daughter was told it would save her father's life, so of course she didn't need to volunteer.'

Latymer saw his medical notes in his mind's eye. 'Clostridium difficile,' they read, 'is a naturally occurring bacterium found in approximately five percent of the population's gut flora. The problem occurs when natural microorganisms are wiped out, clostridium difficile 'overgrows,' causing acute diarrhoea. This usually happens more commonly in people with weakened immune systems. The natural microorganisms have to be re-introduced into the body through the anus. Usually part of a faeces from a healthy relative.'

'I'll drop in on his wife after home visits. See if I can throw any light on it.'

'Yes, it does seem odd that he was poisoned and she wasn't.'

Latymer replaced the telephone into its cradle. He paused for a moment thoughtfully, then went to get the list of home visits from Olive.

She held the paper to her breast as if she wasn't going to let him have it.

'Miss McFadden wants a word.' She paused as if she didn't know quite how to say what it was she wanted to say.

Latymer saw this. 'What is it, Olive?'

She took the plunge. 'I'd just like to say that I'm the soul of discretion, and what you do in your own time is your own affair.'

'It's good to know I can rely on you, Edna, and Bernard.'

She looked nonplussed at this.

'Miss McFadden wants me to ring her?' he asked.

'No.' Olive was a little flustered now, 'She's in the sitting room.'

Latymer walked down the hallway to the sitting room.

The door to McFadden's surgery opened. 'Ah, Latymer, a quick word.' Latymer went into the room and the old doctor closed the door.

It was like stepping back in time. Everything in the room showed McFadden as practising for many years. The furniture was of dark oak. Although austere, there was comfort to it.

McFadden went to his roll top desk and played with his fingers on the edge as though he were beating out the rhythm of a Glen Miller number. He looked at Latymer over his half-moon spectacles.

Latymer knew what was coming.

'A delicate matter, but I just wanted to say.'

'That you are the soul of discretion?' said Latymer.

'Yes. How did you know?' McFadden sounded surprised.

They sat in awkward silence for a moment.

'I'd better get on. Your daughter's waiting for me in the sitting room.'

Latymer left McFadden in his antiquated surgery and went to Gerry.

'Gerry!' Then he saw Susan Harshaw and was disappointed. 'I'm sorry, Miss McFadden, Miss Harshaw.'

Latymer stood there feeling embarrassed because he had sounded like a character out of a Jane Austen novel. 'Is there a problem?'

Susan now looked in complete contrast to a couple of hours earlier. She was clean, dressed, and fed.

'Dad doesn't like dealing with this kind of thing. I hope you won't feel it's a *fait accompli*, but he felt it would be a good idea for you to have a live-in, seven-days-a-week housekeeper. He's offered Miss Harshaw the job.'

'Edna?' Latymer was sure this wouldn't go down well with her. 'What does she think?' He glanced awkwardly at Susan.

'Oh, don't worry on that count. She doesn't lose her job, does just less of it, which I'll doubt she'll mind. And of course, she's in charge.' She emphasised this point as much for Susan's sake as Peter's.

Latymer admired the way Gerry handled all of this. For his young years, Latymer wasn't a stupid boy. He could tell where the guiding hand was. Susan's experience as a servant in Britley's grand house would serve them well. This would give him a clean home and meal on his table every night – he hoped Susan could cook better than Edna. He saw, as well, that it would give Susan a purpose in life.

He didn't know what to say. He sounded rather underwhelmed with, 'I'm happy with that.'

Realising that Latymer wouldn't have a clue in showing a new housekeeper her duties, Gerry said, 'Come on, Susan. I'll show you to Edna and she can tell you what there is to do. I must get off then. Peter? Can you hang on a minute?'

Gerry returned to find Latymer standing, staring mindlessly out of the window.

'Are you all right?' she asked.

'Yes.'

'In the night. Do you remember?' She needed to know.

'I have bad dreams, that's all. Since I was little.'

She knew there was more, but he didn't want to speak about it.

'I have to go back,' she told him.

'Back?' He thought she meant the kitchen.

'To university. I sit my finals in a few weeks.'

'Will you write?' he asked.

Will you? she wanted to ask. 'Do you want me to?'

'Yes,' he said.

She left the room wanting to know why he hadn't asked for her address at university.

***

A few days later, Latymer was talking to the elderly wife of the hospitalised man trying to find out what he had consumed that week. He was getting a lot of unnecessary detail related to the family, but little else.

'My daughter and I and her kiddy went to see my sister Vera and her husband Johnny in Stoke. They've got one boy.'

'Do you know what he ate while you were away?'

'Probably cheese cobs at the Leys. He loves a pork pie as well.'

Now at last they were making headway. Pork Pies and pub food could be lethal.

'Is that all?'

'Oh no!'

This was like the proverbial getting blood from a stone. She should have been a spy. She would have never said a word to the enemy.

'Well, what else then?' Latymer knew he was beginning to sound forceful, but he didn't have the time to waste.

'I left him a stew. I make a very good stew. It lasts two or three days, depending on how much you eat each day.'

'Did you eat any of it?'

'There wasn't a bit left. I didn't expect him to leave me any. Doesn't usually. I said you eat it all up, do you good. How wrong I was there, eh?' She paused waiting for a response and Latymer nodded his head. 'He'd washed up the pan it was in. He's like that, though. Doesn't expect me to do all the running round after him.'

'What did you put in it?'

'What you normally put in a stew.'

'Pretend I don't know.'

'An onion,' she counted off the ingredients on her fingers as if it were an aid to her memory, 'a couple of carrots, potatoes, a bit of cabbage, a parsnip, salt and pepper, gravy salt, and a tin of that lovely meat from Eric's. He's just got it in. Meat, where's he got that from? If only there were more meat available, you know.' She told him as if he weren't aware there was rationing.

'Eric's? The shop round the corner?'

'Yes.'

'And where did you get the vegetables?' he asked.

'My son-in-law grows them.'

'And you all eat those?'

She nodded as if he was a bit on the slow side.

Next stop then would be Eric's.

***

By lunchtime on the day of Susan's appointment as housekeeper to the young, attractive, and available Dr Latymer, the Reverend Lewis sat at lunch with Mrs Lewis. He was wearing an appalled face.

'Can you believe that a man of social standing should allow a wanton harlot to move in with him under the guise of housekeeper?'

As she knew he expected her to, she shook her head in disbelief.

'Nor I. Mind you, the Catholic Church does it all the time. Father Grundy at Our Lady and St Patrick's has probably got children stashed away all over the place, all beget by his succession of housekeepers. The Pope probably has a Vatican full. That is why marriage within the Church of England is a holy blessing overseen by God for the procreation of children.'

Mrs Lewis nodded, though at times she wished the Reverend would forget the procreation bit and get on with the practise of making babies.

***

Doctor Latymer was in Eric's shop looking at row upon row of silver tins. None displayed a label.

'Doctor Latymer.' Eric came around from behind the counter wiping his hands on his apron. 'When did I last see you in here?' Eric looked to the ceiling as if it were a serious question, 'Of course, it is always a pleasure.' He grinned. 'I expect you will be visiting us less frequently for your sherbet dabs, now that you got a new housekeeper.' Laughing at his own silly joke, there was more than a hint of sarcasm in his voice. 'Or has she let you down already?' Eric was always on the lookout for a piece of gossip.

Latymer pointedly ignored him. Gesturing towards the tins he said, 'What are these?'

Feeling a little aggrieved at the rebuff, Eric replied, 'Tins.'

'Tins of what?'

Eric tapped his long nose. He was a small, thin, beaky man who looked permanently unshaven. Very little got past him, and he was always on the lookout for ways of making an easy pound.

Latymer continued, 'I need to know or I wouldn't be asking.'

'Mainly fruit, veg, and meat.'

'How would I know which is which?'

'Look on the bottom.' Eric didn't like these questions and was curt in his reply. 'V for veg, F for fruit and, you may be surprised, M for meat.'

'Why aren't there any labels?' Latymer asked.

'Army surplus.'

'How old are they?'

'No idea. But nothing goes rotten in tins.'

'Hm.' Latymer paused then said, 'Where did you get them from?'

'Can't say.'

'Won't say? Or was it Mr Britley?'

'Your guess is as good as mine.' As he replied, Eric wiped his hands again.

***

Latymer returned to the surgery. He was working out what it was he needed to do next. He should buy a tin of food and have it analysed. He felt a fool, he should have bought all three when he was at Eric's. But what did he have a housekeeper for? He would send Susan later.

Olive came running out of the door towards him. 'Dr Latymer. Thank goodness.'

'What on earth is the matter?'

'A crisis at the school. Dr McFadden and Gerry are there already. They want you as soon as possible.'

Latymer collected his bag. He was surprised that Gerry was at the school. He assumed Olive had made a mistake. But he didn't have time to think about it. Seeing the car gone, he paced as fast as he could. At the school he didn't make any formal introductions, just went straight to the medical room. He was met by Miss Penrose, the teacher he had seen at Amy's funeral.

'What's going on?'

'It just hit the children like a wave.' Miss Penrose was very calm in her response. 'Mainly vomiting. The ones we think are either all right, or who have parents around who can cope, we've sent home. It could be infectious.' But then checking herself so that she didn't appear to be stepping on toes, 'But of course you would know. I don't mean to–'

'No, you took the right action, Miss Penrose. Though I'm quite sure what is causing the sickness isn't contagious.'

Latymer looked around the room. Gerry saw him and nodded in acknowledgement as though they were only acquaintances.

Dr McFadden looked up from the child he was examining, a surprised look on his face. 'You're saying there is no worry that this is infectious? How do you know?'

'I need to talk to you later. I have a suggestion.'

'Go ahead, man,' answered McFadden.

'We need as many dishes as we can lay our hands on for the children to vomit into. If that means bringing them in from the canteen, their homes or even the hospital, then get them here. It goes without saying that we need to make the children as comfortable as possible. We must have plenty of glasses of fresh water. As soon as they can drink, pour as much water into them as they will take, flush out their systems. Soon, hopefully they will start to feel better.'

Mr Beltham spoke up. 'These buildings are a school. I'm going to ring the Leicester Royal Infirmary and have the pupils taken there in ambulance convoy, if necessary.'

Nurse Bullock hobbled into the room heavily on a walking stick, her arm in a sling.

As Senior Medical Officer in the school, my main priority is for the children's health, just as yours is for their education. You'll do no such thing. You'll follow Dr Latymer's instructions,' Dr McFadden told the headmaster.

Mr Beltham turned to the school nurse. 'Nurse Bullock, what do you think?'

'I agree with you, Mr Beltham.'

McFadden spoke very firmly. 'Well, that's because you're both stupid. Now leave us to get on with our job. Miss Penrose, stay and help us, will you?'

'She will do no such thing. She has a class to look after. I have never been so insulted.'

Mrs Bullock agreed, 'I haven't either, Mr Beltham.'

'You surprise me. Mr Beltham, why don't you look after what remains of Miss Penrose's class, rather than sitting at your desk doing nothing?' McFadden was done with his foolishness.

Mr Beltham stormed out of the room, slamming the door.

'Nurse Bullock, we don't need you here either.'

When she'd left the room, Miss Penrose confided in them, 'She keeps a bottle of gin in her handbag.'

'Ah, we all do, Miss Penrose,' said McFadden with a smile.

She looked so shocked that Dr Latymer felt it necessary to say, 'I think he was joking.'

Dr McFadden guffawed, 'Come on to work.'

After twenty minutes things began to settle. Gerry and Miss Penrose brought in water, and tentative sips were being taken. A few parents hearing of the outbreak arrived to take their children home. Often they heard, 'I've been a bit queasy all morning, too.'

Latymer excused himself to make a telephone call. He went out of the medical room and past Mr Beltham's office to use the secretary's telephone. He could hear Mr Beltham's voice and paused outside the door to listen.

'Young pompous doctor, yes Latymer, thinks it's food poisoning. He didn't say as much, but I can put two and two together. You should take them off the shelves. I want no part of it. You can count me out.'

The secretary told Latymer that Mr Beltham was using the telephone.

'He's finished.' He paused. 'No, he's started again. Can you come get me when the line is free? No, I've a better idea. You must have a reliable child here, I'm sure you do. Can you send one of them to Eric's and buy a tin of vegetable, a tin of meat, and a tin of fruit? Then take them to the surgery and give them to Olive. Nothing is to be done to them until I arrive. Here's a pound. Tell the child to keep the change.'

The pupil went to the shop and couldn't find the tins. All he got was the threat from Eric that he would ring Mr Beltham to tell him that one of his charges was a truant. 'I know what you look like. I was a Special Constable in the War,' Eric shouted, 'I'm ringing now.'

The young boy fled and went straight to the surgery where he told them he couldn't find the tins the doctor wanted.

Olive had no idea what he was talking about. She felt irritated with the boy. She went into the kitchen and asked Edna.

'Perhaps something the doctor fancied for his dinner,' said Edna. Susan didn't comment.

At times Olive thought Edna was completely stupid. She could not see Dr Latymer having a school pupil running round the estate buying his dinner. Why, she wondered, couldn't the school send a child with a bit of sense, but she said nicely, 'Well you tried. I'm sure the doctor will get it sorted out. Run along back to school now.' And muttering to herself, 'Let's hope they knock a bit of sense into him.'

Olive returned to the kitchen where Susan was washing the lunchtime dishes. She had quickly got into the routine of the house and was benefiting from a purpose in life.

'What's wrong?' Susan asked.

'Children. We were never like this in my day. Give a child a job and they would do it. None of this mollycoddling. Parents today are too soft on their children.' Then she put her hand to her mouth. 'Oh! I'm sorry, Susan.'

'It's all right. I'd rather people just carried on as normal.'

For Susan, it was quite a victory to see Olive with her defences down.

'Still, it wasn't very sensitive.' Partly to change the subject and because she was puzzled, Olive said, 'I wonder why he sent a pupil from the school to buy the tins and the silly child couldn't see them.'

'Do you want me to go for them?'

'Could you, Susan?'

'I expect you were going to ask anyway.' She smiled. 'What do we need?' Susan folded her apron away.

Edna asked her to get a packet of tea as Dr Latymer drinks it as if it 'were going out of fashion.'

Susan decided she'd need a shopping bag. While she was getting one out of the cupboard, Bernard asked her to get him a couple of ounces of peppermints.

The shop door opened with a jangle of the bell, and Eric came out from the storeroom at the back of the shop.

'Why, Miss Harshaw, Dr Latymer's new housekeep.' Eric couldn't help but sound lecherous.

'Dr Latymer would like a tin of vegetables, meat, and one of fruit.'

Eric reached round the back of the counter and put the three tins on the surface facing her.

'No, the ones without their labels on.'

'He wants me to take the labels off? How's he going to know what's in them, or is that one of the games you two get up to?' Eric was making a poor actor's attempt at sounding puzzled.

'This isn't making any sense. Miss Riley said I'd see them on the shelves, stacks of them without their labels on.'

'Can you see any?' asked Eric.

Susan looked around the shop. 'No.'

'They ain't here then, are they?' said Eric. 'Must have been seeing things.' He laughed wickedly. 'Now, how are you and that handsome young doctor getting on? I bet he sees a few things when he gives you the once over. I bet he doesn't need much persuading. Nor you, either. Lucky bugger.'

Susan left, leaving the door open and without buying the tea or Bernard's peppermints.

Eric laughed as he watched her leave.

***

A week later, on Friday evening before surgery, the two doctors, Olive, and Gerry held an informal meeting in the sitting room. Dr McFadden offered everyone a whisky, all declined, but he took one himself.

Latymer sat opposite Gerry. She was very cool towards him. He had no idea what it was he'd done wrong. She obviously hadn't come to Leicester to see him.

'So, we have a very serious case of food poisoning that could have resulted in a fatality and an outbreak at the school,' said McFadden, stating the obvious.

'Also a number of cases that may or may not be food poisoning,' answered Latymer.

'Though, I would put it down to food poisoning,' said McFadden.

'Fortunately, it doesn't seem to be clostridium difficile,' Gerry replied, showing off her medical knowledge as well.

'No, that was because the elderly patient's immune system was weak.' McFadden asserted his authority.

'There is, of course, the mystery of the disappearing tins,' Latymer added.

'Sounds like the title of an Enid Blyton,' said Gerry with a smile.

'Except, Gerry, now is not the time to be light-hearted,' her father told her, quite firmly.

'Sorry, Dad.'

'Who would want the tins to disappear?' asked Olive.

'Other than Eric and Beltham? Britley.' Latymer said, 'Eric as good as told me.'

'You don't like Britley. You've got it in for him. What did Eric say?' McFadden didn't like members of his club criticised.

'When I said Britley, Eric said 'your guess is as good as mine.' Latymer spoke as if this were the solution to the mystery.

'We need sound evidence, Latymer.' McFadden went for another whisky, but stopped short at Gerry's glare.

'You need conclusive evidence,' McFadden went on, 'the contents of the tins need checking. That's what you were doing, sending people to Eric's to do your shopping?'

'Yes,' Latymer replied. 'I was stupid not buying a tin when I had the opportunity.'

'I feel terrible,' said Olive. 'I accused that boy not being able to find them, thinking he was stupid. It wasn't his fault at all. Eric took them off the shelves. I shall see the boy gets his half a crown.'

'We still need a tin, probably best if it's the meat,' said McFadden.

'The tin of vegetables I bought the other week didn't cause Peter or me any harm,' Gerry told the gathering.

It was the only reference she'd made to him that day, and he wondered if she wished it had poisoned him.

'Would Edna know anyone in the school kitchens?' Latymer asked, looking directly at Olive.

'I don't know. I'll talk to her in the morning.'

'Yes, come on, the patients call.' McFadden ended the meeting by standing up, ready to leave the room.

Olive followed him.

'Well?' asked Gerry of Peter.

'I didn't know that you were here this weekend. I thought you'd gone back to Cambridge to finish your studies.'

'I did as soon as the crisis was over.' She stopped speaking, but he knew she had something else to say. 'Why didn't you say anything while we were dealing with those children? Do you care? You just left. I had no idea where you'd gone.'

Latymer wasn't sure what to say.

'You didn't pick up the phone or write. You've had plenty of time. How were you supposed to know I'd be here today? You didn't even ask for my address. You have to make some effort, Peter.'

He didn't know how to make amends. 'What are you doing here?'

'Not seeing you. So have no fear there. I'm spending the weekend with a friend.'

The colour went from his face.

'Don't worry, female.' She wasn't going to let him suffer too much for his stupidity.

Latymer smiled with relief.

'We could,' said Gerry, 'go to the cinema. She has a boyfriend.'

'Err–'

'I'll see what she thinks and ring you here?'

'I can't,' said Latymer.

'I'm sure Dad will do tonight, if I go and ask him.'

'He is already,' replied Latymer. 'My sister Ruth is here for the weekend. I'm meeting her off the train. Which is where I should be now.'

'You'd better be off then.' Gerry made to leave the room.

'I'll write, I promise.'

Gerry shrugged her shoulders as if she didn't care.

Chapter Seventeen

Ruth travelled from Weymouth to Leicester that Friday evening. Latymer met her at the railway station. A bus took the pair to the estate, where they were dropped off at their destination and took the short walk to Stocking House.

'It's a bit austere,' commented Ruth.

After living there, Latymer was defensive about his new home. 'What do you mean?' he asked.

'Well, it's not Weymouth.'

'No,' he spoke to her as if she were an idiot, 'you're in a different town, Ruth. Remember the train journey?'

They had already begun to behave as they had when the two were children.

She laughed. 'No, I meant the houses are all the same. There's no one about. It's quite scary.'

'There was, and is, a housing problem in the country. Council estates have been built since the end of the last century.'

'Here we go, a lecture from Doctor Latymer.'

'Well you asked.'

'Ay up me duck,' said a man as he passed, 'not on your tod? Nice one.' The man grinned at Ruth, 'Miss,' and touched his cap.

Latymer nodded in response.

'What did he say?'

'Leicester slang for hello and you're not by yourself.'

'Golly, he thinks I'm your girlfriend.'

'Lucky you,' said Latymer.

'Lucky *you*, more like. Have you got a girlfriend?'

Latymer ignored the question. 'Anyway, we just met *someone*. And if I take you into the waiting room of the surgery, you'll meet a lot more. But I won't. There should be a meal ready. Hungry?'

Ruth rubbed her stomach and licked her lips. 'Always hungry.'

'Susan's cooking this evening. I made sure. Edna's attempts leave a lot to be desired. But if you meet, don't tell her.'

Brother and sister went into the house. Latymer took Ruth straight upstairs to the guest room. Ruth looked around the room with pleasure. She took off her coat and laid it across the bed. She was feeling excited about the weekend.

On the dressing table was a small vase of flowers brought in from the garden. Ruth couldn't believe it had been her brother's idea. She went over to have a closer look. 'That's lovely. How lovely.'

'Yes,' said Latymer thinking how Susan had pulled out all of the stops in getting ready for Ruth. She must have been a good maid at Britley's residence.

'There's a note with them, Peter. Is it from you?'

And a written welcome, thought Peter. He smiled, not sure what else to do.

Ruth picked it up and read it.

'What does it say?' Peter asked.

Ruth sounded puzzled as she read the note.

> Thank you for everything.
> I wouldn't be here.
> Susan.

She paused and read the note again to herself as if she hadn't seen it correctly. 'What does that mean, Peter? I wouldn't be here.'

'I don't know. Maybe, no, I don't know.'

'Anyway, everything's lovely.'

'I'll leave you to freshen up. When you're ready come downstairs. The sitting room is the second door on your left.'

Latymer left his sister to unpack her clothes and make herself at home. He poured himself a small whisky and sat by the fire, happy that Ruth liked his home.

Susan came in, 'Dinner is ready, whenever you want it.'

'She'll be down in a moment.'

'Did she like the room? Did she see the flowers and note?'

Latymer was flustered now. 'Er, yes.'

'I'll go wait in the kitchen. I'll hear you.'

Latymer sat for a minute or two more. The door suddenly burst opened and Ruth rushed in.

'You said *left*. You said second door left,' she exclaimed.

'I meant right. Sorry, I should have said right.'

'Yes, you should have.' Having got over the embarrassment and shock Ruth was on the verge of giggling. 'There were all these people in there. One said, My, *you* are going to have to wait, and there was all this shouting, I've got the flu, it's me back, I'm expecting, my leg hurts, I've got a migraine, can't get rid of this cough, until this scary man came into the room looking at them fiercely over half-moon glasses.'

'Dr McFadden.'

'And they all went silent. I ran.'

'Well, at least you've met them all, and Dr McFadden.'

'He'll give me nightmares. I thought Miss Hill at school was terrifying.'

Latymer started laughing.

'It wasn't funny,' said Ruth, 'it was as if they were all mad. Are they?'

Latymer had an image of Reg Fantam in his mind. 'No, not all. Come on, let's eat.'

Brother and sister sat at the table. Susan heard them from the kitchen and took in the soup. She really had tried with the meagre rations that were available. Carrot soup to start with, meat and vegetable pie for the main course, though it contained very little meat, and rice pudding for dessert.

'Miss Harshaw,' said Latymer as Susan entered the room, 'this is my sister, Miss Latymer.' He really could sound pompous at times.

'Oh,' said Susan looking completely nonplussed. 'I was expecting. No, it's all right.'

'Lovely to meet you,' said Ruth. 'My brother reads too many nineteenth century novels. I'm Ruth. Miss Latymer makes me sound like an old maid.'

'My name's Susan. I'm sorry about before. I was expecting Miss McFadden, Gerry, Dr McFadden's daughter. I'll leave you with your soup.'

'Thank you, Susan.'

Susan left the room in something of a flurry.

'Gerry?' said Ruth, 'and who is Gerry?' She knew that she was onto something.

'You heard, Dr McFadden's daughter. Eat your soup before it goes cold.'

Ruth wouldn't let it go. 'Why would she be staying here? Surely she'd spend the weekend with her parents.'

'Her mother died during the war.'

'That's very sad, but it doesn't really answer my question, Peter.'

'Dr McFadden lives in a flat. Probably not enough room.'

They ate in silence for a minute or two.

'Good soup,' said Latymer. 'How are your studies going?'

'Oh dear, now you are sounding like Dad. You know you'll turn into him.'

'Could do worse.'

'This Gerry, then,' asked Ruth, 'how old is she?'

Latymer thought that they had successfully moved away from Gerry. He knew little about the female psyche.

'Oh, err,' he shook his head as if he'd hardly set eyes on the girl, 'I don't know, early twenties?'

'No point in asking me. I've never seen her. Is she pretty?'

'I don't know,' said Latymer taking another spoonful of soup as if it were a very important action to take and needed all his concentration. 'I've never looked.'

'A girl that you've obviously seen, that Susan thought was staying here, so she must have spent at least a night here before, and you don't know if she's pretty or not? Pull the other one. Peter, why are you going red?'

'I'm not.'

'I've known you long enough.'

'I'll tell Gerry, I mean Susan, we're ready for the next course.'

Ruth burst out laughing. 'Tell her I want to know all about Gerry.'

'Don't you dare.' He got up from the table exasperated, wishing his sister was still in Weymouth.

'I'm sure I'll get the chance.' Ruth gave her brother a wicked smile as he went into the kitchen with the soup bowls.

***

On the Saturday morning of Ruth's stay, Latymer had to work morning surgery. He fully intended to complete it as quickly and efficiently as possible.

He left Ruth in her bed. It would be a luxury for her. At home in Weymouth to get up for school on time, his sister would have to be up by seven and out of the house by a quarter to eight. There would be hockey or another sport on a Saturday morning, guides in the afternoon, and their father never let her linger in bed beyond nine on a Sunday.

Ruth woke with a start. Daylight surged into her room. She picked up her watch from the bedside table and saw that it was after ten. She panicked that her father would be stern because she had slept so late. Then she remembered where she was and sank back into her pillow.

Quite a bit later Ruth got out of bed and went downstairs. Susan heard her and met her in the sitting room.

'Good morning,' said Susan kindly, 'or should I say good afternoon?'

Ruth smiled shyly.

'No doubt, you'd like some tea.'

'Yes, but I can get it myself,' said Ruth. She wasn't used to people waiting on her.

'No, no,' Susan told her, 'you sit down. Toast and a boiled egg?'

'Yes, please.'

'One or two?'

When Latymer had finished his morning surgery he found his sister and Susan in the kitchen chatting like old friends, sister to sister.

'Susan was just telling me all about–'

Susan laughed enjoying the companionship of the young woman. 'You'll get me into trouble,' she said.

'Perhaps it's best I don't hear,' said Latymer.

Changing the subject, Susan asked, 'Will you want lunch?'

'After the breakfast you've just given me, I don't think I'll ever want to eat again,' said Ruth.

'No, we'll go out now. Could we have dinner at half past five?'

'What are we doing tonight?' Ruth asked.

'The cinema,' Latymer told her. '*Brighton Rock* is showing at the ABC.'

'And then,' said Ruth sadly, 'back home tomorrow and the grindstone on Monday.'

'I'm sure you'll be here again,' said Susan.

'She will,' Latymer confirmed.

Chapter Eighteen

'Edna wants a word,' said Olive.

In despair Latymer said, 'Have she and Susan been fighting?'

'Dr Latymer, if it were the pair of them arguing, it wouldn't be your business,' Olive told him in a way that meant don't get above your station. 'That would be for Dr McFadden or for myself to sort out.'

Summarily told off, he followed Olive into the kitchen. Edna grinning stood like Jasper Maskelyne performing a magic trick, which she almost was, for there on the table were several tins, all without their labels.

'Edna, you're a genius,' Latymer told her.

'I knew you'd be pleased,' put in Olive to remind him of her part in the act, 'I'll leave you to it.'

'Which do you want to eat then, Doctor?' Edna asked.

'None of them.'

'Oh?' Edna felt disappointed and a little stupid, her willing service crushed.

Latymer picked up the tins one by one. Edna looked on, thinking how strange young people were these days. Finally after inspecting them, when she could see nothing to look at, he said, 'Well done, Edna. You've the whole collection here. Vegetables, meat, and fruit. You got them from Eric's, I take it?'

'I bought them a couple of weeks ago. They were cheap. I like to take advantage of a bargain.'

'Well, they seem to have disappeared off the face of the earth, and I want to know why.' Latymer spoke as if to himself. 'There were shelves full of them at Eric's the other day. The few parents I've spoken to deny buying them.'

He turned to Edna and spoke in a whisper as if there were spies everywhere. She looked around the room. 'Under no account tell anyone that these tins are here. Is there any way we can find out if they were used in the school for school dinners?'

Hesitantly, Edna replied. 'My sister is one of the kitchen ladies who works there.'

'Perhaps you could ask her, sort of normal like,' he said to her.

'Normal like?' Edna was completely puzzled.

'As if it were part of an ordinary conversation. Drop it into your everyday chatter.'

'Yes?' Edna didn't understand.

'Say, shame those kiddies getting ill at school. She'll say, "Yes".' Latymer coached her.

Edna nodded, knowing the likelihood of the conversation taking that course would be remote. They usually spent their evenings grumbling about their husbands or the way prices were going up.

'Then you say, joking of course, probably your cooking, and you'll both laugh.' Latymer laughed to show that it was a joke.

'Why would we laugh?' Edna asked.

'Well–'

'She's more likely to thump me, then her husband 'ull join in and there'll be an almighty row.'

'Just think of a way, Edna,' Latymer was despairing now, 'a way of finding out whether those tins were in the school kitchen and if they've been used for the children's dinners.'

'Why don't I just ask her?'

'Do it your way. Because if she says yes, then bingo!'

'Bingo?'

'Because we'll know what poisoned the children.' Latymer looked at her as if he'd solved the crime of the century.

Edna left the room thinking that this young man had seen far too many mystery films.

Chapter Nineteen

Gerry returned to university. Latymer promised faithfully he would write, but never seemed to find the time. He came to realise that he was also waiting for the letter from her. Rather stupidly, he wondered why. It took him time to realise he was missing her terribly.

After surgery at night when the house felt devoid of company, Susan doing whatever needed doing in the kitchen, listening to the radio made the house seem desolate; he felt very alone.

At times he went out with Racre and James McFadden. Drinking in a country pub, a village such as Woodehouse, the real ale and the log fire. They tried a meal once, but three men out for a meal was odd, and they were too young to be Oddfellows. In the city there was a jazz club and the Inkspots were playing one night.

'I saw them play for troops in a town on the German-French border.'

'What were you doing over there, Latymer?'

'Oh nothing, you know, wine, women, and the–'

'Inkspots?'

The young doctors went along. After the harmony group completed their set, a jazz band took over playing into the early hours of the morning. Latymer loved the music, but he didn't want to take a partner out of the crowd and dance like his friends.

'Come on, man, live a little,' he was told.

***

The skin graft on the airman had been a success. So successful that doctors senior to James McFadden wanted to witness the next operation. It was to be filmed and written up for *The Lancet*. James agreed on condition that these senior consultants only observe. He would stick with his original team where each knew his role in the theatre. That team would include Latymer.

Latymer felt a fraud, but it was insisted upon. He was told he was competent, of importance, he could be relied upon with the physical and mental energy of a young man.

James put it to him, 'That's what I need - young blood, or I'll end up with an interfering busybody sticking his nose in. You know your place. But don't expect Gerry to be there. She's nearing finals.'

'I wasn't.'

'Come off it. You're like a lost puppy. Have you written to her?'

Latymer opened the palms of his hands. 'I've been very busy.'

'You're a fool. Do you think she might be waiting for a letter? Aren't you? Pigheaded, you both could write a tome on it.'

***

Finally a letter arrived. It wasn't the one he wanted; it wasn't from Gerry. It was from the laboratory at the Glenfield Hospital. They sent him a report of their findings. Exhaustive tests showed the food in the tins of meat to contain the germ listeria. This would cause food poisoning, minor to severe, depending on the age and health of the person consuming the food.

Latymer thought about meeting the local MP, Joles, at Amy Harshaw's funeral. He wrote to him expressing his concern about the major outbreak of food poisoning at the school. He told the MP that in his opinion the poisoning had been caused by tins of food bought in from a non-government source, perhaps the black market.

Joles replied that he would be in Leicester the following Thursday to Monday and that Latymer should arrange a meeting with him through Joles' secretary.

It was out of Latymer's realm of experience, making appointments to meet the local Member of Parliament. He didn't know whether he should telephone the House of Commons or try to find the MP's home address, so when in doubt he'd ask Olive to arrange it. She seemed to know how to do everything.

Olive arranged for him to have lunch at Joles' house the following Saturday. Joles lived near Bradgate Park, so Bernard drove him there.

'I know where it is. I'll enjoy a walk round the park. Lady Jane Grey lived there, you know. I like my history.'

'Queen for nine days.'

'That's right. Don't worry, I'll be back to pick you up.'

Joles' house, for a Labour MP, was the house of a hypocrite. It was a mansion. This was a man representing people on a council estate for whom living in a house like this and the kind of money it represented would be a fantasy. For Latymer, perhaps in his naïve, immature way, it seemed wrong for a left-wing Member of Parliament to live this way.

Joles was waiting outside for him; at least there wasn't a butler ready to announce his arrival. The pair shook hands and made pleasantries. Joles asked Bernard to return in five hours, which seemed an inordinate amount of time for a brief meeting.

They went into the house, which did take Latymer's breath away in its beauty. Lightwood and stone. Modern art hung on the walls. Latymer recognised a Bacon and what could have been a Picasso hanging next to a Matisse.

He was introduced to Mrs Joles who was very country. 'She dropped her title,' Joles said.

Latymer nodded, lacking real understanding, and Mrs Joles smiled as if she regretted the loss of her "lady."

Latymer realised where the money was and who owned the house. The small party of three made their way into the drawing room, where Latymer was quite overwhelmed to find at least twenty people present.

'You look surprised.'

'Pleasantly.' He knew his manners and lied to Mrs Joles, 'I was expecting a brief meeting with your husband.'

'Lunch, Dr Latymer, enjoy yourself. Business can wait until later.'

'Peter, please.'

She touched his arm. 'Peter it is.' Though that afternoon he never knew her other than Mrs Joles.

'Sherry, dry?'

He took the drink.

'Let me introduce you to a few people. I'll try and avoid the boring ones, which could be difficult here. I don't know where his lordship finds them; politics, deathly dull.'

There was a polite ripple of laughter from those who overheard, believing that the comment didn't refer to them. They were obviously a little afraid of this formidable woman.

'Ah Cecilia.' Mrs Joles addressed a young woman.

Both smiled at Latymer. MP Joles seemed to have vanished.

Latymer felt he was now disappearing into a well of the social swirl of Leicestershire upper crust society and he felt out of his depth.

'Cecilia doesn't have a boyfriend,' Mrs Joles told Latymer whilst Cecilia and the small group around her listened in. The attractive eighteen-year-old went crimson.

'Oh dear, I've embarrassed you.' She touched the girl's arm in an act of contrition, but she didn't honestly mean it. She was enjoying playing the game. Mrs Joles went on, 'Are you married, Dr Latymer?'

'No.'

'Oh dear,' she feigned drama, 'I was worried that we'd left Mrs Latymer at home.' The lady of the house paused and smiled at her own little joke. 'I'll leave you two then.' And she busied off elsewhere.

Latymer felt embarrassed. He didn't know what to say. 'I–'

'Don't worry,' Cecilia interrupted him, 'she's always like that. It's her way.'

The pair stood in silence.

'Shall I get you another drink?' asked Latymer.

'I'll fall flat on my face if I have more than one sherry.'

So he went for the obvious question. 'What do you do?'

'I'm going to university in September.'

'I think my sister is as well. Where will you be studying?'

'Edinburgh,' Cecilia told him.

'That's a long way. What to study?'

'Literature.'

'I love reading,' Latymer said.

'So do I.'

'I would hope so.'

They both suddenly saw the funny side of what was said. Because of the tension of the social occasion they found it difficult to stop giggling.

When Cecilia had gathered herself, she asked Latymer, 'Who's your favourite author?'

He reflected for a moment and then said, 'Cowper-Powys.'

'Mine's Austen.'

The gong rang for lunch.

Cecilia and Latymer weren't seated together, so Mrs Joles' matchmaking came to nothing.

Mrs Joles sat Latymer next to her, saying, 'I wanted to sit next to this young man who is so interesting.' Whilst they were eating their soup she went on, 'You've been involved in groundbreaking plastic surgery, I hear.'

'If you mean the skin grafts, well, I was in the theatre the same time as it was happening.' Latymer spoke modestly because that was what he genuinely felt.

'You keep your light under a bushel, Dr Latymer.'

'Peter.'

'Mr Joles and I are Jewish.' It was an announcement she made, and a few heads turned as if they didn't know. Mrs Joles intended to attract the other diners' attention for the statement that followed. 'We're aware of your other work in Europe at the end of the war.'

Now, Latymer felt very uncomfortable. 'I'm sorry, but I would rather leave those experiences in the past.'

This comment, that was bordering on being rude to his hostess, raised more faces from their bowls of soup.

'I understand. But from the bottom of my heart, my total gratitude on behalf of the Jewish people.'

Latymer looked down at the porcelain, aware that the comments were making him the hero he didn't want to be.

'Now then,' she looked up and down the table for a new topic of conversation, 'Mr Beltham, what do you think of our new young doctor?'

Latymer was shocked. Beltham, what was he doing here? Beltham was a friend of Joles'? In fact, at the funeral, they seemed anything but. It took Latymer time to learn that all invites weren't necessarily for social reasons. There were other political manoeuvrings that went on as well.

'A fine young man, Mrs Joles,' the headmaster lied as he carried on slurping his soup. Beltham obviously wasn't going to add anything else. He said what was expected of him. Conversation resumed and the meal took its course.

At the end of the meal there was an easy atmosphere. The guests enjoying the aftertaste of their lamb cutlets. A few of the guests lit cigarettes. Brandy and port were passed and taken by a few, but the women didn't leave the room. That wasn't Mrs Joles' way. Latymer didn't take any more alcohol than the two small glasses of wine that he had with his meal. He wanted his head to be clear when he spoke to

Joles. He made polite, if meaningless, conversation with the few people across the table.

A man, who Latymer later learnt was Joles' secretary, came and told him that his car was waiting. He spoke loudly as if he wanted the whole room to hear.

Mrs Joles expressed her dismay, 'Oh, you're leaving us so soon.' Beltham looked smug. One or two guests said their farewells and what a pleasure it had been to meet him, though nothing of any note was spoken.

Latymer was confused. Joles hadn't been present for the lunch. He heard Mrs Joles mentioning an important phone call her husband was taking. It didn't feel right. There was more going on than met the eye, so he mumbled his goodbyes, played the polite young man and followed Joles' secretary.

Mr Beltham turned to the guest sitting near him. 'Young upstart. I'll have another glass of port before I see Mr Joles.' The headmaster greedily took a swig of the drink. The alcohol was making him jolly and sure of himself. 'Mr Joles,' Beltham spoke as if Joles were a close confidant, 'invited me here, you know, to discuss my appointment as an education adviser in the government.' Beltham nodded importantly. 'Mr Joles is known for recognising talent when he sees it.'

Mrs Joles simply smiled and watched the play unfold.

Known only to Mrs Joles when he left the room, Latymer was taken straight to her husband's study. There Beltham would be expected to explain to Joles and Latymer how the tins of food from Britley ended up in his school's kitchen.

Joles smiled pleasantly when Latymer entered the room.

'Take a seat. Have you enjoyed yourself?' he asked.

Latymer replied, 'I have. Many thanks for you and your wife's hospitality.'

'We'll do it again, perhaps in more pleasurable circumstances. I'm sorry I didn't see more of you. Still, I expect that my wife introduced you to the lovely Cecilia?'

Latymer smiled.

Joles continued as if the smile encouraged him to do so. 'She can't get the matchmaker tradition out of her system.' He turned to his secretary. 'Stay please, Briggs.'

Briggs disappeared into the shadows. 'A drink?'

'No, I need to keep a clear head.' Latymer smiled again.

'Good idea. We both need to. I think we have solved our problem.'

'Yes?'

'The tins of food in the school,' he paused as if to make sure that he explained the fraud clearly enough, 'the most worthwhile, most nutritious, and often the only hot meal of the day that the children eat is in the school.'

Latymer could still taste the four lamb cutlets he'd just eaten. He felt guilty and wondered why the privileged classes were able to have access to that kind of food.

'The government, with all party support, decided that the best-quality food that we could provide should be given to schools and other public institutions. Rationing hurts, people don't like it. And they like it far less when they see the children not given the best. We can only believe that Beltham has been buying army surplus for his school. We have to now think why and where from.'

'Eric, the local shopkeeper.'

'Quite. Eric, as you know him, has been buying it from the forces. Which one we don't know, it probably doesn't matter. But they were very cheap. The fiddle may have worked, except the contaminated ones ended up in Beltham's school. The nurse and Beltham told cook that the tins were very high value, vitamin enriched foods. They would take the proper wholesome vegetables and meat away, which they duly kept and sold on the black market.'

'Incredible.'

'We'll see Mr Beltham now, Briggs.'

'One minute, is Britley involved?'

'You don't like him, do you?'

Latymer gave a rueful smile.

Joles went on, 'Well, let's find out.' Briggs left the room. 'He'll deny it, of course. But I'm determined to stop this food scam and whoever is behind it.'

Beltham's jaw dropped when he was shown into the room expecting a government job offer from Joles, and he saw Latymer sitting there.

Joles was correct, Beltham did deny everything. But that was no surprise.

Beltham protested his innocence. 'I was led to believe,' the whiny headmaster said, 'that Sir Brian Britley provided Eric with the tins as a goodwill gesture to his workers on the estate. That Sir Brian, out of the good will of his heart, recognised that the people were short of good quality food.'

Joles, Latymer, and Secretary Briggs could see that the little man was writhing now.

'And that it was all in the interest of the children, healthier for them.' He now firmly made a statement as if it would convince them all. 'You have the word of a gentleman, if I'd known otherwise, I would have never got involved,' Beltham protested.

'And what happened to the fresh food?'

'I don't know,' he whined, 'perhaps cook sold it on.' Beltham spread his hands in innocence, happy to put the blame elsewhere. 'You know what these people can be like. No moral fibre.'

'You mean scheming and nasty?' Latymer said.

Beltham blanched.

Joles gave a look to Latymer to keep under control. He wanted Beltham to be able to say that he had been treated in a cordial manner.

'If we checked your bank balance,' Joles asked, 'a man like you would have a bank account?'

'My bank account is a private matter.'

'So you would object?' Joles questioned. 'What do you have to hide?'

'There is nothing to hide.' Beltham tried to be firm in his answer.

'We'll see.'

'What do you mean?'

Firmly Joles told him. 'You can go now, Mr Beltham.'

'A car was sent for me, so I assume it is waiting outside?'

'I don't know how you're going to get home,' Joles said.

'Mrs Beltham will worry.'

'Dr Latymer, what do you think?'

'The walk would be very good for your health. An excellent prescription, plenty of exercise and time to think.'

With the sulk of a schoolboy after a telling off by his headmaster, Beltham left the room, purposely leaving the door open behind him.

'Perhaps that whisky now, Peter?'

'A small one.' Latymer replied.

Briggs stepped forward from the shadows and poured the amber liquid into their glasses. 'And close the door, Briggs.' Joles perused his drink as if he'd never drunk whisky before. There were other matters on his mind. 'Where did the tins come from, Peter?'

'Eric's.'

'I know that, but he didn't pluck them out of thin air.'

Latymer was a little confused. 'Surely Britley was buying them cheap and passing them onto Eric.'

'Possibly, but buying tins to pass onto one shop in Leicester? I doubt it. There wouldn't be enough money in it for him. Have there been other outbreaks of food poisonings in the Midlands?'

Latymer said, 'I haven't heard anything.'

Joles swallowed his drink in one gulp. 'I should see my guests. I think we've frightened one little man enough this afternoon. He won't be doing that again in a hurry.'

Latymer grinned, 'I agree. I should get home.'

'See if Dr Latymer's car is here.' Joles spoke to the shadow and Briggs left.

The pair made polite conversation. There was nothing to dwell on or delight in relation to the wrongdoings of Mr Beltham. Bernard was waiting. Joles walked Latymer to the front door.

Latymer got into the front seat beside Bernard. Without a word, Bernard put the car into gear and pulled away.

They were less than a mile away from Joles' when they saw a figure walking in the roadside.

'Pull over by him, Bernard, I think that's our Mr Beltham.'

'You mean Mr Beltham from the school?' Bernard was puzzled as to why the headmaster should be wandering around the Leicestershire countryside.

'Yes.'

'What's he doing?' Bernard asked.

'Taking the long walk.'

Bernard stopped. Latymer wound down the window and spoke to the little man. 'Beltham.'

The headmaster turned, scowling.

'Only, oh I'd guess, seven miles to go,' Latymer told him.

'Nearer ten, I'd say.' Bernard added, speaking to himself, but clearly enjoying the situation Beltham found himself in.

'Did you hear that? Would you like a lift?'

Beltham made to get in as Latymer got out. 'Hold your horses. Eric and the tins, tell me everything you know.'

'I don't know anything.'

Latymer got into the back of the car. 'Drive on, Bernard.'

Bernard went to pull away.

'Wait.' Beltham shouted.

'Well?' Latymer asked.

'Okay.'

'Get in and we'll talk.'

Beltham sat obviously waiting for the vehicle to move. His face was set and grim. 'Well? Aren't we going back home?'

'After you've told me the whole story.' Latymer said.

Beltham sat, still in silence.

'Out you get then,' Latymer told him. 'Enjoy the walk.'

'Want help there, Dr Latymer? Help to get him out?' Bernard was enjoying himself and would have a great tale to recount to Edna that evening.

'This is only what I've heard.' Beltham began slowly. 'Of course, I'm not actually involved.'

'If you say so,' said Latymer. 'Just buying cheap, inferior food and keeping the best for yourself to sell on.'

'It wasn't like that,' said Beltham.

'From where I'm sitting it looks like it was exactly like that.'

'Mrs Beltham is disabled, in a wheelchair. She also has terrible breathing problems.'

Latymer wanted to say spare me the sob story. But it could be true and could explain why Beltham was a bitter man.

'I wanted the money to put the deposit on a small house next to the sea in Devon. This way of making extra money was too good to miss. Everybody was doing black market stuff.'

'I wasn't. Were you, Bernard?'

'Well,' Bernard found it difficult to tell a lie.

'Wrong, I know,' said Beltham, 'and now I'm paying for it. I expect I'll go to prison. I don't know what will happen to Mrs Beltham then.'

'Tell me,' Latymer replied, 'tell the police. Perhaps they won't press charges. How many times have you done this?'

'Only once.' In his shame Beltham was whispering. His bravado dissipated and with it dreams of cottages by the sea and posts in government.

'Any idea when it will happen again?'

'Eric told me to expect more tins next Wednesday.'

'Tell me the details,' Latymer insisted.

'I think,' said Beltham, 'that they'll bring them along to the school cookhouse during the day. Like I say, it's only happened the once. That's the truth.'

Latymer knew that Beltham had given him vital information to pass back to Joles.

'Take us home then, Bernard.'

'Right you are.' Bernard was more than ready to get home and tell Edna all about his afternoon.

Beltham sat silently, looking downward. When home, he got out and didn't look back. His shoulders were slumped and his gait heavy.

Chapter Twenty

Milly was sitting at the kitchen table. The room needed repainting. There were still traces of green showing through the blue where Reg had painted over it. All the rooms were painted green when they moved in. It was the only colour paint left after the war; the colour of camouflage as though they were hiding the inhabitants away.

Reg might have to completely decorate the small bedroom, though. She would love to buy all the furniture, just the correct wallpaper, and hang the fripperies like she saw for sale in Lewis' store where she worked. But all of that took money. She saw the kind of people with money to spare to buy the luxuries. They didn't live here on the estate, but at the other end of the city, Stoneygate, up the London Road.

She felt tired from being on her feet and smiling at people all day. Usually, with her effervescent character, she loved it. She was the perfect shop assistant, ever helpful, ever cheerful. The managers were looking at her for promotion to supervisor, as long as she didn't get herself in a family way. It was two months and well into the third since her last monthly. She was due again next week. She and Reg wanted a baby. They'd been trying hard enough. It was many months since Reg had bought 'something for the weekend, sir?' from the local barbers. A baby, they would love it. It might make Reg grow up and be more responsible. At the moment he was the baby in the family.

She could hear the football results on the radio. The announcer's sonorous voice, 'West Bromwich Albion, one,' she knew the way he said 'one' that they'd lost. Then with a high tone as though he wanted Arsenal to win he said, 'Arsenal, two.' And so it went. She knew Reg would be holding his breath waiting for the Leicester City result.

He would have loved to have gone and seen them play Manchester United; instead, he was lining Britley's pockets. He'd go to the factory in the morning as well on a Sunday. Still, they would need all the money they could get soon, especially if Milly gave up her job. And now he sat there listening to two numbers as if nothing else mattered.

She was going to enjoy teasing him, call him, and tell him that she believed she was expecting.

'Reg,' Milly called.

'Hang on.' He spoke with a painful whine. 'I'll only be a minute,' telling her as if she didn't know that the most important event of the week was about to take place, 'it's the football scores.'

'Reg, it's important.'

He begged. 'Oh please?'

She didn't know whether he was speaking to her or the radio.

Here it was. 'Manchester United, four,' said the announcer.

Milly knew who'd won from the tone of the announcer's voice, but Reg needed it confirming.

'Reg,' Milly shouted again.

'Leicester City, five.'

'Yes!' The scream came from thousands of living rooms across the city.

Britley, the rich man with friends in the right places and the leisure time to be at the game, knew, of course. He'd been sitting in the director's box with a bottle of champagne and chicken sandwiches, shaking hands and congratulating the team after the match, being presented with an autographed shirt for his son.

'Yes. Yes.' Reg came running into the kitchen waving his arms above his head like the overgrown schoolboy he was.

'Reg. I'm expecting.'

That shut him up.

'At least I think I am.'

'Expecting?' He said the word as if it were a phenomenon he wasn't aware of. 'How did that happen?'

'What do you mean how? You know how.'

'I need a cup of tea,' Reg said. He spoke weakly. 'Have we any strong spirits in the house. I need to sit down.'

'No, Reg. You look after me now,' she paused and smiled, 'and the baby. There'll have to be other changes as well. Saving money, decorating.' She paused for a moment. 'We need to go see Dr Latymer next week.'

'Shall we go and tell my mum?' he asked.

'No, we tell nobody's mum. Not yours, not mine. Nobody until Dr Latymer confirms that I'm expecting.'

'Yes.' He agreed. 'Go and sit in the living room and I'll bring you a pot of tea.' Reg guided her towards the door with his hand as if she didn't know the way.

'And tonight, Reg, we'll go out to celebrate your football, but that will be it for a while.'

He held her carefully and kissed her. 'I'm expecting and Leicester thrashed Manchester United. I won't forget this day.'

'Well, it's me that's expecting and Leicester hardly thrashed them, but I'm pleased as long as you're happy.'

Milly went and curled up on the sofa by the fire, the radio murmuring, and dozed to noise of tea being got ready as though it were a four course meal. She felt very secure. Finally Reg appeared with the teapot, cups, and tray. 'I found a packet of biscuits as well. You need to keep your strength up at time like this.

Chapter Twenty-One

When he reached home, Latymer sat and thought about what Beltham had told him. He didn't really know what to do with the information. He did feel convinced that Beltham wouldn't do anything as stupid again, but what if the net were wider? If there were others involved? He decided to telephone Joles. Briggs, his secretary, answered and went to get Joles.

'Dr Latymer? So soon. Did you get home safely?' asked the Member of Parliament.

'Yes, yes, everything is perfect. I'm sorry to have dragged you away from your guests.'

'Don't worry, most have gone. Now, what can I do for you?'

Latymer recounted what had happened on the journey back to Stocking Farm when he and Bernard had met Beltham.

'Yes,' said Joles. 'I can see why you called. That does throw more light on the situation. Leave it with me.'

'Okay.'

'Don't worry about it anymore. If it needs following up, I'll deal with it.'

***

Joles thought, took advice, and finally met with the British Military Police, telling them his concerns relating to the tins of poisonous food. He further told them that the food may be coming onto the black market from the armed forces, nearly causing one fatality.

Because of the potential food poisoning risk, it was decided to put a watch on Eric's shop twenty-four hours a day before and after the day Beltham said there would be a consignment arriving.

'If they want to keep the operation secret, they are more likely to commit an illegal act under the cover of darkness.' The military policeman told Joles, 'Once we catch them making the delivery, then we can trace it to the source.'

How wrong they were. As if it were the most normal delivery of foodstuffs, a sky-blue Britley's Bedford van pulled up outside Eric's on the Tuesday morning.

The police who were watching the shop swung into action. They approached the van as the driver got out of the vehicle and identified themselves. The driver was a short, chubby man wearing a brown overall. He looked at their warrant cards and asked in complete innocence, 'How can I help you?'

Without wishing to appear at all aggressive, so that the driver wasn't put on his guard, one of the policemen said, 'What do you have in the van?'

'Foodstuffs. Tins of food. A delivery from Britley's to Eric here.' He gestured in the direction of the grocer.

'Mind if we take a look?'

The driver opened the back doors of the van. 'Be my guest.'

The uniformed officer looked inside and wrote down the details of the vehicle.

'SAY 743,' he said to himself.

Inside the van, neatly stacked, were brown cardboard boxes. There was nothing either written or printed on the outside. The policeman took a closer look, though in the bright daylight it didn't seem necessary.

'Here,' he called across to his colleague who was just getting details of the driver's name and address, 'Len, come and have a look.'

'Yeh, what?'

'Look, in the corner of the box a small letter 'V.' I can tell you that one's a box of tins of vegetables. The rest will have an 'M' for meat and 'F' for fruit. Guarantee it.'

'You should have been a detective.'

'I reckon we'd better take this lot away,' the policeman said.

The driver was completely flustered, lost for words. He could only say, 'You can't do that.' It was a very feeble attempt at authority.

At that point, seeing a commotion, Eric came out of his shop. The grocer wiped his hands on his apron in nervous anticipation. He had a feeling he'd been rumbled. He decided his best course of action was to play it innocent.

The population, who relied upon the radio for their entertainment, was gathering a crowd. Though six or seven people could hardly be called a mob and it was unlikely that a riot was going to take place.

'What's up then, mates?' Eric asked innocently.

'Van full of black market stuff,' one of the watchers shouted out.

The policeman decided to ignore her and spoke instead to Eric.

'And who are you, sir?' The officer was more formal in his approach to the suspect.

'Eric Stokes.'

'And?'

'And?' Eric played the confused man.

'You just happen to be passing, do you?'

'No, no. I got the shop over there. Just wondered what was going on. I'll get back in. Customers, no doubt.' Eric gestured towards the building with a nod of his head as he lit a cigarette and added 'Mate.'

'Stay where you are, Mr Stokes. Were you expecting a delivery this morning, tins of food?'

'I get deliveries all the time in my line of work,' Eric said.

The policeman asked the driver for the delivery papers. The man was nervously polishing his glasses on his grubby overalls. He leaned into the driver's cab and took out a sheaf of papers clipped to a board.

'Here we are,' the driver read from the sheet, 'thirty-six boxes each containing two dozens tins of a variety of food for Eric's Grocer and Greengrocer, Marwood Road, Stocking Farm.'

'Well that's me. Where have they come from?'

'I'm sure you know,' the policeman said.

'Britley's,' the driver was honest, wanting nothing to be held against him.

'Best speak to him then,' Eric said, 'to Britley.'

Recognising a liar, the policeman said, 'Mr Stokes, we have reason to believe that this merchandise has been stolen.' A gasp of horror went through the small gathering as if Eric were exposed as a Nazi convict, 'And may be the property of His Majesty.' He forgot to point out that it was stolen from the forces. For more than one person there was an image of the King having nothing to eat for his dinner that night.

'The King'll have to come shop at Eric's then, like the rest of us,' one man shouted out.

Eric laughed out loud and arrogantly shook his head.

'I'll take the van, its contents, and the driver to base for further investigation and return here.' Speaking to his colleague, the policeman told him, 'You wait with Mr Stokes. He can continue with his business.'

'Thanks for nothing.'

'Don't let him out of your sight,' the military policeman said.

'But what if I need the toilet?' asked Eric.

'He'll go with you.'

'I ain't done nothing wrong.' Eric went back into the shop under guard, protesting his innocence.

The MP and the driver walked towards the van; the driver was saying, 'I've got other deliveries to make. How do I get back? My missus will worry.'

Business was never better for Eric that day as people came to have a look at him serving under armed escort. Seizing the opportunity, he refused to let them inside the shop without buying at least one item costing more than one shilling.

Chapter Twenty-Two

Whilst the events at Eric's were taking place, Latymer was conducting his surgery. He sat for a few moments before he called in his next patient. He felt very happy. Some days were good and this one was exceptional. Latymer would be finishing surgery early that evening, leaving the rest of the patients to McFadden, so he could meet his sister from the train station. But that wasn't the only reason. He slid open the drawer to his desk, gazed lovingly upon the envelope that lay there. It was navy blue, his name and address written in small, but neat handwriting, 'Dr P Latymer.' He would treasure it forever. The lovely missive arrived that morning. He'd been eating buttered toast lightly spread with marmite when Edna appeared in the doorway.

'Dr Latymer,' to get his attention she said the words quite loudly. She was holding aloft a small silver tray, though it was certainly not genuine silver and it hadn't seen a polish in a good while. 'Is everything to your requirements?' she asked.

He heard a giggle, stifled; 'Is Susan there?' he asked Edna and footsteps hurried away.

With a resigned air, playing her game he said, 'Edna what do you want?'

'You have a letter, Dr Latymer.'

'Yes? I get letters just about every day. Nothing new in that.'

'We think that this one is from a lady.' She then went hurriedly, 'Well, Susan and I definitely do from the handwriting and the selection of stationery used. Bernard was in doubt until he smelt it and he's right, there is a definite scent of gardenia. Which, you may be aware as Susan and I are, is the favoured perfume of Miss McFadden.'

'Do you read, Edna, books?' Latymer asked.

The question caught her off guard. She stood stock still for a moment as if remembering what a book was. 'Er, Mills and Boon sometimes. Why?'

'Nothing. It doesn't surprise me. Would you like to bring the communication over here so that I may see it?'

Edna bore the tray and envelope into the presence of Dr Latymer.

'Will all my post be delivered this way in the future?' he asked.

'Susan said this would be suitable as it was from a lady.'

'Does she think then that the letter has been passed from silver tray to silver tray since it was placed in the post box?'

'I wouldn't know, Dr Latymer. I will ask her and give you her reply, if you wish.'

'Don't bother.' He smiled quietly to himself as to how well he got on with the staff.

Latymer took the envelope from the tray and Edna stood as if awaiting further instructions. He passed the envelope beneath his nose, an inch or two away as he was aware of Bernard's proboscis having been in the same proximity. He was careful to keep the vellum clean from grease smears and the stickiness of his breakfast. 'There is a distinct scent of perfume, but I don't know which,' he mused.

'Yes, Bernard is invariably correct. He believes he was a St Bernard dog in a previous life, and that's why he's called Bernard,' Edna told him.

'Just as well he wasn't an orang-utan, or goodness knows what he would have been called.'

'Yes, I often think that.'

'Do you?' Latymer asked.

'No,' came the reply, then she said, 'Aren't you going to open it?'

Latymer turned the envelope over and reached for the clean knife from the tray. He was ready to slit the paper when he realised he ought to dismiss Edna. 'That will be all, thank you.'

'I can wait whilst you read it, in case any action needs to be taken.'

'Tell you what, Edna, I'll read it, pass it onto you, so you can read it out loud to Susan and Bernard.' She nodded approval. 'Later on you can read it to everyone in the waiting room.'

'That won't be necessary, just Susan and–'

'Edna, I'm sure you have work in the kitchen. Tell Susan I'd like fresh tea. This,' he gestured towards the cup, 'has gone cold.'

The door opened and Olive entered the room. 'And me, Edna, I'll have a cup,' said Olive. 'Morning, Peter.' Olive saw the tray Edna held to her side as she left for the kitchen. 'What have you got there, Edna?'

'It was to bring Dr Latymer's letter in on.'

Olive didn't understand, but nodded all the same.

Edna whispered to her in conspiratorial tones, 'A letter from Miss McFadden.'

'Oh, I see.' Olive giggled with Edna following suit. 'What did it say?'

Latymer sighed. 'I don't know who it's from. I haven't opened it yet. It's probably from my sister.'

'Yes, Dr Latymer, of course it is,' said Edna.

'Morning, morning, morning. A bright and fresh day to you all.' Dr McFadden breezed into the room.

'Good morning, Dr McFadden. Can I get you a cup of tea?' asked Edna.

'Aye, with a wee dram in it.'

All eyes turned on Dr Latymer.

'Dr Latymer's received a letter,' said Olive, enjoying the fun.

'From your daughter,' said Edna being more forthright with the old doctor than she normally dared to be.

'She never writes to me,' said McFadden. 'What does she have to say, Latymer?'

'He hasn't opened it,' said Edna.

Latymer stood up and picked up the letter. 'I'm going upstairs.'

'Shall I bring your tea there?' Edna asked.

'No.'

'Young love.' Olive seemed to be remembering a lost dream.

'Have you ever been in love, Miss Riley?' asked Edna.

'Yes.'

'Damn that war!' Dr McFadden's fist hit the table, angry at what was lost. With Edna's thoughtless question his good mood dissipated.

And what had the letter said? Latymer read the words again and smiled. He loved her and, he believed, from the double entendre, that she loved him.

***

Latymer brought himself back to the next patient. Looking at the notes on his desk he saw that Milly Fantam was next. He went to his door and spoke in a normal tone, 'Mrs Fantam, please.'

Dr McFadden showed a completely different attitude. He would throw open his surgery door and boom the patient's name. Latymer wondered if it were possible for a patient of Dr McFadden's to book in and then go back to the comfort of their home, waiting for the call. He felt sure that the old doctor's voice could be heard across half of the housing estate.

'Ah, Mrs Fantam, this way.' Latymer smiled as he watched Reg help his wife to her feet in the waiting room. She shook him off, as if he were an irritant, and then they proceeded to walk hand-in-hand to Latymer's surgery. Everybody present knew why they were there from the way the couple was behaving.

'Come in, have a seat,' Latymer said to them.

Before they'd sat down Reg exclaimed, 'We're expecting!'

'No, I'm expecting,' said Milly, and then correcting herself, 'I think I may be expecting.'

Latymer feigned surprise and asked the usual medical questions.

'I've missed my monthly for two months, nearly three.'

'Hm, hm. Any sickness in the mornings?' asked Latymer.

'Oh yes, I feel queasy.'

'I see.'

'My breasts are a bit swollen and quite tender.'

'Yes, I've noticed that,' interjected Reg.

'Reg!' Milly looked at him and glared.

Latymer couldn't help but smile.

Milly went on with her symptoms, 'And I know this may sound silly, but I feel like I'm expecting.'

'No, no, you may be correct,' Latymer said. 'Often it's the things you can't actually measure that have as much relevance.'

Reg nodded as if he thoroughly understood.

Quite seriously, Reg said, 'I feel like I'm expecting as well.'

'Oh, Reg.' Milly was embarrassed for them both in front of the clever doctor. She wished that she'd left him at home. 'You can't possibly feel pregnant' she told him.

'I feel different.' Reg sounded as if he meant it.

'Very possibly.' Up to a point Latymer wanted to encourage Reg. At least the father was present, caring, and interested. The male attitude can be that it's just up to the mother to get on with the pregnancy and look after the children.

'I feel more grown up.'

Milly gave Reg a despairing look. 'Well, I wish you'd go back to being a ten-year-old again.'

'Don't you want me to grow up? You're always saying that.'

'Now then,' Latymer brought the conversation back on track, 'I'll complete an examination of you tonight, Mrs Fantam. You won't need one, Mr Fantam.'

'I see.' He nodded seriously.

'That was a joke, Reg.' At times it was impossible for Milly to resign herself to Reg's stupidity.

'Mrs Fantam, can you provide me with a urine sample, then we can confirm whether you're expecting.' He gave her a small glass container. 'You know where the toilet is?'

Milly got up to leave.

'If you'd like to wait outside for your wife, Mr Fantam?'

'I'm all right here.'

'I'd like Miss Riley to help me with the examination. I don't think she'd be comfortable with you present. Can you tell her I'd like to see her? We won't be long, then you can both ask any questions you have.'

Ten minutes later Milly and Reg were back in the surgery.

'Well, the sample will confirm the pregnancy, but from a physical examination I would say you were pregnant.' Mr and Mrs Fantam beamed.

'How long will it be before we have the results?'

'Come in, say, next Tuesday, and I'm sure we'll know by then.'

They left the surgery a contented couple.

Reg returned every day until he got the thumbs-up from Olive when he entered the waiting room, then he went home with the good news.

Chapter Twenty-Three

Peter was sitting opposite his sister at the table eating a meal at Stocking House. James McFadden had told Peter about the Christmas party at Bruntingthorpe Airbase, *bring anyone you like*, he'd said. Latymer thought how his sister would love it. Away from staid Weymouth and Aunt Enid, seeing something of the wild life. Now he was regretting it, taking his sister into a possible den of iniquity. What if his parents found out?

'You won't say too much about tomorrow night to Mum and Dad, will you?'

'What do you mean?' asked Ruth.

'Well, it might be a bit wild.'

'Oh, goody.' Ruth clapped her hands together in delight.

'That's not what I told Dad when I asked him if you could go.'

'A lie?'

'A white one.'

'What did you tell him?' asked Ruth. She put down her knife and fork in excited anticipation of the answer.

'I said it was a dinner dance with Gentlemen Officers and their wives at an RAF mess.'

'And?' Ruth wanted to know.

'It'll be a party with a bunch of airmen, WAFs, and the lot.'

'Yes! This is the best Christmas present you could give me.'

'That saves me some money, anyway. Just don't tell Mum or Dad. They'd have a fit.'

'Mum's the word.'

The Doctor, The Plutocrat, and The Mendacious Minister

***

The following day Ruth and Peter went into Leicester town. There were far grander shops in the town than in Weymouth. Latymer was patient to his sister's wishes to look and admire the newest fashions in the shop windows.

They realised as well that it was an opportune time to begin Christmas shopping, or better still, start and finish it. They had few to buy for, mainly being their parents and Aunt Enid. It was pointed out to him by Ruth, the correct gesture would be to buy a small gift for the staff at Stocking House. It would have never occurred to Latymer.

'Well, I can think of a few things I'd like to give to Aunt Enid,' said Latymer.

'Leave her to me. I'll get her something from both of us.'

'I think I'll get Dad *Weymouth Sands*.'

'Is it a history book?' asked Ruth.

'No, a novel by Cowper-Powys.'

Brother and sister walked through the market area to the bookshop Tantalus on Cank Street. This was one shop that Latymer had visited previously. Once there Latymer purchased the book which Ruth would take home to wrap. Latymer knew already that he wouldn't be with his family for Christmas. Dr McFadden had made that clear. Latymer would be manning the practice probably alone for a couple of days whilst McFadden had his family around him. Latymer was resigned to that.

'Perfume for Mum, I think,' said Ruth, 'can't go wrong there.'

On their way back to Lewis' they heard a shout. 'Peter!'

A man ran across the road to them, weaving in and out of the buses.

'Peter, well, I didn't put you down as a shopping man.'

'No, this is one of my first times in the town,' said Latymer.

The man appraised the woman standing with Latymer, looking her up and down.

'My sister, Ruth,' said Latymer answering the man's unspoken question. 'Ruth, this is my friend, Dr James McFadden.'

Ruth and James gave each other a nod and formal shake of hands.

'You surprised me there for a moment, Peter. I thought you had a new girlfriend; but of course it's your sister. Ready for tonight?'

Ruth smiled and gave a nod. 'Can't wait. There's going to be so much to tell the girls about at school.'

'That's what's worrying me. Won't be too wild, will it?'

'Let's wait and see.' James laughed. 'We live in hope. I must fly. Tonight then.' Without another word he walked briskly away. Then he turned and shouted, 'I'll send a Jeep at about seven!'

Latymer sighed, wishing he'd never suggested his sister come down for the party. 'Okay, Lewis', then we'll find somewhere for lunch,' said Latymer.

'Brucciani's.'

'Coffee and cake?' he asked.

***

They entered the large store and took the lift to the third floor where perfumes could be found.

Ruth said, 'That friend of yours, James, said "new girlfriend." What did he mean?'

'No idea. Now let's get on with what we have to buy here.'

'He's Gerry's brother, isn't he?'

'As they have the same surname, more than likely. But who knows? Perhaps not.'

'You remember, I heard about her last time I was here.'

Why do women have such good memories? thought Latymer.

They approached the counter displaying a range of bottles in shapes, sizes, and colours meant to entice the discerning customer.

'Right, you choose,' Latymer told his sister.

She went off and was looking and smelling, and Latymer could tell it was going to be a long process. He looked around the store to see if there was anything of interest for him to peruse. There wasn't really. It was a floor full of women's goods. He wanted to buy Gerry a Christmas present, but he didn't want to share that with Ruth, as much as he loved his sister. He would have to return by himself on his next days off.

'Hello, Dr Latymer.'

He turned and saw Milly standing behind the counter.

'Hello, Mrs Fantam.'

'Perfumes, is it? Let me help.'

'I, my.' Before he could get the words out Ruth busied over with a couple of bottles for him to smell.

Mrs Fantam registered surprise.

Ruth read it in her face. She was an outspoken girl, when she wanted to be. And if she wanted to know something, she asked.

'I'm Ruth, Dr Latymer's sister. I'm not his girlfriend. When I've been in Leicester, people have been mistaking me for her. Tell me, who is his girlfriend?'

Milly knew better than to let on, but Reg, who had appeared on the scene after finishing work early, didn't know any better.

'Dr McFadden's girl is Gerry. The whole estate knows. Didn't you know, Milly? I thought you did. We was talking about it the other night.'

Why don't you go and get trapped in a lift somewhere, thought Latymer.

Shopping finished, they travelled home by bus. Ruth teased him all the way.

'That man,' she said, 'Mr Fantam.'

Latymer whispered stories about him and she laughed all the more.

'And Gerry,' Ruth asked, 'what's the big secret?'

'I really don't want to talk about her. It's just gossip. I don't see how she could possibly like someone like me.'

'Well, I'm your sister, I know, but don't underestimate yourself. You see something, then go for it.'

***

Back at the house they went their separate ways for a while. Latymer disappeared into his surgery. Ruth walked the large house, exploring, looking at the rooms, and out of the windows. Finally she ended up in the kitchen. Susan was sitting at the table, idly looking through the *Leicester Mercury*. She folded the paper shut and held it out to Ruth to read. Ruth shook her head.

'Cup of tea?'

'Yes, please.'

Susan got up to get it.

'No, I'll get it.'

'It's easier for me. I know where everything is. Sugar?'

'No. I got used to not having it in the war.'

'We got used to not having a lot of things. Lovely man, your brother. And I'm not a good judge of men.'

Ruth wondered what she meant. 'Yes?'

Susan told her all that she felt he had done for her, trying to find the wonder drug for Amy and the funeral. It was good to unburden herself.

'I don't want a man,' said Susan, 'but I could marry your brother.'

157

'You never know,' said Ruth, though she knew her words were idly meant.

'Me!' exclaimed Susan. 'A girl from round here? I don't think so.'

'Well, I've hardly met you, but I think you're lovely, and I'm sure Peter does as well.'

'You're too kind,' said Susan quietly. She turned away, pretending something needed sorting with the dishes, feeling very emotional at the sentiments expressed.

There was silence as Ruth sipped her tea. 'What about this Gerry?' Ruth told Susan about what had happened with Reg Fantam at Lewis'. How he had let the cat out the bag about her brother and Gerry.

Susan turned to face her, grinning. 'Reg is what we call a character. Your brother? He's sweet on Gerry and she on him. I'm not sure they both realise it.'

'Tell me more.'

'Well...'

Some time later, Latymer found his sister in the kitchen with Susan sitting over a pot of tea and enjoying each other's company. When he came into the room Ruth looked at her brother and was uncontrollable with her giggles.

Susan got up, took the cups, and busied herself at the sink.

'Ruth,' he spoke in his serious voice, 'the Jeep will be here presently.'

'The Jeep will be here presently,' mimicked Ruth.

Susan stood, facing away, her shoulders shaking with laughter.

'You'd better get ready.' He attempted to ignore her sarcasm. 'Susan, you know we're going out?'

'Yes, your sister said. I won't wait up for you.'

'Do you live here then?' asked Ruth.

'Yes.' Susan nodded as if the answer was obvious.

'Sorry, I was having a snoop earlier. I didn't touch anything.'

'Don't worry. I don't have anything worth having.'

Ruth left the room to change for the party, thinking how Susan sounded desperately lonely.

***

After their evening at the base in Bruntingthorpe, the Jeep dropped them back at Stocking House at one in the morning. Ruth was breathless with excitement as she stood in the sitting room. The room was still warm as the ashes of the evening died away.

The Doctor, The Plutocrat, and The Mendacious Minister

'I'll find some cocoa,' she said.

Latymer let her.

When Ruth went into the kitchen, Susan had left two cups out on the table ready, just needing hot milk added. She returned to the sitting room with the drinks.

'That was quick.'

'Yes, Susan had left everything out.'

'I think I'll take this to bed. Your train at?'

'Twelve minutes past ten.'

'Goodnight then, Ruth.'

'Goodnight, Peter. I've had a wonderful time.'

He kissed her on the cheek. 'Anytime. James certainly had an eye for you tonight. My turn now, you see. Who's your boyfriend, Ruth?'

'Peter.'

But he had turned to leave the room. 'Yes?'

The moment had been lost. 'It doesn't matter.'

Ruth sat and drank her drink, staring at the fire. She heard the door open and close, and turned her head to see Susan standing there.

'Sorry if I startled you,' whispered Susan, 'I wanted a drink.'

'No, no, you didn't. I was just finishing my cocoa. Thank you for leaving it for us.'

Susan smiled and went into the kitchen. After a few moments she returned. 'Goodnight then,' she said.

'I always wished I'd had a sister,' said Ruth.

Susan perched on the edge of a chair. Unsure of whether to sit properly. Not knowing if her company was wanted.

'My sister,' said Susan, 'was a bit older than me, and we fought like cats and dogs.'

'Peter and I did sometimes. I remember when I broke his train. That's the maddest I ever saw him.'

'We didn't have any toys. Amy should have had so much more.'

Susan paused, but Ruth didn't want to question.

'How was the night at the airbase?' Susan changed the subject.

'It was wild. Mum and Dad would be horrified if they knew what had gone on.'

'Shock me, then!'

Ruth told her about the evening. The dancing and the drinking. 'And they have such wonderful food! I've never seen anything like it. Where do the Americans get it from?'

159

'America, I suppose.' Susan pondered for a moment. 'I just wish they'd share a bit more with us.'

Both girls thought about what it would be like to have what they wanted on a plate.

'What's your favourite food?'

They talked and laughed until finally Susan said, 'Look at the time! Twenty past two. We'd better get you to bed, or you'll never be up for your train in the morning.'

They made their way to the stairs. Ruth turned and whispered, so as not to wake Peter, 'I've had such a wonderful time, Susan. I can't wait to see you again.'

Chapter Twenty-Four

Nothing could be found to press charges against Eric Stokes, the greengrocer. The seedy man merely bought with confidence in the seller. They were goods that Eric believed were legal and above board. That was his story, anyway, and he stuck to it.

Everyone on the estate knew that Eric was always on the lookout for making a 'fast buck' and would happily be part of a scam. But away he went, back to his shop, brimming with his new-found righteousness, the wronged man.

To customers who would listen, and there were plenty, he would tell tales of how he was interrogated for twelve hour stretches, suffered sleep deprivation, put in a cell where there was only a cold concrete floor to sleep on, the light was never switched off, and he was only given stale bread and water as any form of nourishment.

In truth, Eric was taken to a Military Police base on the afternoon of the initial delivery and was back in his shop by four o'clock, with the proviso that he may have to answer further questions.

Eric asked the Military Police, 'Shall I surrender my passport?'

'That won't be necessary.'

'I haven't got one, anyway,' Eric said. 'Where would I go? Germany? I don't think so. Am I wearing my stupid face?'

***

A military policeman paid a visit to Latymer at Stocking House. He wanted to know what the doctor knew about the whole situation regarding Beltham. He learnt that as unpleasant as Beltham was, there were circumstances in his life which led to his actions.

'His wife is ill, confined to a wheelchair. I don't think he has it easy.'

'I understand,' the MP said, 'but a lot of people cope with difficult circumstances. We can't leave it there. What he did was theft, and as it turned out, dangerous for the innocent children, as well as the old man.'

'Maybe you can just speak to him?' said Latymer.

'Don't worry, we'll do that all right,' said the MP. 'But we still may have to press charges.'

***

In the end they didn't press the full force of the law onto Beltham. The commanding officer sent two of his policemen into the school for an interview with the headmaster. It was a very formal occasion. One of the officers was a good deal over six foot in height and as broad, without an ounce of fat on him. Their truncheons hung from their belts. The pair filled Beltham's office.

Beltham began the meeting with his usual sense of pompous bravado, but by the time the officers left the room, Beltham was grey faced and shaking. He didn't recover for at least three weeks, and for the following six months was seen to smile at children, who became more frightened of him when he did. They were happy when he had recovered his former composure; though, he was never quite the same man as before.

As a matter of courtesy the Military Police passed all the written reports about Britley, and the sale of the tins of food, to the Civil Constabulary in Leicester. Inspector Ron Hovan read through the reports. It made interesting reading, but he couldn't see that anyone was to blame. Yes, Beltham was an idiot, Stokes was probably an odious little man, and he knew Britley from the Oddfellows. The pair passed the time of day and Britley gave Hovan the occasional bottle of whisky. Hovan never ask where it came from.

Inspector Hovan believed Britley to be a fine, upstanding member of society. Britley was perhaps even caring enough to pass the tins of foodstuffs onto Stokes, so the inhabitants of Stocking Farm had good food in their bellies during this time of rationing. Accidents happen; no one knew when a misfortune like the food poisoning would occur. It was nobody's fault.

However, Ron Hovan felt it important to keep his force busy and saw no problem in sending out one of his officers to have a look at the contract Britley had made with the government. He sent an officer who could do the least damage.

***

Detective Constable Harry Brabbins of the Leicester Constabulary entered Sir Brian Britley's outer office unannounced. The policeman stood, looking at the attractive secretary. He smiled just as he'd seen Robert Mitchum do in many films. Brabbins expected it to melt her heart. Later she would tell a friend, 'That copper liked to think he was a film star. Honestly, his face was like a deformed hamster.'

'I'm here to see Sir Brian Britley,' the Detective Constable informed her.

'Do you have an appointment?' she asked. She knew there were no meetings scheduled for Sir Brian that morning.

'Perhaps I should introduce myself.' Brabbins took from his pocket a wallet, flipped it open in one swift move. He'd practised the move many times in front of his mother's full-length mirror. Brabbins was convinced the action looked impressive. 'Plainclothes Detective Brabbins of the Leicester Constabulary.' He paused to let the gravity of the situation sink in. 'Further to enquiries of national importance, I'm here to question Sir Brian Britley. I don't need an appointment.'

Sir Brian's secretary stood up and said, 'I'll tell him you're here.'

The woman went to Britley's office door, knocked quietly, waited for a few moments, then entered. She closed the door behind her.

The detective could not hear the conversation between Britley and the woman. The door to his office was undoubtedly sound-proofed. Brabbins took his silver nickel cigarette case, a present from his mother the previous Christmas, and lit a cigarette. He stood near a low coffee table, staring intently at prints of racing cars from the Silverstone circuit. He turned as he heard the door to Sir Brian's office open.

'Sir Brian will be out in a few moments,' the secretary informed him, 'he's just completing an important business call.' Although she believed Sir Brian was keeping the policeman waiting, Brabbins took her at her word.

Britley took that time to use the Oddfellows network and telephone Inspector Ron Hovan to find out what was going on. The policeman receiving the call told Britley that Hovan was in a meeting with the Chief Constable and under no circumstances could he be disturbed.

Britley said, 'What if I was reporting a bloody murder?'

'We have other policemen who could deal with your problem.' The policeman responded calmly, 'Would you like to be connected to one of those?'

Without replying Britley slammed the telephone headpiece down. The policeman at the other end stared at the receiver as if it were an object he'd never seen, before carefully placing it back into its cradle.

Sir Brian was furious. He had to be in control. Nothing could disturb the equilibrium of his power base. At best, the policeman's visit would be a general enquiry concerning the new Factories Act, recently passed through Parliament. At worst, the warehouse full of black market goods present on the factory site. But every month or so he passed Inspector Hovan a bottle of fine whisky, nylons for Hovan's wife, and chocolate for his children; it was a gentlemen's unwritten agreement. Scratch my back, I'll scratch yours.

Maybe it was about buying the army surplus from the government. Britley could flannel his way through that. What concerned them was probably the tins of food. But that wasn't his fault. How was he supposed to know they were poisonous? He would offer to pay for a kiddies' Christmas party and be "Mr Benevolent."

Feeling calmer, Britley got up from his desk and went to the outer office to receive his visitor.

Britley knew that he would play the psychological advantage, if he went to greet the policeman. He went out smiling, arm extended ready for a handshake.

'Detective Brabbins,' Britley said.

Brabbins quickly put out his cigarette. They shook hands.

'A pleasure to meet you,' Britley went on. 'Now how can I help? Won't you come into my office?'

'No, no. I'm maybe wasting yours and my time. Probably nothing.'

Good, Britley wanted to say out loud. Let's hope so.

'Just the items you bought from the government.'

Britley nodded.

'Army surplus, I believe it was.'

'Yes, there was an unfortunate incident with food poisoning, and I plan to make it up to the children at the school by paying for a Christmas party for them.'

'I'm sure that will be much appreciated, Sir Brian,' said Brabbins. 'No, it wasn't that, but another matter.'

Britley instinctively went on guard then.

'The police,' said Brabbins full of importance in his voice, 'wanted to have a look at the contract that was drawn up with the government.'

'Ah,' said Britley. He knew he needed to sound full of confidence. 'That is in the government files.' He paused to show the importance of where they were lodged. 'In London. You would need to apply there.' As soon as he got rid of this buffoon, he could get onto Wakeham, with whom the deal had been made, and warn him.

'I see,' said Brabbins. 'No problem. I'll tell my Chief and I'm sure he'll see to it. I'll be on my way.'

The pair went to shake hands again.

'Sir Brian,' the secretary said, 'don't you remember? We filed a copy.'

Britley tried to nod and smile as if he'd forgotten all along.

She went to the filing cabinet and retrieved the document from the second drawer. She passed it to Sir Brian.

'That's the one, isn't it?' she said to him.

'Yes, of course it is. What would I do without you?'

'May I take it?' Brabbins asked whilst attempting to look at them.

'Of course. You'll let us have it back when you've finished?'

'Without doubt. Thank you, Sir Brian. You've been very helpful.'

***

Britley was sitting behind his desk, staring at the wall. He was thinking, why had his secretary been so stupid as to pass the document over? She didn't know. Why had he put in all the correct figures, the amount that he had agreed to pay Wakeham and Norrington? He should have told a lie and pocketed the rest, just as the crooks in government had done. Because it was his way, he needed to know precisely what came in and what went out, that he had written the full figures.

***

Brabbins decided to take the initiative. Perhaps it irritated his superiors that he forever asked them what the next course of action should be. He'd been sent on the mission to find the contract, he had retrieved it. He had no idea why, but he assumed that now Inspector Hovan would want to see the contract from the government. He would telephone his Member of Parliament, Solomon Joles; he would know how to find the government copy for him.

The detective left his office and went into the typing pool. He smiled his hamster smile at the youngest and prettiest female. He knew this would impress her when he said, 'Could you find me our Member of Parliament's telephone number and bring it along to me?'

Brabbins went back to his office and waited. After a few minutes the number was brought along to him. He looked at the piece of paper. It contained four numbers.

'Is this all I need to get through?' he asked the woman.

'Yes.'

She made to leave. She didn't want to be asked out and have to lie that she must wash her hair that evening.

'There's a new John Wayne film–' but she'd already left and closed the door.

***

He picked the receiver up and dialled the number.

A well-spoken female voice answered, 'Mrs Joles.'

Brabbins was thrown. He expected to be speaking to a person at the Houses of Parliament, and rather stupidly he believed them to be all men. Perhaps Mrs Joles acted as the MP's secretary.

Attempting to sound confident he said, 'I wanted to speak to Mr Joles, the Member of Parliament.'

'And you are?' replied Mrs Joles.

'Oh, I'm sorry. I should have introduced myself. I'm Detective Brabbins of the Leicester Constabulary.'

'What does this concern?' That for one moment her husband had got up to anything he shouldn't have, Mrs Joles couldn't imagine, but she was always careful to avoid a scandal.

'I'm not at liberty to say.'

'I see. Well, he's in the House.'

Brabbins was completely baffled. 'Haven't I telephoned the Houses of Parliament?'

'No,' she was impatient. The cockers needed walking, 'his home.'

'Where are you then, in the garden? Do you have a phone in the garden?'

This man is a complete nincompoop, she thought. It was hardly surprising that criminals got away with what they did, if he was a prime example of a policeman. 'The House,' she was trying to control her temper, 'The House, as in Houses of Parliament.'

'Oh. I'm sorry, Mrs Joles. I've been given the wrong number.'

'I can give you the Commons number. Do you have a pencil?'

'Yes.'

'And paper?' She wanted to make sure the idiot was completely at the ready.

'Yes.'

'And the pencil's sharpened?'

He looked at the point. 'Yes.'

She gave him the number. He thanked her profusely.

The Detective Constable dialled the number she'd given to him. He felt excited at the prospect of ringing the House of Commons, the British seat of power. Again the telephone was answered quickly.

'Commons, reception.'

'I wish to speak to Mr Joles, MP for Leicester East. I'm Detective Brabbins of Leicester Constabulary.'

'Could I ask what it concerns, sir?'

He was not a clever detective, so he wasn't prepared for the man's question. Brabbins glanced down at the papers he'd taken from Britley and saw the word defence, and said, 'A defence issue.'

'I see. I'll connect you.'

Brabbins waited and waited. There was only a faint hum on the line. He wondered whether he'd been disconnected. At last the voice said, 'Mr Joles isn't in the building. But Lord Wakeham has just passed. He is of the Defence Department. He is willing to take your call. I'm just waiting for him to reach his office.'

Brabbins felt sure that was perfect.

'I'm putting you through now.'

'Lord Wakeham.'

'Detective Brabbins.'

'How can I help you?' said the Peer.

The Detective explained all that had taken place with the food poisoning, the involvement of the Military Police, and how he, Detective Brabbins, a Civil Policeman, had been sent that morning to Sir Brian Britley's factory to have a look at the contract made with the Defence Department of the government.

'I see,' said Lord Wakeham, 'and you have the contract in front of you.'

'Yes.'

'Well, I'll pass all this on to Mr Joles.'

'I think my chief wanted to see the contract the government made?'

'But you have it. It won't be any different. I think you've been sent on a fool's errand, young man. Tell your chief that.'

'Well, thank you, your Lordship.'

'Hm. Good bye, Mr Brabbins.'

Brabbins sat and looked at the receiver. He'd spoken to Lord Wakeham. He was enjoying this. He couldn't wait to tell his mother.

***

Two days later, Brabbins was working a late shift. Inspector Hovan had never asked him about his meeting with Britley. The police station was silent; too early yet for the Friday night drunks. Brabbins sat twiddling a pencil. Should he telephone Mr Joles to see if His Lordship had spoken to him? He didn't know what to do. He decided he would try like a lottery. If Joles was at home, he would tell him, if he wasn't, he would drop it and send the document back to Britley on Monday.

Brabbins picked up the receiver and dialled. It rang out for a long, long time. Finally, it was picked up.

'Joles,' a man's voice said.

Brabbins introduced himself.

'How can I help?'

The Detective could hear the noise of guests in the background. The man sounded impatient.

'Have you communicated with Lord Wakeham? I rang the House of Parliament and spoke to him.' Brabbins couldn't help but sound proud of the fact.

'No,' asked Joles, 'should I have done?'

He heard a woman's voice ask then, 'Who is it?'

Joles hissed at her, 'A man called Brabbins.'

'The man's a complete idiot,' the woman said, who Brabbins now took to be Mrs Joles, 'get rid of him.'

'No, Mr Brabbins, Lord Wakeham hasn't said anything to me. What did it concern?'

The detective went through the whole story. Joles, in spite of his wife, listened patiently.

'And you have the contract with you?'

'In front of me now.'

'And could I take it away for a few days?' asked Joles.

'I should think so, sir.'

'Tomorrow? I'm rather tied up now.'

'Tomorrow,' said Brabbins, 'I work an afternoon shift.'

'Right ho, I'll come along to the station at, say, three o'clock and collect the document.'

***

Britley was optimistic. He heard nothing from the police. He waited for his contract to reappear. When it was back in his hands, no one would ever see it again. He didn't want to go chasing it up, that could point to guilt. He would bide his time.

For the moment Eric was the one who suffered the most. At the surgery there was a notice stating that the tins of unlabelled food from Eric's may have caused the outbreak of food poisoning. In the shop, customers shunned other items as well. Eric's sales dropped until the local populace became too lazy to make the mile walk to the next greengrocer.

The *Leicester Mercury* got hold of the story. They interviewed Eric who in his opinion was the wronged man. They spoke to Latymer who added very little. Britley was unavailable for comment. Believing there was nothing to it, they let the story die a natural death.

Chapter Twenty-Five

The following day McFadden finished his morning surgery and was out on a home visit, so Latymer knew there must be money to make in it. Peter was rounding off with his final patient. A mother sat with a child, aged five, standing by her side. The boy looked afraid as if Latymer were about to perform major surgery on him, there and then. She asked Latymer about immunisations for the child.

'It is important that you have the child immunised, but you don't really need to see me, the school nurse gives them.'

The mother nodded, but didn't respond verbally. She didn't look convinced. He could see there was something more troubling her.

Latymer went on, 'If you go to the school, you can make an appointment for Nurse Bullock to give the injections.'

'Oh.'

'Is there a problem?' asked Latymer.

'Nurse Bullock. I don't want her near my child. She'll terrify him for life.'

'I see.' He thought if he did it for one, he'd have a queue down the road. He wasn't sure he had the time for that.

'I'd rather you gave them to him,' said the mother.

'You'll need to make an appointment with Miss Riley, so that I have the vaccinations in the surgery.'

On cue the door burst open and Olive rushed in. 'Ah, Miss Riley, can you?'

Olive didn't listen. 'Something terrible has happened at Britley's factory. They want you there immediately. A car is waiting outside.'

'What's happened?' Latymer asked.

'I don't know. Just go,' she ordered.

The woman put her hand to her mouth and said, 'Oh God.' The child began to cry.

'Have they called an ambulance?' Latymer asked.

'I don't know. I should think so. Just go.'

Picking up his bag and without any formalities, Latymer left them worrying what the extent of the accident was. Did it involve one man, an explosion injuring many, or a fire wiping out the whole factory? Pulling the blinds aside, Olive looked out of the window in the direction of Britley's. All was peaceful there, as if there were no trauma within the building.

Latymer quickly got into the front seat beside the driver, and he sped off without waiting for the doctor to settle himself.

'Any idea what's going on?' Latymer asked the driver.

'Only that a bloke is trapped under machinery.'

'Has an ambulance been called?'

'I would hope so,' said the driver. ''Tis a pretty hopeless lot if they haven't.'

Latymer didn't comment.

Upon his arrival at the factory, Latymer was hurried to the scene. It appeared that a man was crushed from his torso down by a falling piece of machinery. He was conscious, but could barely breathe, coming in laboured gasps.

'Dr Latymer.'

Latymer took the man's hand. The doctor was very calm. 'Reg. What have you been up to, then? We'd better get you up and about for that baby of yours.'

'Yeh.' Reg could hardly breathe the word.

There were two ambulance men present. They were ineffective in the circumstances. 'We were waiting for you,' one of them said as if to excuse their uselessness.

'He needs freeing from here.'

'There's a cutting crew from the fire service on their way,' the other officer said.

'Okay, Reg, I'm going to give you an injection to make you more comfortable.'

Latymer injected morphine into Reg's inert body. The last Reg remembered, as he went into unconsciousness, was the concerned eyes of his doctor.

Finally, Reg was freed from the machinery and taken away in the ambulance.

A middle-aged rotund man in a blue suit approached Latymer. 'You are going to need a cup of tea, and a stronger drink as well, I shouldn't wonder. Come with me.' The man took Latymer to an office. He held out a hand. Latymer shook it. 'Ray Williams. Sit down, Doctor. Whisky?'

'No thanks,' said Latymer.

'Two teas then, Grace.'

The door closed and the two men sat in silence absorbing the shock of the dreadful event, until the lady returned bearing a tray.

Latymer stirred his tea.

Ray pushed a piece of paper over to him.

'If you'd be good enough to sign this for us, Doctor.'

Latymer picked up the paper and began to read.

'Nothing important,' Mr Williams was saying. Williams was trying his hardest to sound brisk and business-like, but there was a worried edge to his voice. 'Just saying you were present and witnessed what went on. For the records like.' Williams was now grasping at straws as he saw the anger developing on Latymer's face. 'For the accountants. You know what they are like.'

'For the accountants? Don't lie to me, whoever you are. Britley's lackey? Read it yourself.' Latymer thrust the paper back across the table. 'But, come on, you know what it says. To sum up, that no one here was negligent. While that man lies there. This accident will be thoroughly investigated. Expect the factories inspectorate.'

Latymer pushed back his chair, stood up, and left the room. His tea left to grow cold.

Chapter Twenty-Six

When Milly Fantam learned what had happened to Reg, she collapsed. One of the pair of factory officials delivering the news ran to the nearest phone box and rang for an ambulance. Milly was taken to the hospital. There in the maternity ward it was touch and go as to whether she would miscarry the baby. She would have to wait it out.

***

Latymer heard about Milly Fantam from Susan when she brought him his tea.

'I'll get you a bite to eat.'

'No, I'll manage,' Latymer told her.

'You should,' said Susan.

'You the doctor now?'

Considering the situation, they both managed a weak smile which acted as a kind of relief. For a moment they became aware that their roles were reversed.

McFadden came into the living room. He went straight over to the whisky decanter and poured himself a glass. It was an excellent whisky. The liquor they'd drunk during the War was a poor quality. Latymer didn't think where it came from or who it was that kept the decanter filled. But he'd seen enough of the world to know that magic didn't exist.

Latymer was firmly told by McFadden, 'I'll do surgery tonight, Peter.'

'No, I'll carry on.'

'No, young man. You're in no fit state. Listen to your jazz and have,' he waved the glass around, 'one or two of these.'

It felt like an order, so Latymer resigned himself to it.

McFadden drank, standing, humming to himself as if there were something on his mind. 'Ah yes, I remember now. Joles wants you to ring. Olive left the number by the phone.'

Latymer got up and went into the hall. He dialled and a woman's voice answered. He asked for Mr Joles.

'Whom shall I say is calling?'

'Dr Latymer.'

'Dr Latymer, it was I who wanted to speak to you. Mr Joles is here and also our son, Sebastian, who is home from school. Poor Sebastian is in bed feeling poorly with a high temperature. Can you come and have a look at him? If it was one of the cockers I'd know what to do, but you know how it is.'

Latymer didn't know about cockers, but all the same he said 'Yes, I'll come along now.'

'So kind. Stay, and eat with us.'

'I couldn't possibly.'

'Mr Joles insists.'

Latymer went into the kitchen to tell Susan that he wouldn't need a meal.

Bernard was with her. 'Where are you going, Doctor?' Bernard asked, 'If I may be so bold.'

'Mr Joles'.

'I'll run you. I'd enjoy the drive.'

It was as if they were being especially kind because of the trauma that he had encountered earlier.

'No, I couldn't ask you. They've asked me to stay for dinner. It would be a long wait.'

'I'll come back here,' said Bernard.

'And you can eat what I've made for Dr Latymer.'

Bernard looked pleased at that prospect, as Susan's cooking was superior to his wife's.

'You ring when you're ready, Doctor. I'll come and pick you up,' said Bernard. 'You should have a chauffeur when you're visiting a posh house.'

***

On the way in the car Latymer commented that the whisky decanter never seemed to get empty.

'That's 'cus I fills it,' said Bernard.

'Oh. I see.'

'It's like this, Dr McFadden brings in a bottle. I think he gets it from Mr Britley. I take what's left in the decanter, and fills it with the new one.'

'Britley? Why does he buy it from Britley?'

Bernard tapped the side of his lengthy nose. 'Black market. You can get all sorts from Mr Britley. Soap, nylons, chocolate…didn't you know? Eric keeps it under his counter. But we all know it's Britley really selling it to us.'

'I didn't know.'

'You won't tell him I keep a drop of the whisky like, will you?'

'No, your secret is safe with me, Bernard. One of your perks.'

***

Mrs Joles greeted him at the door. She took him straight upstairs to the patient. When Latymer saw Sebastian in the bed, he smiled properly for the first time in quite a few hours. The boy in the bed gave a weak smile like an ill patient should.

'Physician heal thyself,' said Latymer.

Mrs Joles looked startled. Was this man a lunatic, whom her husband misjudged?

'You're the doctor from the railway station,' said Sebastian.

'You've met?' asked Mrs Joles.

'We've met,' said Latymer. 'He helped me treat a patient, this one. Gave a second opinion when it wasn't asked for.'

'Yes, a precocious child, my son.'

'Like his mother.' Joles' quiet voice came from the doorway.

'Like his father, pompous and precocious.'

'It's needed to be a politician. Though knowing when to be humble is also a good quality.'

'True,' Mrs Joles said.

'Dr Latymer,' said Joles, 'when you've finished with our patient here, I'd like a word.'

'He's staying for dinner.'

'Can you bring him down to the study first?' Joles asked his wife.

After Latymer diagnosed a mild influenza and bed rest for twenty-four hours, he sat in Joles' book-lined study, swirling a small whisky in the bottom of a glass. Their talk related to Beltham and the food poisoning. The pair knew greater crimes had been committed; Beltham was just a fool in the thick of it.

'Do you know a policeman named Brabbins?' Joles asked him.

'No,' said Latymer, 'should I?'

'To be fair, I can't think why your paths would cross. The man seems a bit of a idiot.'

'Well?' Latymer was puzzled.

'Well, for whatever reason the Leicester Police sent this Brabbins chap to Britley's office to pick up the contract between Britley and the government. I honestly can't think why.'

'As I understand, the matter was in the hands of the military police,' said Latymer.

'Quite. Anyway, to cut a long story short, I've got the contract now. I don't know what I'm going to do with it, either. I think I will compare it with the one in the Commons Library. Who knows what it will throw up? Come on, dinner. I think we have a pheasant each tonight.'

Chapter Twenty-Seven

Joles walked in the corridors of power in London, Parliament. Joles ran a small government department, wheels within wheels subsidiary to Trade and Defence. There was no axe to grind with Britley, as far as Joles was concerned. The Member of Parliament for East Leicester put himself above personal animosity. For him, clashes with opponents were fought over ideological differences, abuse of the law, the system or the power a person may hold. Joles could have an argument with an opposition party member in the Commons, and eat or drink with him afterwards as a friend.

Regarding the deal with Britley, Joles harboured his doubts. It may turn out to be totally kosher. A search of the office at Britley's factory in Leicester by Detective Brabbins uncovered the account for the sale of the army surplus goods bought from the government. Joles procured a copy of the invoice from Brabbins. He knew precisely the payment made by Britley to the government. Nothing now would look amiss him searching documents relating to Britley and the incumbent government. Joles ought to find these in the Commons Library.

Firstly, he asked one of his research assistants to bring all of the documents from the Commons Library relating to Britley. Very surprisingly, that drew a blank.

Joles looked across his desk at Ted, his assistant, who'd been sent on the straightforward errand and asked in disbelief, 'There's nothing there?'

'Nothing,' Ted told him.

Ted thrived on efficiency. Success for him was finding nothing because he knew that there was nothing there to find. It told him as much as if he'd found a sheaf of papers.

'You're sure?' Joles looked quizzically at Ted. 'Of course you're sure. I shouldn't have insulted you by asking the question.'

Joles put the tip of his thumb in his mouth, which he did when he was deep in thought, then asked Ted to draft a letter to the Minister of Defence, Henry Norrington.

'Hm,' said Joles pensively, 'Go for the food poisoning aspect.' He paused, 'Say that I am concerned that this Britley fellow has been buying illegally from the forces and that this matter should be looked into. Get one of the backbenchers to sign the letter, so he won't know it's from me. Get the idea?'

Ted always did.

Joles received a reply from an MP within Norrington's team who felt that the backbencher wasn't important enough to bring the letter to the attention of the Minister himself. This member of Norrington's department, believing that he could fob off a man of no importance, said that there were no irregularities. Nothing more.

Joles decided to go for the jugular. He briefed a trustworthy opposing Member who would ask the first question concerning the Britley matter. Then Joles would take over. The House was poorly attended that afternoon.

The corpulent figure of Henry Norrington, Minster of Defence, stood up when called by the Speaker in the House of Commons. He pushed his fat frame into position. He was an ugly man who followed almost every statement he made with a guffaw, whether it be happy or sad, as if he were practising to be Father Christmas in a next life.

Norrington made a statement appertaining to the strength of Britain's forces, their role in Europe and the rest of the world. To the more perceptive members it was the same usual drivel that they'd come to expect. To others though, it was Winstonian and there was a feeble waving of order papers.

Norrington sat down satisfied; full of money and status, he didn't want for much more. His piece was followed by an innocuous question regarding how soon troops in Singapore would be sent extra supplies for Christmas. A junior member of Norrington's team had been 'set up' to ask this question to put the minister in benevolent light. Norrington was ready with the answer. He told them of the delights the soldiers could expect to receive on Christmas Day, then guffawed.

This drew a few more feeble 'hear, hears' as if the MPs always received the generous quarter bottles of rum themselves in their Christmas stocking.

An Opposition Member stood up for his allotted query. He asked, 'Have sales of army surplus stock taken place since the end of hostilities in 1945?'

The question threw the minister, but he liked to believe he could bat any ball thrown at him. He replied in his pompous voice with a jokey bluff, 'We can expect the opposition to waste valuable time by asking irrelevant questions, ho.' He looked around and was satisfied to see that a few of the old duffers were laughing along with him.

The Member stood up. 'A simple answer, Minister, yes or no?'

The Minister couldn't remember information that he preferred to forget, so he went for the old standby, which he always did on occasions like this. 'I'm sure there has been, but for reasons of national security, particularly in sales to foreign nationals, I'm sure you'll understand for various reasons, I'm unable to give a specific answer now.' The Minister was waffling and everyone knew it.

'Thank you for enlightening us,' the MP said, and resumed his seat.

The Members seemed satisfied. Minister Norrington wanted to leave now. He glanced at his watch, a few minutes of this session left. He was wily enough to know that there was something amiss, and he wanted to get out of it. He would find out the problem when he got back to his office. He did not want it on his mind when he dined with Lord Marlborough that night. He fully intended to enjoy the evening. The Oliviers were expected and he loved beautiful women. His mind wandered briefly. He looked around and that seemed to be the end.

Norrington made to rise and leave the chamber when the Speaker called out 'Member for East Leicester.' Norrington was puzzled for a moment. He wasn't expecting this, but at least Joles was one of his own Party. Whatever the man wanted, it would be soft. He could leave on a high. Norrington happily waited for the question.

Joles spoke, 'I can answer the Member's question.'

The Speaker interrupted him, 'You should be asking the question.'

Joles acquiesced with a bow of his head. The Speaker looked at his watch. Joles waved documents in the air as though they were order papers. 'These are from the offices of Sir Brian Britley, an industrialist in my constituency. They are the invoices for army surplus, bought from the Honourable Member's department. Why are there no contracts in the Commons Library relating to these?'

Norrington became flustered. He began to panic and went again for the old chestnut, 'National Security.'

Joles was back on his feet before the Speaker could stop him for having run out of time. 'It's in the public domain. I have them here in my hand from Sir Brian Britley, who bought the army surplus. He was happy to pass them over to the police. Why are the contracts being kept secret from Honourable Members in the House?'

The Minister grunted. The Speaker, seeing the seriousness of the situation, asked for a more voluble answer from Norrington.

'The documents will be placed there, Mr Speaker, by the end of the day.' This wasn't followed by his usual guffaw. Norrington knew the game was up, simple. He should have covered his tracks more carefully or at least checked that the man Britley wasn't a fool. Why did he leave it all to Wakeham? Well, if he was to be hung, Wakeham was going to drop with him.

The minister left furious, furious with his own member.

From a boring session, the Commons was abuzz, and those who were absent regretted it.

Chapter Twenty-Eight

Olive spoke to Dr McFadden. She told him that Latymer needed a few days break.

'He's put up with a great deal here.'

Dr McFadden wasn't as understanding. 'Don't we all, Olive? Day after day.'

'There was the death of the child. He took that hard.'

McFadden made sympathetic noises, so she knew she was on the road to winning.

She went on, 'And then all that business with the food poisoning.'

'He could have asked me for more help. I'm the older, more experienced man.'

'But you aren't always that approachable. Your children say that,' Olive told him.

'My children talk to you?' he asked, surprised.

'Well, Gerry does,' she answered.

'Ah.' He said it in such a way that he knew James would never confide in her, 'she misses her mother.'

'You should remember that,' she told him.

'We all miss her mother.'

'I know.' She wanted to reach out and take his arm, but they didn't have that kind of relationship. She already was overstepping the mark. 'Anyway, Dr Latymer?'

'Hm, hm. Perhaps you're right.' Olive knew then that she was grinding him down to victory.

McFadden twiddled his thumbs in his waistcoat pockets, took out his watch, looked at the time, as if that would help him make a decision. He put it back into his pocket. 'Tide and time waits for no man, or whatever the saying is. I've notes to write up.' He made to leave the room.

A respite now for Latymer could not slip from her grasp. 'Dr McFadden,' she asked again, 'Dr Latymer? What are we going to do for him? He needs a rest.' She was trying hard for the young doctor. She decided she may need to restrain herself a little.

'London. Send him to London.' McFadden almost succeeded in making it sound like a punishment. 'That's where we loved to go during the war, even though the bombs were falling and you knew it would be dangerous. You believed you'd be safe in a cathedral.'

***

With the blessing of McFadden, Latymer booked into The Georgian House Hotel, close to Westminster. It was a short taxi ride from St Pancras Station, which was the London destination for trains from Leicester. Olive suggested the hotel. 'Mother and I stayed there when we went to see a show before the war. Will you go to one?'

'By myself, I don't think so,' said Latymer.

Latymer hoped that the hotel lived up to her memory; but it didn't matter that much. He argued, albeit politely, against going and leaving McFadden alone until the kindly doctor informed him, 'I managed without you for long enough, so don't be thinking you're indispensable. Anyway, you don't need reminding, I shall be expecting you to work by yourself over the Christmas period. Always a bad time of the year. Especially afterwards when the great day is over.' Neither knew then how bad it would be on the mood of the populace of the estate. 'So go away and build up your strength,' McFadden told him.

Latymer settled into his seat in the corridor coach at London Road Station Leicester, waiting for the engine to haul the train away. He sat looking out of the window. There were few people on the platform, one or two porters uniformed, WH Smiths, and he wished that he'd purchased a newspaper. He wondered whether he'd time to get off and buy one, but decided against it. Just his luck that the train would pull away punctually.

A female face passed the window glass, holding a small suitcase. She waved. He raised his hand in acknowledgement, though she was gone too quickly to be certain as to who it was. The coach doors started to slam, and the thuds and echoes made him remember Reg Fantam and the time that had passed since that first night in Leicester. It was a few months, but it seemed like a lifetime ago. The whistle blew. He felt the strain of the engine as it pulled its loaded carriages, passengers, and mail, to St Pancras in London.

Latymer determined to enjoy himself, but how he wasn't sure. He hadn't made any plans. There was a black cloud when he grasped that doing everything alone was a bit bleak.

He settled into his seat, smiled, and tried to put a jolly aspect on his situation. He prepared himself to enjoy the delights of the countryside from the window. He was very happy that there was no one else in the carriage to make polite conversation with, he told himself. Then the door slid open.

'There you are.'

He looked up in surprise. 'Gerry?' Latymer was well and truly shocked.

'Didn't you see me?'

'You?'

'I waved to you.'

'That was you? I saw a woman waving at me out there, but–'

'Am I that forgettable?'

'No, it's just that,' he fumbled for words, 'I just didn't expect–'

'Do women wave at you all the time?'

'No,' and in his self-righteousness, 'of course, they don't!'

'Hm,' she said. 'Do I believe you?'

'What are you doing?'

'Well, at the moment I'm trying to get in here with my suitcase and put it onto the luggage rack, but there doesn't seem to be a gentleman around to help me.'

Latymer leapt to his feet and took her bag. They stood staring at each other.

He was the first to speak. 'I meant, where are you going?'

'London.'

'London? So am I. What a coincidence.'

'Oh, Peter, for a clever man you are completely stupid.'

'Ah.'

'My father told me where you were going. He said he'd pay for my weekend away, if I needed a break from my studies and finals. It seemed like a good idea, the rest and a weekend with you. I thought it would be what you would want as well. Looks like I got it wrong. You're probably sitting here wishing it was another female waving at you.'

'Gerry, this is wonderful. I couldn't want for anything more. This calls for a bottle of champagne.'

'I think we'll have to make do with a cup of tea and last week's pork pie until we get to London.'

***

For the ninety-minute journey to London their talk was garrulous, and afterwards they went into spells of silence, as if exhausted by their conversation. When they reached the outskirts of London, Gerry hooked her arm through his and held his hand, as if it were the most natural way to be in the world.

He turned his head and kissed her on the cheek.

'That was what I was expecting when I came in the compartment,' she told him.

'I was just thrown. It was a shock. As I've already explained.'

'You looked as if I were the last person in the world you wanted to see.

'Nothing could be further from the truth.'

'Then why have you never kissed me?' she asked.

'I just did.'

'Peter, I expect you gave Olive, Susan, and Edna a kiss when you left.'

The memory of his excitement when he left the house that morning. Shaking McFadden's and Bernard's hands; kissing the rest. Standing at the front door they waved as the taxi pulled away, as if Latymer were making a trip to the other side of the world.

'I was fairly free with my kisses, yes.'

'And I assume you don't want to spend the weekend away with them.'

'Particularly not Edna,' said Latymer.

'Then kiss me, Peter.'

They went into a passionate embrace. As their temperatures were rising, the compartment door slid open and the guard stood there.

'Oh, I'm sorry,' the guard said. In his embarrassment the official was lost for words. He just slipped into his usual formula as if nothing was going on. He said to them, 'London in a few minutes. On your honeymoon? I hope you'll be as happy as me and the missus. Well,

The Doctor, The Plutocrat, and The Mendacious Minister

happier, I hope.' The guard left without looking at their tickets and the door slid shut.

Peter and Gerry broke apart, smiling broadly.

***

They took a taxi to the hotel and booked into their rooms. As soon as they were ready, they arranged to meet for tea downstairs in the hotel foyer. Latymer sat by himself waiting for Gerry. He expected to be first down, and preferred it that way. He felt that it was what a gentleman should do. The waiter came and asked for his order. Latymer replied that he wanted to wait until his friend appeared.

'Is there anything you'd recommend seeing in the West End, you know, a show?' Latymer asked the waiter.

'In all honesty, I don't. People assume that because we live here, we go to the theatre all the time.'

Latymer saw Gerry appear. He stood up, so she could see him.

She came across and sat down.

'I was just asking about us seeing a show,' Latymer told her.

'That's a lovely idea,' Gerry said. She looked at the waiter as if he would provide them with the idea for their evening's entertainment.

'There were guests staying earlier in the week and they'd enjoyed a play they'd seen. I'll see if I can find out the title for you,' the waiter said.

'Many thanks.'

'Would you like tea now?' he asked.

Gerry and Latymer nodded their approval.

'I'll bring cakes as well,' the waiter said. They liked the sound of that.

'A show would be nice tomorrow. Perhaps a walk today to get our bearings, then dinner,' Latymer said to her.

'Sounds a good idea to me.'

Latymer sat back in the leather, content and relaxed.

The waiter wheeled a trolley over with a white envelope on it.

'He's bringing the bill? How odd,' said Latymer, 'Don't you normally settle up when you leave a hotel?'

'Which reminds me, we are going Dutch.'

'No,' said Latymer.

'Yes,' said Gerry. 'Dad's given me money.'

'No. And that's final.'

'You are Dr Latymer?' asked the waiter.

185

'I am. Is someone unwell?'

Gerry looked around as if she expected to find a body lying on the floor.

'No, no, nothing like that. A letter arrived for you.'

'Oh, the second letter for me delivered on a silver tray,' said Latymer. Gerry looked at him puzzled. 'A long story involving Edna. Don't bother yourself with it.'

The waiter set down the tray on the table, the letter propped against the teapot. Gerry was beside herself to know its contents.

The waiter stood as if he were to make an announcement. 'The play is *Deep Are The Roots*. It's a talky, not a sing-song. The chef has seen it and rates it highly, although he is a coloured gentlemen.'

Neither could see the connection, but it did make them more intrigued to see the performance.

'I can contact the box office for you and see if they have tickets. You can pick them up at the theatre.'

'That would be very kind. For tomorrow night?' said Latymer.

'I'll let you know or you can ask at the desk.'

The waiter left them to their tea.

'Shall I pour?' asked Latymer.

'No, open the letter. I'll pour. I wonder who it's from. Who knows you're here?'

Latymer started to list the names, counting them off on his fingers. Gerry looked at him as if restraining her exasperation and saying, *get on with it.* He picked up the letter. It bore the crest of the House of Commons.

'Hm, I think I know who this is from.' He took a knife from one of small plates that were for the cake. After slitting the envelope, he took out the contents, unfolded the paper, and scanned it. A frown appeared on his forehead. Gerry wondered what the matter was. He glanced through its contents again, refolded it and returned the letter to the envelope. He put the whole lot into the inside pocket of his jacket and said, 'Where's that tea then? I'm parched.'

Gerry watched him in disbelief. Wasn't he going to divulge its secrets?

'Who was it from?' she said to him. She was trying hard to give the appearance of not being over inquisitive.

'Its contents are top secret, for my eyes only. When I am alone I must destroy the letter. The reasons, before you ask,' he looked around the room furtively to make sure no one else was listening, 'are for the security of the nation.'

Gerry was close enough to the war to believe that kind of claptrap. Her eyes opened in surprise. There was obviously a secret life to Peter that she didn't know.

'No. We're invited for lunch with Joles tomorrow at the House of Commons. A car will be sent at midday.' Latymer was smiling broadly.

'Peter, you idiot. I could pour this pot of tea over your head.'

'Drink it instead, and let's have that walk.'

***

The pair stood outside on the steps of the hotel. Peter looked up and down the street for inspiration. He drew a blank. It was what it was, a street that could lead to anywhere in London. London wasn't waiting for them on the steps of the hotel.

'Do you know where to go, Peter?'

'No.'

'Have you been to London before?' she asked.

'No. Have you?'

'Twice,' she replied, 'with my parents. So it was awhile ago.'

'Best you lead the way then.'

'I don't want to be bossy,' Gerry said.

'Okay, but neither do we want to walk down a load of blind alleys pretending we are seeing the sights.'

Gerry decided, 'Trafalgar Square then. We'll start there.'

'Which is where?'

'On the underground, over there. We'll find it in a jiffy.'

'What,' said Peter with a smile, 'would I do without you?'

'What, indeed!'

She put her arm in his and they started down the road for their London adventure.

***

The following day at noon they were waiting on the steps of the hotel, when a black car drew up. Latymer went to get in, but Gerry held his arm and whispered, 'It could be for someone else, and then we'd look silly ending up where we don't want to be.'

'True.' Latymer stepped back and waited.

The driver, dressed in a dark suit, white shirt, and plain tie, but lacking the traditional uniform of a chauffeur, got out and came up the steps to them.

Addressing them he said, 'Dr Latymer and Miss McFadden?'

They answered in the affirmative and he went on, 'Mr Joles sent the car for you.' He made off back down the steps and opened the car door for them. Latymer followed Gerry into the back seat. They motored through the light London traffic until they arrived at the forecourt of the House of Commons.

Latymer went to open the door. Again Gerry put a hand on his arm to restrain him. She'd obviously done this before.

The driver came round and opened the door on Gerry's side. 'I believe Mr Joles is waiting for you at the entrance.'

As they looked across the courtyard they saw Joles making his way across to them. They greeted one another and went inside the old building.

'Have you been here before?' Both replied in the negative. 'After lunch we'll do the tour. The House doesn't sit until three. I can put you in the public gallery where you can watch the proceedings. I think you will find the session interesting. Anyway, let's eat. Sadly, too cold for the outside terrace today and the views of the Thames.'

They sat in the oak dining room and took Joles' recommendations as to what to eat. He insisted that they have wine. He wouldn't join them, as he was working and the afternoon was particularly onerous.

'I wanted to have this opportunity to speak to you, Peter.' He looked at Gerry.

'Don't let me bother you,' said Gerry, 'Don't think of me as the little woman who can't keep up with men's conversation. I'm intelligent enough to find it very interesting.'

'I didn't mean anything like that,' Joles apologised. 'There are plenty of men here who can't keep up.'

'You'll see, we'll have a woman Prime Minister one day,' laughed Gerry.

'When we land on the moon,' grunted a man as he passed their table.

'Anyway, Peter, are you up to speed on what Britley was doing?' Joles asked.

'No. News doesn't always reach us in the deepest depths of a Leicester council estate,' Latymer replied. 'And I suppose we have different priorities,'

Joles began, 'Britley drew up a contract with the government to buy army surplus after the war.'

'So he was committed to buy everything?' Latymer said.

'Yes, but it was the scrap he wanted to use. The metals for the manufacture of cars.'

Listening without comment, Gerry looked from man to man as they spoke.

'How did he get rid of the rest?'

'Oh,' Joles waved an arm around as if the action explained everything. 'Businessmen have ways. Different outlets, as simple as that food going to that shop near you, and others like it. You may have noticed Army and Navy stores opening up.'

Latymer wasn't aware of any, but he nodded all the same.

'It was all quite legal,' Joles went on, 'Except for one slip-up in the normal democratic processes.'

Latymer looked puzzled.

'The contracts weren't available for the members at Westminster to see. Ironically, Britley kept all his accounts present and correct for audit or whatever. But if anyone compared what he paid for the army surplus with the amount the government received, a schoolboy would notice the difference.'

'Especially your son.'

Joles smiled. 'Yes, doesn't miss a thing, that boy. Anyway, Britley was bribing the Minister to receive the contract. There must have been fierce competition for it, or it was never put out to tender. We shall probably never know and it doesn't matter now. This afternoon the Minister Henry Norrington will be making a statement in the Commons. After that he will resign. You'll be able to watch it from the public gallery. Lord Wakeham of Budleigh, who is complicit in the scandal, will never be allowed to speak again in the Lords. He can still draw his daily allowance, but he has lost his respect and status. Though I doubt whether the whole affair bothers him at all. It would be nice to think he does care for his own and the government's reputation; I hope so, but somehow I doubt it. The Prime Minister has distanced himself from the affair, or it could have brought him and his government crashing down.'

'And Britley? He gets away scot-free I expect, knowing what a snake he is.'

'Goodness, no. The contract was and is illegal. I imagine that Britley will have to return all the goods and money. If he challenges it, his assets will still be frozen. This will finish him.'

Latymer gave a self-satisfied smile. 'I'll drink to that,' and took a sip from his glass.

'And on top of everything, this terrible accident at the factory. No, Britley's businesses will go bankrupt and close. There will be a lot of unemployment in the area. How good is that for my constituents? But there was no other way. Corrupt government cannot be allowed to exist.'

Joles leaned over the table and clapped him on the back, although there was nothing to applaud.

'Come on, let's eat.'

Later that afternoon in the Commons, Latymer watched Henry Norrington resign his post as Minister. Peter found observing the downfall of democracy very sad, though he had yet to grasp the full extent of what he had witnessed.

***

After the curtain closed on the play *Deep Are The Roots,* the cast left the stage and the applause faded.

Gerry and Latymer sat in the bar of the theatre, soaking up the after-production atmosphere. Latymer was concerned whether it had been to Gerry's taste, that she might have preferred a musical.

He became conscious that he didn't know her well enough to know her likes and dislikes. He was also thinking where to take her for dinner, wishing now that he had booked in advance. He was more aware of how much he lacked experience in matters of the heart.

He said, as an opener to the conversation, hoping that it elicited the correct response, 'I'm sorry that wasn't a West End musical.'

'Why should you apologise?' Her tone was very firm in her reply.

'Don't women like that kind of entertainment the best?'

'Well, here's one who doesn't,' she said to him. 'I much prefer my distractions to be thought provoking, than the mindless entertainments to keep the populace happy. Don't you?' She was now checking that they were both on the same wavelength, and that he was a thinking man rather than just a scientist who could pass exams.

'Yes. A war has just been fought in Europe to get rid of the Nazis. Yet, if that play is to be believed, in America it is still happening against black men and women.'

The pair sat in silence for quite a few minutes. It was difficult for them to switch from a matter so serious to frippery and banter.

Gerry leaned forward, touched Latymer on the knee and whispered, 'Peter, at the hotel, please stay in my room tonight.'

He contemplated the full meaning of her statement before he replied. Feeling embarrassed, he said, 'I have nightmares.'

'I know. I stayed at Stocking Farm the night that elderly man was taken into hospital with food poisoning; the start of all this drama with Britley. I heard you screaming. I got into your bed and held you all night.'

He looked bewildered. 'I don't remember you being there.'

As soon as she said that, it was as if it made his words flow like a confession.

'At the end of the war, the government asked for medical volunteers to go to Europe. Such was the demand for doctors and nurses that they took those who were still training. The forces, when they got into the camps, saw the dreadful state of the inmates. Any medical care these people from the concentration camps could get was needed. We were clueless. We simply volunteered. We knew it was for prison camps, but we thought it was going to be like criminal prisoners we kept under lock and key here at home. How naïve we were.

'Throughout the war most of us were too young to volunteer. Those who could weren't allowed because after the war, Britain would need a new generation of doctors. So we did our duty and went to Europe in this other way. We believed that we would be part of the victory with the wine, the flowers, and the girls. We were so stupid. We had no idea.

'We were flown to, I don't know where, in Eastern Europe. I was attached to the Coldstream Guards. A day or two before we arrived the soldiers liberated Belsen. They told us what that was like. I'll spare you the details. We didn't see Camp Commandant Kramer or his deputy, Irma Grese. I didn't witness how the officers lost control of the ordinary British soldier who attacked the German guards.

'No, there were no flowers, no wine, no girls or any that resembled girls, or for that matter looked human. Any humanity that they'd possessed had been cruelly stolen away from them.

'It was a case of treating those that might survive and allowing those who were to die, to do so as peacefully as they could. With dignity. They were skeletons in striped uniforms. A doctor called me over and said, "Feel this man's stomach." I pressed my hand on the man's belly and could feel the bones of his vertebrae.

'The graves were full of the bodies they'd gassed or shot. They were so many bodies that it grew to infinity. I became numb to the horror. It was all too much to take in. It was like a coping strategy. This should never happen again. And yet tonight that play we watched– already in America the black men and women who fought for the allies against the Nazis, to stop the horrors of prejudice against the Jews, Gypsies, the mentally and physically handicapped–is starting to happen all over again because they are black.'

'Peter, I'm sorry.' Though she knew an apology was useless. 'I had no idea that it was so horrifying.' That was a problem, a lot of people didn't know. She knew that she had to be strong enough to keep her emotions within herself. It would be of no help to him if she broke down.

'No. Nobody does,' he said. 'There are thousands of men and women who were witnesses to the horrors. No, we didn't return with physical wounds. People believe they can understand when they can see a scar.'

'Perhaps in time?'

'I don't know. Right now, I don't think so. Come on, this is getting too maudlin. Let's take a walk, eat, and go back to the hotel. See where that takes us. Back to work tomorrow for both of us.'

Chapter Twenty-Nine

Within a few weeks, production at Britley's factories across the Midlands ground to a halt. Those who worked for him became unemployed. Only a few found work in the short term, and those were mainly clerical staff. The knock-on effect began to be felt across the cities, particularly Leicester, where retail shops began to stock cheaper items, but at least they provided employment. Smaller local shops, like Eric's, continued to exist, but mainly on credit, and he saw to it that his interest rates were high and fully paid up on benefits day.

For many, it was a downward spiral. The children looked healthy enough because the school provided one hot meal five times a week. Local pubs like the Beaumont Leys could be full, but little was being spent, and more than one man was heard to say, 'All of this only happened when that Latymer came here. Why couldn't he leave well enough alone? We'd still have jobs.'

The working man and woman didn't have a care whether Britley was honest or a thief. They didn't understand capitalism. They just wanted to be able to put food on their family's table.

Latymer's honeymoon was definitely over in Leicester. He was no longer the miracle worker.

***

At the vicarage, the Reverend Lewis told his wife that the situation they were in was like the thirties. Though, in his privileged upbringing, the Reverend Lewis had never known poverty.

'The people will look to us more, Anne,' he told her.

She was surprised at his socialist tone and wondered whether Adam was going to provide manna from heaven.

Over grace at meal times the Reverend would say, 'O Lord, we thank you for this bounty. We remember, as we eat, those who are without. Teach them, O Lord, that physical sustenance is not always necessary to fulfil our needs and that there is spiritual sustenance to nourish our bodies and minds also.' Then he forked three large potatoes from the serving dish. Ann noticed that her husband was growing corpulent. A little more spiritual sustenance seemed needed.

They, Drs McFadden and Latymer, were eating lunch at the medical practice. Edna cooked a nameless, tasteless stew.

'Dreadful this, isn't it, Latymer?'

'Don't let her hear you say that. A lot of people out there would love it.'

McFadden took a forkful and grimaced. 'Did it all turn out the way you had it planned?'

'Planned? What do you mean? There was no plan.'

'No, but you didn't like Britley from the moment you met him. I saw it in your eyes that evening at the Oddfellows. Anyway, now you're happy. He's bankrupt. Penniless. We're led to believe.' McFadden chuckled, putting the food in his mouth and chewing slowly.

'I didn't plan this.' Latymer said again. He grew annoyed at the inference.

'No. All right, I'm sure you didn't sit and plot it as a campaign, but you didn't think of the consequences.' He waited for a response from Latymer and received none. McFadden laid down his knife and fork. 'You didn't have to get Joles and the Military Police involved. Very dramatic. Oh yes. Why not ask me to have a quiet word in Eric's ear? The man would have never stepped out of line again. Word would have got back to Britley. Old boy's network.'

'Oddfellows.'

'It has its uses. That's the problem with the young, they believe they know everything and learn less as they grow older. The opposite is true, my boy. They won't thank you for this out there, out on the estate.'

Latymer got up from the table. 'I'm going to write to Gerry.' As he left the room he turned and said, 'Shall I give her your love?'

'No, Latymer. I can do that for myself.'

Chapter Thirty

The council estate roads were deserted on the rain-swept, early December afternoon. The streets were empty because it wasn't yet the age of the motor car. Sir Brian's vision of the Britley Runaround remained a dream.

On Stocking Farm Estate in December 1948, there was nowhere for anyone to go. The people didn't have the money. The children were in school warm and secure during the day. The husband and wife sat at home beside a meagre fire, sniping at one another.

'But there is no work,' the man of the house would say for the hundredth time, feeling feeble and inadequate.

Neither was it the age of imaginative cooking. The wife and mother had little idea of what to do with yet another lot of vegetables from the garden. She felt better fed during the war.

The festival of Christmas would be here soon. The nation believed that as victors there would be prizes. The housewife expected her rewards would be good food, nice clothes for herself, a radiogram for her husband, a doll's house for her daughter, and a train set for her son. But all of these, she now knew, were a delusion. The stockings at the end of the bed would contain little more than fruit and perhaps a small bar of chocolate with a cheap toy, a game, or jigsaw puzzle. They would play the game and pretend to enjoy the day. Christmas, a time of miracles, but there would be no miracles for them.

***

Sir Brian Britley rode in his chauffeur-driven car that afternoon. Up and down the streets of the council estate, the tyres hissed against the rain. He was deep in thought, planning for the future.

Britley tapped on the glass dividing him from the driver. He said to the man in the peaked cap, 'Take me home.'

The chauffeur nodded.

As the black car headed out of the estate they passed a deserted factory. The building still bore the sign, Britley's Sheet Metals.

Britley called out, 'Slow down.'

The chauffeur ground to halt.

'Okay, carry on,' Britley said.

Britley smiled a self-satisfied smile. Christmas is soon upon us. The people have no money. He knew where they would get the money from, Britley's Charity Bank, and when they'd signed on the dotted line, it would be as if they'd sold their soul to the devil. Charity? These pitiful souls would be so easily fooled. Britley let it be known there were loans to be made that very day.

A man out with his dog looked at the grand Daimler and said to his hound, 'Good to know the lucky bugger Britley's got money.'

***

Amongst the patients that Dr Latymer was due to see Friday evening was Milly Fantam. Latymer requested that she see him every three weeks. Usually a midwife would be giving a pregnant woman all the care she needed. Sometimes a doctor was necessary. Latymer knew that with her recent trials, Milly needed a lot of extra care.

After all the usual checks he asked, 'And how are you feeling in yourself?'

'I'm fine,' she replied, as if she didn't want to give anything away.

'Yes, physically you are. I believe you will give birth to a healthy baby. But how are you coping?'

'Well enough. I miss Reg.'

At least now, he thought, *there is truth showing itself.* He knew it was important to get a person to speak out. Once they began to unburden themselves, then the healing process could begin.

'Reg,' asked Latymer, 'how is he?'

'How do you think?' Her tone was aggressive.

Latymer knew. He'd contacted Reg's hospital where he was being cared for earlier that day, still unable to move.

'I'm sorry, Dr Latymer.'

He reached out and took her hand. Human contact in situations like this is undervalued.

'That's all right, Milly.'

'I'm so angry.'

'Yes.'

'He might as well be dead.'

Dr Latymer did not reply.

Close to tears she spoke. 'He can't walk. What sort of dad is he going to be? Not the man Reg wanted to be. Playing football, walking the kid. Playing all those games kids want to play. He was a big kid himself. They would have got on well together. Reg would have made a lovely dad.'

'He still will, Milly.'

'Hu, from a wheelchair?' She gathered her bag and made ready to leave. 'There's others you've got to see. Sitting here talking about it won't make it better.' She got up to leave. 'Thank you for being here.'

'I'll always be here.'

As she reached the door, she turned, hand resting against the panel as if she needed the support. She looked directly at her doctor.

'Oh Doctor, why can't we just go right back to the beginning and the silly, great fool traps his arm in a carriage door?'

Dr Latymer looked down. There was no reply he could make.

'You're a good man, Dr Latymer.'

He realised then that he couldn't wish for greater praise.

Milly left the room, closing the door behind her.

Latymer reached for his papers to see who was his next patient.

Later he would be going to the railway station to meet his sister, Ruth. Back to where it all began.

Acknowledgements

My gratitude goes to the following people for their help in producing this novel: Liz Bone, Kate Beswick, Stephen Butt, BBC Radio Leicester, David Robinson, Karalyn Hubbard, Kate Simpson, Michael James Treacy, Mary Edington, Sue Guiney, Anita Beery, Nadine Laman, and Jill Pope.

This is not a work of history or a medical book. It is a novel. The historical events described about the British government never happened. The story is fiction. Stocking Farm of Leicester, England, exists, but none of the characters existed, nor any of the events ever happened. They are completely of the author's imagination. I was given medical advice, but the interpretations and mistakes are my own.

Glyn Pope
Deux Sevres, France, 2010

About the Author

Glyn Pope grew up on a council estate in England. He studied theology at Nene University. In addition to writing short stories and novels, Glyn interviewed Bob Marley the night before Marley cancelled his UK tour and went back to the warmth of Jamaica. Glyn has published articles for both Leonard Cohen and Bob Dylan fan magazines, and has won a short story competition in the magazine *Devon Life*. He has two novels published. A few years ago, he and his wife and daughter moved to France, where he pursues a full time writing career.